RAISING
CAINE

RAISING CAINE

WILLIAM W. JOHNSTONE

AND J.A. JOHNSTONE

PINNACLE BOOKS
Kensington Publishing Corp.
www.kensingtonbooks.com

PINNACLE BOOKS are published by

Kensington Publishing Corp.
119 West 40th Street
New York, NY 10018

PUBLISHER'S NOTE
Following the death of William W. Johnstone, the Johnstone family is working with a carefully selected writer to organize and complete Mr. Johnstone's outlines and many unfinished manuscripts to create additional novels in all of his series like The Last Gunfighter, Mountain Man, and Eagles, among others. This novel was inspired by Mr. Johnstone's superb storytelling.

All Kensington titles, imprints, and distributed lines are available at special quantity discounts for bulk purchases for sales promotion, premiums, fund-raising, educational, or institutional use.

Special book excerpts or customized printings can also be created to fit specific needs. For details, write or phone the office of the Kensington Sales Manager: Attn.: Sales Department. Kensington Publishing Corp., 119 West 40th Street, New York, NY 10018. Phone: 1-800-221-2647.

First Printing: April 2022
ISBN-13: 978-0-7860-4898-4

10 9 8 7 6 5 4 3 2 1

Printed in the United States of America

CHAPTER ONE

Sheriff Dan Caine looked out of his office window into the dusty main drag of Broken Back, a Texas cow town precariously perched on the crumbling edge of nowhere.

Across the street, outside John Taylor's mercantile, Mrs. Jean McCann and Mrs. Blanche Baxter were in deep conversation, though what they found to talk about was beyond Dan's comprehension since a burg as small as Broken Back generated little gossip. Mrs. McCann was pregnant again. What was it, her third or fourth? Dan had lost count. He watched Frank Lawson, the local gambler, dressed in his usual black frock coat, white shirt, and string tie, touch his hat as he passed the ladies and then continue on his way to Ma's Kitchen where he breakfasted every morning on coffee and three fingers of bourbon. Lawson had once worked the Mississippi riverboats but that was a dozen years ago and he'd fallen on hard times since then, fallen so far and so fast in fact that he'd landed with a thud in Broken Back where the stakes were low, and he counted his winnings in nickels and dimes. Lawson carried a silver-plated Remington derringer and the talk was that across the card tables he'd killed several men with it. But he'd

never drawn down on anybody in Dan's town. Just as well.
Dan Caine had little tolerance for shootists, especially
homicidal, washed-up gamblers.

Mrs. McCann and Mrs. Baxter's conference had drawn
to a close and they hugged and went their separate ways.
A dust devil spun in the street and then collapsed in a puff
of dust, and the risen sun burned away the shadows and
opened a furnace door that blasted waves of dry heat over
the town.

Dan Caine sighed and reread the letter again. It was
from Toby Reynolds, a rancher who'd once hired a much-
younger Caine as a puncher and had kept up a desultory
correspondence with him for years. The missive was badly
spelled, painstakingly written in block letters, and the news
it imparted was straight to the point and all bad.

DEER DAN. I HAVE BAD NOOS ABOUT YOUR
FREND DICK MEDOWS. HOW IT CAME UP
HE WAS MURDERED AFTER NOOS GOT
AROUND THAT HE HAD STRUCK IT RICH
AND HIS CABIN WAS FILLED WITH GOLD.
AS WE BOTH NO DICK NEVER HIT PAYDIRT
IN HIS LIFE. THREE MEN WAS ARRESTED
FOR HIS MURDER THE SONS OF THE BIG
RANCHER BARTON CLAY. BUT THANKS TO
THEIR PA HAVIN MONEY AND INTIMIDATIN
THE JURY THEY WAS FOUND NOT GILTY.
DAN, THEM THREE BOYS CELEBRATED IN
THE SALOON AND LAFFED ABOUT HOW
DICK HOLLERED WHEN THEY HELD HIS
TOES TO THE FIRE. FOLKS AROUND THESE
PARTS NO THE CLAY BOYS GOT AWAY WITH

MURDER BUT THEIR PA HAS HIRED RUBEN
WEBB THE TEXAS DRAW FITER TO KEEP
OUR TOWN AND USELESS CITY MARSHAL
IN LINE. THE MARSHAL IS A DARN FOOL.
CLAY RANCH IS EAST OF TUCSON AT THE
FOOT OF THE RINCON SKY MOUNTINS.
I JUST THOT YOU WOULD WANT TO NO.—
TOBY REYNOLDS ESQ.

Dan dropped the letter and his eyes went to the street
again. Nothing stirred except for John Taylor's yellow dog
that flopped down outside the mercantile's door and glared
balefully at Sophie, Dan's calico cat who was sunning herself on the boardwalk. That dog, his name was Ranger, had
chased Sophie seven times, caught her once and never
tried it again.

Dan's attention went back to the letter and its disturbing
contents. He built a cigarette, thumbed a lucifer into flame
and smoked as he remembered . . .

Snake River Dick Meadows was not by any stretch of
the imagination a nice old man. He was rattlesnake mean,
cranky, violent in drink, and he hated people with a pas-
sion, avoiding them in the same way ordinary folks walked
wide around skunks.

But when Dan Caine was just six years old, Meadows
had saved his life. He'd found the boy alone, hungry, and
frightened in a ramshackle cabin in the New Mexico Territory, clinging to the body of his mother who'd been dead
for three days, casually killed, along with his father, by a
passing Apache war band.

The old man made a meager living as a tinpan and wandered far and wide, but he called a small stone cabin in

the Arizona Territory's Mogollon Rim country his home not-so-sweet home. His attitude to Dan was one of indifference, once staking the boy out to call in a grizz that had been prowling too near his workings. But Meadows kept the growing youngster fed and taught Dan how to hunt, fish, and shoot, including tutoring him in the ways of the Colt revolver.

Dan struck out on his own when he was sixteen, mounted on a ten-dollar horse, carrying a Springfield carbine, Model of 1877 in .45-70 caliber that he could shoot ten times in a minute with accuracy. He and Meadows shook hands and promised to keep in touch, but they never did.

Until the letter came.

Dan's deputy, a half Scottish, half Apache breed, walked into the office from his bunk in one of the cells. His father had taken his offspring's name from a bourbon bottle and called him Old Crow, though Dan just called him Crow. Suffering from the effects of last night's overindulgence at James Logan's saloon, Crow wore only fire engine–red long johns and, a holdover from his early days as a drover, his battered hat, the front brim curled up and secured with a pin he'd received from the Women's Temperance Guild of Kansas. Crow had been drunk at the time and could never remember which of the ladies had given it to him, but nonetheless it was a prized possession. He stood beside Dan's desk, scratched his belly and yawned.

"Speak, thou dreadful specter," Dan said.

"Coffee," Crow said, his voice breaking on the word.

"You know where it is," Dan said.

Crow shook his head and held up two shaking hands. "Get it for me, Dan."

"Who was it this time?" Dan said, rising to his feet.

"Same as usual," Crow said. He sat gingerly on the chair opposite the sheriff's desk. "Eleanor Martine."

Dan poured coffee into a thick white cup. "Eleanor Martine . . . her real name's Ellen Martin," he said.

"Gimme . . . gimme . . ." Crow said, reaching out with both hands for the cup.

"What was the drink?" Dan said. "Or can't you recollect?"

"Champagne," Crow said. He tested the coffee. "Ow . . . ow . . . hot."

"What kind of champagne?"

"French, from France. Oh, my head. Frog . . . fail . . . fall . . . how come when I say a word starting with f my head hurts worse?"

"Try fake, false, fraud . . . like the French champagne you guzzled last night. It's made in Fort Worth out of raw alcohol, ginger ale, and apple juice, and Logan buys it by the barrel, bottles it himself and charges top dollar."

"But Eleanor drank it."

"No, she didn't. When you weren't looking, she poured it out, and you were too drunk to notice."

Crow groaned. "Three dollars a bottle and we drank about nine or ten. A month's wages gone. Pfft! Just like that."

"Was she worth it?"

"Who?"

"Ellen Martin."

"I don't know."

"You were too drunk to know."

"I woke up in my bunk. I've no idea how I got there." He held his head in both hands and groaned. "Dan, put me out of my misery. Just shoot me."

"Sure, I will, but later. In the meantime, I've got something I want you to read."

"Read? What time is it?"

"It's just gone nine."

"In the morning?"

"Seems like."

"Nobody reads at nine in the morning. It ain't Christian."

"You will." Dan tossed Toby Reynolds' letter across the desk. "Wrap your eyeballs around that."

"Do I have to?"

"Only if you want to keep your job."

Crow picked up the letter. "You're a hard-hearted man, Dan Caine."

"And you're one complaining Injun."

"It's only the white part of me that complains, not the Injun half."

"And if you don't eyeball the letter right now, both halves of you will be out of work."

"I'd shake my head at you if it didn't hurt so much," Crow said.

He read the letter, rubbed sleep from his eyes and read it again. Then he said, "Dan, I'm sorry."

"Don't be. Snake River Dick Meadows was a disgusting human being, and I owe him nothing but my life. But I reckon that's enough."

"Enough for what?"

"Enough for me to head to the Arizona Territory's rim country and see that the three men who murdered Meadows pay for what they did. I want them to hang."

"Dan, a rich man's sons are gallows-proof, you know that," Crow said. "Money talks in a courtroom. The hundred-dollar bill is the West's best defense lawyer, and that's a natural fact."

"Then I'll find another way to punish them. I'll be wearing a gun."

"Ah . . . then you haven't heard of Ruben Webb, the Amarillo drawfighter that Reynolds mentions in his letter, huh?"

"You're correct, I haven't had that pleasure."

"Well, the talk is that when he was seventeen, he put the crawl on John Wesley Hardin."

"The loose talk in the saloon?"

"Yeah, from men who . . ."

"Heard it from other men who heard it in another saloon."

"Something like that. Dan, I know you set store by Wes Hardin."

"Yes, and I still do. As you know, I did some hard time in Huntsville with him and I can tell you this . . . Wes never backed down from anyone, even Wild Bill Hickok. And if a two-bit, wannabe gunman like Webb says otherwise then he's a damned liar."

"All right, I'll try a different tack. Have you told the fair Helen about Dick Meadows?" Crow said.

"Some of it," Dan said.

"How long have you been married?"

"Six months."

"And now you're going to leave her and lay your life on the line in the Arizona Territory?"

"That's how it shapes up," Dan said. "What I aim to do has to be done. To do otherwise would mean I could never again hold my head high in the company of men."

"Maybe, and probably only in the Arizona Territory, nowhere else." Crow said. "Dan, you can't go up against those Clay boys as a lawman. Your sheriff's star won't shine in that neck of the woods."

"Then I'll go as a vigilante and do what the law should've done in the first place."

"You're bucking a stacked deck. Taking on a big rancher with three sons and who knows how many punchers riding for his brand are mighty long odds." Crow held his head and whimpered. "Oh, dear God, even thinking about it is making my white-man headache worse."

"White-man headache?" Dan said.

"An Apache doesn't get headaches. Didn't you know that?"

"Well, I guess they don't get them often, unless like you, they drink too much tiswin." Dan got to his feet. "Hold the fort," he said. "I have to speak with Helen."

"She doesn't know about the letter?"

"No. The Patterson stage pulled in early this morning and Buttons Muldoon and Red Ryan brought it to me. Helen doesn't know about it yet."

"When do we leave?" Crow said.

"You're not leaving," Dan said. "This is a job I'll handle by myself."

"That's a hell of a thing to say to me, Dan," Crow said. "You're the sheriff of Broken Back and I'm your shadow. That's how it's been since you first pinned a badge on me. You head for the Territory and I'll be right behind you." Dan opened his mouth to speak, and Crow held up a silencing hand. Dan thought he looked like a cigar store Indian in long johns. "Besides . . . oh my poor head . . . I know the country south of the Mogollon Rim, well some of it at least."

"How come?" Dan said.

"You don't want me to answer that. It happened a couple of years ago before I got civilized."

"Tell me," Dan said.

"You won't like it. It ain't about what you would call churchgoing folks."

"Go ahead. I'll try my best to bear it."

"Are you sure?"

"Sure, I'm sure. Have at it."

"Well, it was some years after my father died when I was living on the San Carlos with my ma and her new Chiricahua husband. She was a nice lady and last year I heard that she'd died way too young of the cholera."

"I remember that," Dan said. "And I was right sorry."

"Anyway, how the Mogollon Rim thing came up, me and a couple of other young Chiricahuas, Tarak and Delshay, nice fellers, heard that an army payroll wagon had left the reservation on its way north to Fort Apache, so we planned on robbing it. You sure you want to hear this? It ain't respectable."

"Yeah, I'm sure. Now get to the exciting part."

"There is no exciting part. Unbeknownst to us, the wagon was met with a cavalry patrol from the fort and they cut loose on us. Tarak got a thumb blown off and Delshay took a bullet to his left leg, broke the knee that later left him with a limp. At least that's what I heard."

"And you didn't get hit?" Dan said.

"No. Maybe them soldiers thought I was a white man. Well, anyway, when we got back to the reservation old Geronimo, a nice enough feller but death on Mexicans, asked me to join his war band, but right there and then I decided to leave the Apaches behind me and walk the white man's path."

"You do look like a white man, you know," Dan said.

"Yellow hair and green eyes, how could I look like anything else?"

"Back in the day you must've seemed a mighty strange kind of Apache to ol' Geronimo and them. Hell, what am

I talking about? You even look like some mighty strange kind of white man."

And that was true.

Crow's straight, fair hair fell over his shoulders except for two braids that framed his face. He'd inherited his wide and high cheekbones from his Apache mother and his six-foot-two height and stubborn chin from his Scottish father.

And he was being stubborn now.

"Sheriff Caine, I'm a very sick man this morning, close to death, but you're not going to the Arizona Territory without me, so put that in your pipe and smoke it."

"Who can I leave in charge of law and order in this wild and wooly town?"

"John Taylor."

"He's a grocer, for God's sake."

"A grocer who'd like nothing better than to get out from behind his counter and strut around town with a star on his chest."

"Now I study on it, maybe you're right. At town meetings Taylor's a man who likes to puff out his chest and talk and brag, all the time poking holes in the air with his finger."

"A banty rooster boasting on a dung heap," Crow said.

"I'll talk to him," Dan said.

"What are you going to tell him?"

"That you and I are going on a hunting trip into the Arizona Territory after mule deer."

"He'll want to load you up with cartridges."

"That's all right. Where we're going, we'll probably need them."

CHAPTER TWO

His cat tucked under his arm, Dan Caine crossed the sunbaked street and took the alley between the mercantile and a land office that led to open ground and a small limestone cabin with a wood shingle roof and wraparound porch. Dan bought the cabin from a dentist who'd called it quits, closed his practice, and headed for Austin where there were more folks with bad teeth than in Broken Back.

That summer Dan Caine was in his early thirties, a brown-eyed, broad-shouldered, good-looking man with jet-black hair and eyebrows that were slightly too heavy for his lean face. He had a wide, expressive mouth and good teeth, and women, respectable and otherwise, liked him just fine. Dan Caine looked a man right in the eye, holding nothing back, and most times he had a stillness about him, a calm, but of the uncertain sort that had the brooding potential to suddenly burst into a moment of hellfire action. He seldom talked about himself, but as a young man he'd served three years in Huntsville for an attempted train robbery. He'd spent the first four months of his sentence in the penitentiary's infirmary for a bullet wound to the chest he'd taken during the holdup. At some point during that time, probably in the spring of 1880 according to most historians, he was befriended by John Wesley Hardin. Prison life had tempered Hardin's wild ways, and Wes convinced the young Caine to quit the outlaw trail and live by the law. Released early in the summer of 1882, Dan Caine drifted for a couple of years, doing whatever work he could find. He arrived in Montana in January 1884, the year the citizenry, irritated by the amount of crime in the Territory, appointed hundreds of vigilantes to enforce the law. Hard-eyed hemp posses dutifully strung up thirty-five cattle and horse thieves and an even dozen of just plain nuisances. Dan didn't think Montana a good place to loiter, and in the fall of 1885 owning only his horse, saddle, rifle, Colt revolver, and the clothes he stood up in, he rode into the town of Thunder Creek, missing his last six meals. The sheriff, Chance Hurd, a former outlaw himself, liked the tough, confident look of the young man, fed him steak and eggs and gave him a job as a twenty-a-month deputy. Now Hurd was dead, and Dan had moved on to Broken Back where he was offered the job of town sheriff.

Dreading what he was about to tell his bride, he stepped into the cabin and Helen greeted him with a wide smile. Dan was again struck by how pretty she was and how lucky he was that she'd consented to marry him. Helen was teaching a class that day, eight kids between the ages of six and twelve crammed into a tiny cabin reserved for that purpose by the town fathers, and she was dressed for work, wearing a plain, brown cotton dress with white collar and cuffs, her dark hair pulled back in what she called a "schoolmarm's bun."

Dan set down Sophie and returned his wife's smile. "You look as pretty as a field of bluebonnets," he said. "And that's a natural fact."

Helen dropped a little curtsy. "Why thank you, kind sir," she said. "There's coffee in the pot and some leftover yellow cake in the cupboard. And now tell me why you're back here so early in the morning. It seems that you just left."

Dan held out the letter. "The Patterson stage just delivered this, Helen. I think you should read it."

A frown wrinkle appeared between the woman's eyes, and she said, "Dan, you're such a man of mystery." She took the letter from his hand, read it, read it again, and then said, "You told me about Dick Meadows. He was not a nice man and sometimes he treated you cruelly, but I guess I should be sorry he's dead."

"He saved my life, Helen. I owe him."

"I think you paid back what you owed him many times over. Judging by what you told me, he treated you like a slave."

"I would've died in my folks' cabin. It was cold and there was no food and I was six years old and I'd been trying to wake my dead mother for three days. Dick took me out of there and gave me a home." He hesitated and then added, "Of a sort."

"Well, I'll mention him in my prayers tonight," Helen said. A pile of blue covered textbooks under her arm, she said, "Now I must get to school." She moved toward the door, stopped, kissed Dan on the cheek, and then said, "See you later, husband. Don't forget the cake and take a slice to Deputy Crow."

"Helen, wait," Dan said. "We have to talk about this."

"Talk about what? The cake?"

"No, about the men who murdered Dick Meadows."

"I don't want to talk about that," Helen said. A gleam of irritation lit up her eyes. "The old man who saved your life and then abused you is dead. Well, it's sad. Now let it go."

"I can't. I want to see that the men who killed and then escaped justice are punished. I owe him that much."

"And what do you owe me, Dan?" Helen said. "What do you owe your wife?"

She was angry. Dan saw her body stiffen, white knuckling the hand holding her textbooks. It was the first time Dan had seen Helen angry, and it shocked him. She was ready to pit her bird and he needed to step carefully.

"I love you, Helen," he said. "And I want to spend the rest of my life with you."

"A life that could be cut short in the Arizona Territory . . . and all for a dead old man you didn't even like. Is he really worth dying for? Dan, you're not making any sense. It's as though you're talking nonsense to me in a foreign tongue, Mandarin Chinese maybe, and I can't understand a word you're saying."

"Helen, the dead can't cry out for justice, only the living can do that. I'll get Dick Meadows the justice that was denied him."

"Why? For heaven's sake, why?"

"Because it's my duty. It's that simple. Helen. Duty calls and I can't turn my back on it."

"Dan, the star on your chest means that your duty is to this town."

"And if I showed yellow and didn't do what has to be done, I could never wear this star or any other ever again." Dan touched his wife lightly on the cheek and said, "If you can't understand why I'm doing this thing, at least tell me you'll stand by me."

"I can't do that, Dan," Helen said. "I can promise you nothing." She shook her head. "I think you're a fool, and I think you're throwing our marriage away like you'd throw away dirty dishwater. Yes, dirty dishwater, Dan. That's what our marriage means to you."

"Miz Caine, are you all right?"

The voice outside belonged to twelve-year-old Nat Campbell, Helen's star student.

"Yes, I'm just fine. Go back to school, Nat," she called out. "I'll be right there."

"You ain't sick, ma'am?"

"No, Nat, I'm not sick. Now go back to school like I told you."

"Yes, ma'am."

Helen opened the door and said, her voice like melting ice, "When will you leave, Dan?"

"As soon as me and Crow saddle up. I expect we'll head for San Antone and catch a train to the territory."

"Dan, I'll tell you one thing you shouldn't expect," Helen said. "Don't expect me to be here when you get back. If you get back."

"Helen, wait . . ." Dan said.

But his wife was gone, striding, back stiff, toward her waiting class.

CHAPTER THREE

Give or take, there were three-hundred-and-seventy miles of railroad track between San Antonio, Texas, and Tucson in the Arizona Territory and Dan Caine winced when he paid fifteen dollars for his and Crow's fare, plus another three to put their horses in the boxcar. The fare, on a rare midnight cannonball, was the cheapest he could get, hard bench seats in what the Southern Pacific called "emigrant class."

Earlier, the thirty-mile ride east from Broken Back to San Antonio had passed mostly in silence. Even after they changed trains, Dan seemed preoccupied, and Crow was careful not to mention his wife. But now as the train hurtled through the night toward Tucson and the windows were rectangles of inky darkness, Crow decided it was time to speak his mind.

"Dan, how did she take it?" he said.

"Huh?"

"How did Helen take it?"

"Badly."

There were a dozen other people in the carriage, but wrapped up in their own uncomfortable misery, and used to gun-belted men, they dozed off and on and paid little heed to Dan and Crow.

"How badly?" Crow said.

Now Dan looked his deputy in the eye. "Helen told me I'd thrown away our marriage like dirty dishwater."

Crow shook his head. "That was bad. A woman says something like that it's serious and a bunch of flowers ain't gonna fix it."

"Yes, it was bad. And what's worse, I think she meant every word of it."

"She'll forgive you. Women always do . . . eventually. All it takes is time."

"I don't think she'll be in Broken Back when I return. I think she'll just pick up her stuff and leave. Helen thinks I deserted her, and she'll never forgive me."

"You'd be surprised what women will forgive."

"How do you know?" Dan said.

"Somebody told me that. All right, I don't know first-hand because I've never given a woman cause to forgive me."

"Nor me, up until now," Dan said.

"There's a first time . . ."

". . . for everything. Yeah, I know."

"I can tell you don't want to talk about it, Dan."

"You're right. I don't."

"Then let's cuss and discuss what we're gonna do in Tucson once we get there," Crow said.

He was dressed much like Dan in canvas pants with wide suspenders worn over a blue shirt and spurred boots with two-inch heels. His only concession to his Apache heritage was the bear-claw necklace he wore for protection and good health.

"No use in discussing anything until we get there," Dan

said. "But I guess our first order of business will be to track down the Clay brothers."

"And then what?"

"And then I don't know."

The clack-clack-clack of the rails was loud in the silence, and the other passengers were mostly hidden in shadow, the carriage's only illumination a few oil lamps that hung from its ceiling and cast little light.

"We aiming to gun them one by one?" Crow said.

"Not we, Crow, only me, and I won't go the gun unless I have to," Dan said. "I plan to have the Clays arrested again and this time see that they get a proper trial."

"According to the feller's letter, you can't count on getting any help from the local lawman."

"I reckon there are enough honest citizens in Tucson who will want to see justice done. Those are ones I'll talk to about arresting the Clay brothers and arranging for a new trial, maybe with a circuit judge. The local sheriff doesn't enter into my thinking. He failed Dick Meadows once, he'll fail him again."

Crow turned his head and pretended to look out a window black as a chalkboard and then said, "Ruben Webb."

"What about him?" Dan said.

"He's good. Maybe the best there is."

Dan smiled. "You heard that in the saloon, huh?"

In the gloom, a man coughed, coughed again, and the woman with him whispered some soothing words that only he could hear.

"I saw him kill two men," Crow said. "A year ago in a Laredo saloon."

"Why did you pretend you'd only heard of him?"

Crow shrugged.

"Because you thought you'd scare me?" Dan said.

"Maybe something like that. I don't know."

"All right, tell me what you saw in Laredo?"

"I was at the bar in the Silver Garter saloon and like everybody else in the place I watched Webb, him being a named shootist an' all. Well, I was on my second beer when Webb got into it with a couple of Lazy-T punchers who called him out for cheating. Now I was told later that both those boys were drawing gun wages and one of them, a tall, redheaded feller by the name of Collins or Rawlins, I never did get the right of it, grabbed Webb's wrist and said, 'Show your hand. If you got more than five cards, I'll kill you.' Well, sir, Ruben Webb opened his fingers and six cards dropped onto the table. Collins or Rawlins was as good as his word. He stood up so fast, his chair fell over, and he went for his gun. Lordy, Dan, that cowboy was almighty sudden. But he wasn't fast enough. Webb didn't even get to his feet. He skun his iron and shot across the card table. Pow! Pow!" Two shots into Collins' or Rawlins' chest, and him with his gun still coming up. Meantime the other cowboy's hand, I never did get his name, was dropping for his gun. To this day I'll always remember it was one of them fancy Smith & Wesson Schofield revolvers, you've seen the kind I'm talking about. But the man never even cleared leather. Pow! Pow! Webb's shots hit him, one in the chest, the other in the throat. Listen, Dan, this is funny . . . well, it ain't funny, but it's interesting. That last bullet went clean through the puncher's neck and hit Robert E. Lee, who was hanging on the wall, right between the eyes." Crow elbowed Dan. "Listen up, the thing about all that is that Webb barely moved. Hell, he didn't even get out of his chair." Crow snapped his fingers twice. "Fast as that, he killed two men. Now that's what you'll be facing in Tucson, and I don't want to scare you none. I'm just putting you on your guard, you understand."

Crow got no reaction and then saw why . . .

Dan Caine was sound asleep.

CHAPTER FOUR

Dan Caine led his horse out of the Tucson train depot into a drab, dusty little town that's boom days still lay two decades in the future. He and Crow stood at the junction of Toole Avenue and Congress Street in the early evening light and looked around at rows of adobe houses, none of them finished in plaster, dirt streets without boardwalks and a few saloons and restaurants gathered into plazas. To the east of downtown, the Santa Cruz River that gave Tucson its reason for being, sometimes flowed with water and sometimes didn't, but that summer in places it overflowed its banks. Like a painted ceiling, the sky was bannered with streaks of crimson and jade that imparted a rosy glow to the town and hid most of its warts.

"Well, Sheriff Caine, now what?" Crow said.

"Now we find a livery and put up the horses and then book into a cheap hotel and finally go on the hunt for some grub."

"I've got fifteen dollars," Crow said.

"And I've got twenty. Between us it's enough, but we'll need an advance on our wages when we return to Broken Back." Dan's eyes stared into nothing, seeing a picture in his mind. "When we return to Broken Back . . ."

"She'll be waiting," Crow said.

Dan shook his head, clearing his thoughts. "Mount up," he said abruptly. "There's got to be a livery in this burg."

The livery stable was on Cemetery Street, owned by, as a sign said above the wide doorway, Josiah Crumb, prop. Crumb, small and wiry with a bad limp, had been a Texas Ranger and had fought both Comanches and Apaches and he was a talking man.

Dan sounded him out, hoping to learn more about Barton Clay and his three sons.

"Who's the biggest rancher in these parts, Mr. Crumb?" he said.

"That would be Barton Clay of the Clay Land and Cattle Company," the man said. "He owns most of Pima County and I reckon he has a notion to take over the whole damned territory, Tucson included."

"Does he come into town often?" Dan said.

"Nah, not often." Crumb laid down the feed bucket he carried. "There's a settlement called Wheeler's Crossing, if you can call a mercantile that doubles as a saloon, an abandoned blacksmith's forge, a sawmill, and a scattering of adobe cabins a settlement. More like a whistle stop except there ain't no trains. But what it does have are whiskey and whores. A feller by the name of Luther Wheeler owns the mercantile and he runs the ladies, usually half a dozen of them but they come and go. Most Friday nights you'll find of a crowd of Clay's punchers in the Wheeler place, drinking and whoring. They're a hard bunch."

"What about his sons?" Dan said.

Crumb shook his head. "Now those boys just ain't been tamed. I mean they ain't civilized, and you'd be well advised to stay away from them. All three of them are good with guns, especially Decker, the youngest, and they're wildcat mean. Yeah, they use the bar and the brothel and they keep upstairs rooms at the mercantile to bed down when they get too drunk to ride home. The Clay boys are wild animals and they're pure pizen. The only one who can do anything with them is their pa. I heard he whales on them with a riding crop when they cross him."

"Dang, I was gonna ask Barton Clay for a job," Dan said, lying smoothly.

"As a rider?"

"Yeah, as a puncher."

"Don't do it. Sure, Clay has punchers and maybe they work cattle now and then, but he brought them up from Texas and he pays them drawfighter gun wages. I was a Texas Ranger for a number of years and I know a professional gunman when I see one, and Barton Clay has a dozen of them." Crumb took a step back and studied Dan from the toes of his scuffed boots to the top of his hat, lingering on his face for long moments. Finally, he shook his head and said, "Mister, you don't fit the bill. You don't look like a hardcase gunman to me and I guarantee you won't to Barton Clay either. There are other ranches to the west of us. Try one of them." Crumb added quickly. "No offense."

"None taken," Dan said. But the man's words rankled.

Crumb gave the same attentive inspection to Crow and after a while he said, "Now you might pass muster. You got hell in your eyes and the look of the breed about you, but if Clay pegs you as a gun, he won't hold that against you. He's already got a couple of Mexicans working for him, and I'm sure one of them is a breed. What name do you go by?"

"Crow to my friends."

"And to your enemies?"

"They don't call me anything. They're all dead."

Crumb laughed and said to Dan, "Hear that? Now that's the kind of talk that brings gun wages in Pima County."

"Talk's cheap," Dan said, irritated. Crow seemed to be enjoying this. "Can you recommend a cheap hotel?"

"Ah, cheap and good," Crumb said. "Your best bet is Mrs. Dale's Boarding House for Christian Gentlemen. It's just down the street and the rooms are clean and Mrs. Dale cooks a nice chicken stew and offers a boiled wash for clothing. You'll be just in time for supper."

"How much?" Dan said.

"One dollar a day," Crumb said. "That's fifty cents cheaper than the Palace Hotel and grub is not included."

"We'll give Mrs. Dale a try," Dan said. He picked up his Winchester and saddlebags. "Crow, I never took you for such a dangerous gunman."

"Me neither," Crow said.

CHAPTER FIVE

Mrs. Gertrude Dale, a widow for half of her fifty years, was a plump, plain-faced woman with steely gray eyes and a thin, intolerant mouth, not an attractive female . . . except for her head of magnificent auburn hair that she wore piled up in glossy waves and cascading ringlets, all held in place with silver-and-turquoise pins. Mrs. Dale had the face and body of a washerwoman and the hair of a Brothers Grimm princess.

When she came to the door and looked over Dan Caine and Crow, she seemed less than impressed. "Did you have a recommendation?" she said. Her voice was of the loud, booming sort, and Dan figured the woman could never keep anything secret.

"Josiah Crumb . . ." Dan said.

"At the livery stable," Mrs. Dale said. She made a face. "He loves to tip a jug, that one."

"I wouldn't know about that," Dan said.

"Well, he does," Mrs. Dale said. Then, still standing in the doorway, "My rate is a dollar a day and that includes two meals. Breakfast is served at seven sharp, dinner at eight. The rules of my house are few and I expect them to be obeyed. Payment in advance. Spurs not to be worn in bed. No ladies in the rooms. No pissing in the cuspidors and no discharging of firearms in the rooms. Not a rule, but I expect you to wash your face and hands before meals. Soap, water, and a roller towel will be provided. Have you any questions?"

Dan shook his head. "No, ma'am. I think you pretty much covered everything."

"Separate rooms or will you double up? The double-up price will be a dollar-fifty each."

"Two rooms," Dan said. He smiled and tried to lighten Mrs. Dale's mood. "I've heard Crow's snores."

"Your name is Crow?" the woman said.

"Yes, ma'am. I'm half Apache,"

Mrs. Dale's hand flew to the top of her chest. "Oh, dear Lord, will we all be murdered in our beds?"

"No ma'am," Dan said. "He's very tame. And he's half Scottish and loves to dance little jigs."

"If you say so . . . Mister . . ."

"Caine, ma'am. Dan Caine."

"Then you'd better come in and I'll show you to your rooms," Mrs. Dale said. She looked askance at Crow and added, "He can do little Scottish jigs if he's quiet about it, but please, no Apache war dances. I don't want to scare my other guests."

Including Dan Caine and Crow, five guests sat at Mrs. Dale's and shared a repast of mutton broth, roast beef with baked sweet potatoes, and apple pie for dessert. The beverage was a small glass of beer. Dan, always a picky eater, disliked the salty mutton broth, found the beef tough and the pie passable. Crow, his appetite the product of a hungry childhood, ate, with obvious relish, everything in sight.

The other three guests introduced themselves as Wilbur Thatcher, a drummer in ladies' undergarments, Israel Roberts, a local print shop owner and the youngest of the three, George Cole a bookkeeper with a strangely flat personality. But lingering over his beer, the young man took it on himself to warn the others about the perils of demon whiskey and loose women.

"Beware of dancing girls in the saloons," he said. "They're clean and pretty enough, but don't trust them if they offer you something more than a dance."

"Damn right," Thatcher said.

"Language, please, Mr. Thatcher," Mrs. Dale said.

"I beg your pardon, dear lady," Thatcher said.

"Well, anyway," Cole said, "many a poor fool has taken them up on that offer and woken the next day with an aching head, no clear memory of what happened, and a lot less money than he started out with. The girls always claim the man had too much fun and passed out from sheer exertion, but in fact they were drugged, dragged into an alley, and then rolled."

"Then it becomes a matter for the law," Mrs. Dale said, touching her beautiful hair.

Dan took the opportunity to sound out the woman on Bill Roche. With wide-eyed innocence, he said, "Who is the local sheriff?"

"City Marshal," Mrs. Dale said. "His name is Bill Roche."

George Cole said, "He loves the ladies, the shady kind."

"Is that a fact?" Mrs. Dale said. "I knew he was fond of drink, but I never heard that he's a bustle chaser."

"Some claim he came up from Texas under a cloud," Israel Roberts said. "I heard that not a week ago."

"Yes, I was told about that," Mrs. Dale said. "But as far as I know it's never been proved that he committed any crime whatsoever in Texas."

"Never proved, maybe, but mighty suspicious all the same," Roberts said.

"What happened, or is said to have happened, in Texas?" Dan said. "A shooting?"

Roberts said, "As I heard it, the story goes that when Roche was a lawman him and another sheriff's deputy by the name of Byron Woods rode into the Texas badlands in pursuit of three train robbers. A week later Roche showed up again without a scratch on him but there was no sign of Woods. Roche said they'd been bushwhacked and Woods had been killed. But there were rumors that the deputy had been lusting after Woods' pretty young wife and there was talk that he'd murdered Woods to get him out of the way. And worse was to come. When Mrs. Woods turned down Roche's offer of marriage, he later burst into her bedroom at night and raped her."

"Rape. What a horrible, harsh word that is," Mrs. Dale said, shuddering. "I hate the very sound of it."

"And so you should, dear lady," Roberts said. "It's a very serious offense, so serious that Roche narrowly escaped a lynch mob and ended up here in Tucson."

"Apaches give such men to the women of the tribe for punishment," Crow said. "The females use fire and sharp steel, and they are patient."

That last caused a lull in the conversation, every man present seeing disturbing images in his head. Dan filled the silence with another question.

"Did Roche investigate the murder of Dick Meadows, the old tinpan?"

Another lull, but this time more of a shocked silence.

The three men at the table quickly said their goodnights to their landlady and scattered like quail.

Dan smiled. "Was it something I said?"

"Some topics are not for conversation and are better left alone," Mrs. Dale said.

"Why? Because of Barton Clay?"

The woman looked as though she'd just been slapped. "Mr. Caine, feel free to use the parlor and you can smoke in there if you're so inclined." The woman rose to her feet and began to pick up plates and sighed. "I sometimes think my work is never done."

After Mrs. Dale left for the kitchen, Crow said, "I'd say there are a lot of scared folks around this burg."

Dan nodded, his face grim. "Seems like."

CHAPTER SIX

After a breakfast of bacon, beans, and soda biscuits, Dan Caine and Crow agreed that their first order of business was to talk with Bill Roche and state their intentions. It would be interesting to hear what the man had to say. If possible, Dan wanted to work within the law to ensure that the Clay brothers got the punishment they deserved. Talking to the city marshal and offering him their protection just might set the wheels in motion, depending on how nagging was the lawman's guilty conscience.

It should be noted here that most historians agree that Dan Caine miscalculated badly that day . . . a mistake that would come almighty close to costing him his life.

Before he and Crow left, Mrs. Dale told Dan that City Marshal Roche's office was in the courthouse at the corner of Court and Pennington streets, a two-story brick building on a stone foundation adorned with fancy gables and a flag-flying cupola. The building not only housed the court but also space for federal and Pima County officials and the city jail. She said that Dan couldn't miss the place since it was the only brick building in town and was within walking distance of the boardinghouse.

"Mr. Caine, I'll say one thing and one thing only," the woman said. "Bill Roche is not a nice man and one way or another he's getting rich off the county's three Cs . . . cattle, copper, and cotton, turning a blind eye to any and all wrongdoing. No respectable woman is safe around him, and he's mean enough to piss on a widow's kindling. So if you talk to him, mind your p's and q's and for your own safety, please don't wear your guns." Her homely face shut down. "That's all I have to say."

Dan and Crow walked through a new-aborning morning that was coming in clean before freight wagon wheels had a chance to lift the mustard-colored dust that blanketed the city. The courthouse would not have been impressive in a larger city, but in Tucson it dominated a surrounding landscape of small adobe houses and modest-sized plazas.

As they neared the building, Crow said, "Mrs. Dale doesn't think very highly of the marshal. We could be wasting our time."

"We'll give him his chance," Dan said. "Maybe he's changed his ways."

"Do you really believe that?"

"No."

"I've got my knife."

"Good. If Roche draws down on us, stick him in the belly."

"I've never stuck anybody before."

"There's a first time for everything. Shall we go in?"

The courthouse interior was surprisingly cool and still shadowy, yet to be fully illuminated by the rising sun. A roomy foyer, hung with portraits of old men with Rip Van Winkle beards, each with a small brass nameplate at the bottom of his picture frame, opened into a large, rectangular open space with office doors lining its walls. A wide staircase opposite the foyer led to the upper story and more offices. There was no sign of the jailhouse, and Dan guessed it was probably somewhere in the rear of the building. The place smelled musty, of stacked books and ancient documents and the ever-present odor of boiled cabbage that seemed to permeate every official premises in the West.

Dan and Crow stood in the middle of the floor at a loss, so many doors, so many painted names and titles, but a woman, dressed in a tan skirt and white shirt with puffed sleeves, came out of one of the doors, closed it softly behind her and said, "Can I help you, gentlemen?"

The expression on her haughty face betrayed the fact that she didn't consider a half-Indian wearing a bear-claw necklace and a man who dressed like a drover to be men of the gentler sort.

"We're here to see City Marshal Roche, ma'am," Dan said, touching his hat brim.

The woman visibly winced before she pointed to the far wall. "Third door on the left."

She gave Dan a withering glare and then stepped away, her heels clacking on the polished marble floor before she disappeared into one of the offices.

"I think she likes you, Dan," Crow said.

Dan grinned. "You noticed that too, huh?"

"What can I do for you gents?" City Marshal Bill Roche said. He was a big man, well over six feet, beefy across the shoulders, thick-lipped, heavy browed, sporting the huge dragoon mustache that was then popular among Western men. "Are you bounty hunters, and who did ye bring in?"

"No, we're not bounty hunters. My name is Dan Caine

and I'm the sheriff of Broken Back, a town in central Texas and this here is Crow, my deputy."

Roche smirked and put his inherent meanness on display. "And I'm supposed to be impressed by that?"

"No, you're not," Dan said. "Broken Back is a small town, but we believe in law and order."

"Unlike Tucson," Crow said.

Roche scowled. "You're a breed, ain't you? I never could abide a mouthy breed." Then to Dan, "State your business."

"My business is to get justice for an old man by the name of Dick Meadows," Dan said. "Does that name ring a bell?"

"Can't say that it does," Roche said, too smoothly.

"He was murdered by the Clay brothers."

"Who are they?"

"They're Barton Clay's sons."

"The rancher?"

"You know it," Dan said.

"All I know is that he's county. I'd advise you to speak with the Pima County sheriff, a man named Tucker Steele. Maybe he's heard of your man Meadows. I sure as hell haven't."

"Where is Steele?"

"Right now, I believe he's in Fort Worth. He has a sister there who keeps poorly and is like to die from consumption." Roche shrugged his massive shoulders. "I don't know when he'll be back."

"The Clay brothers were charged with murder and went on trial in this courthouse," Dan said, his uncertain temper barely under control. "You don't recollect that?"

"A lot of lawbreakers go on trial here," Roche said. "I

can't keep track of them all. So an old tinpan dies, who cares?"

"How did you know Dick Meadows was a tinpan?" Dan said.

"You must've said it."

"No, I didn't."

"He didn't," Crow said.

"Then maybe I heard something about an old miner being killed. At the time, I didn't pay it any heed."

"Maybe you paid heed when you heard that the Clay brothers murdered him."

"I think . . ." Roche frowned. "Yeah, I seem to remember something about a crazy old coot threatening folks with a shotgun for trespassing on his property. Somebody killed him sure enough, but it wasn't Barton Clay's sons. Yeah, that was it, I remember now, they were put on trial and then acquitted after the real murderer confessed."

Dan was surprised. "The real murderer?"

"Now I'm thinking on it, the man was drunk and talking loud in the mercantile bar at Wheeler's Crossing, just a few miles east of here," Roche said. "He told Luther Wheeler that murdering old man Meadows was the dirtiest trick he ever played. He figured the tinpan had a stash of gold hidden away in his cabin, but he never found any."

"What was this man's name?" Dan said.

"Well, since it was a county matter, I wasn't paying that much attention, but I think it was Bowman or Boland, something like that."

"Where is he now?" Dan said.

"Dead."

"Was he hung?"

"Hell, no. There were a couple of Barton Clay's punchers at the bar and they heard everything the man said. So they figured to make a citizen's arrest, but Bowman, if that was his name, was having none of it. He cursed them out for being low-down eavesdroppers and went for his gun. But the punchers were way too quick for him and shot him down, ending his dirty tricks forever."

"Besides the Clay punchers, who else witnessed this?" Dan said.

"Luther Wheeler and a couple of his whores. They heard the man's confession and then saw him die in the gunfight."

"Convenient," Dan said. "Maybe too convenient. I suppose the Clay brothers were immediately released."

"The guilty party had confessed to the murder, so they were innocent. Why hold them?" Roche said.

"Innocent. That's a joke. Later, right here in Tucson, the brothers boasted about killing Dick Meadows," Dan said. "How many people witnessed that?"

"Mister, you're starting to bore me," Roche said. "What's your interest in the death of the old man anyway?"

"He saved my life and then he raised me. He didn't raise me right, but I owe him," Dan said. "I believe some drunken drifter was shot in or near Wheeler's Crossing by Barton Clay's gunmen and witnesses were paid or frightened into saying they heard the man confess to murder. Justice wasn't done and I'm here to see that the Clay brothers pay for their crime. And I'll start with Luther Wheeler. And then this man here."

Dan took the letter from his shirt pocket and tossed it across Roche's desk. "He's a rancher named Toby Reynolds wrote that. Read it, Marshal."

"Damn, Caine, but you're persistent."

"Read it, Marshal. Hear what Reynolds has to say."

Roche picked up the piece of paper with his fingertips as though it was an unclean thing. He read the contents and said, "Toby Reynolds owns a two-by-twice spread a few miles east of town. He's long been jealous of Barton Clay's Lazy C brand and is suspected of now and then rustling a few head from Clay's range. He's never been caught, but he's lucky Barton always laughed off the loss of a couple of unbranded mavericks and hasn't hanged him." He tossed the letter back to Dan. "It's not worth the paper it's written on. Reynolds hates the Clays, and I wouldn't believe a word he tells me about them."

Roche watched a brewer's dray unload beer barrels at the saloon next door and then said, "Talk to Reynolds, talk to anyone you want, just don't expect any help from me. I don't get involved in county matters."

Dan shook his head, his eyes cold on the marshal. "How can you live with yourself, Roche? You're a sworn lawman, yet you stood by and did nothing while you watched three guilty men get away with murder."

"My conscience doesn't bother me none, and I sleep well o' nights," Roche said. "Now take your breed and get out of my sight before I lock up both of you."

"On what charge?" Dan said.

"Don't worry, I'll think of something," Roche said.

After Dan Caine and Crow left his office, City Marshal Bill Roche sat at his desk, staring at the wall, his eyes unfocused, thinking. The hick sheriff was bad news. He could cause trouble unless he was stopped. It was probably not a good plan to kill him, that might raise awkward questions, but he could be scared into leaving Tucson. Like a man tarred and feathered, he'd never come back. Roche reached a decision.

It was time to talk with Barton Clay.

CHAPTER SEVEN

"He's nothing," Barton Clay said. "A hayseed from a one-horse Texas town. I can't believe you made me call my sons in from the range for him. What's his name again?"

"Dan Caine. He's the sheriff of Broken Back," Bill Roche said.

"Never heard of him or his town," Clay said.

He was a tall, well-built man with a sensitive, intelligent face and alert blue eyes. He wore a full beard and a thick shock of blond hair that gave him the appearance of an Eastern college professor. But looks were deceiving. In his time Barton Clay was responsible for the deaths of fifty-eight men, not counting Indians or Mexicans. He had hanged or shot nesters, rustlers, outlaws, wannabe gunmen, chicken thieves, and unfortunates who'd had the bad luck to get in his way. But as historians of the more knowledgeable sort will attest, Barton Clay was unique in the annals of the West in that, despite the death toll, he never once pulled the trigger on a man or put a rope around his neck.

Killing was a dirty job he left to others.

Roche sighed. "Mr. Clay, Caine is trouble. I can sense it. He says he won't rest until he sees your sons hang for the murder of Dick Meadows. Right now, he's more than willing to muddy the waters."

"Pa, I can gun him, get him out of the way," Decker Clay said. He was his father's youngest son, his good looks spoiled by green, reptilian eyes and a hard, cruel mouth. He had killed three men, a couple of nesters, and a San Antonio bartender over the affections of a loose woman.

Barton Clay looked at Roche. "What do you think?"

The marshal shook his head. "I'm not in favor of it. Hick town sheriff or not, Caine is a lawman, and gunning him could lead to complications."

"What kind of complications, Roche?" This from Ben Clay, the oldest son. A drunken brawler, it was him who had the idea of holding Dick Meadows' toes to the fire. Like his brothers Decker and Pete, he was a handsome man but fancied himself a hard case and at twenty-eight years old he was in line to inherit the ranch when his pa retired or passed on. He was hell on horses and women, and the whores he frequented were afraid of him and his violent, thunderous temper.

"I'm sure there were men in his town who knew where he was going and why," Roche said. "If he doesn't return, they could come looking for him."

"So what?" Ben Clay said. "We can take care of them rubes too."

"No, Ben, the marshal is right," Barton Clay said. "Things could get messy and questions asked. The last thing I want is somebody prying into the drifter we killed."

"The sacrificial lamb," Pete Clay said. He was much cleverer than his brothers, did all the ranch's bookkeeping, and his father depended on him to keep track of twenty-five thousand cattle and two hundred quarter horses.

"He was a no account who saved your lives," Barton Clay said.

"As I said, he was the sacrificial lamb," Pete said.

"Boys, I shouldn't be listening to this," Roche said.

"Yes, you should," Pete said. "You're in as deep as the rest of us."

"I still don't understand why you had to murder old man Meadows in the first place?" Roche said.

"Murder is a strong word, Bill, maybe too strong," Barton said.

"Then what word would you use?"

"Accident. There was some horseplay, and my sons accidentally punched his ticket." Barton sighed. "Somebody else confessed to the crime, now let's all forget it."

"Mr. Clay . . ."

"Soon to be Governor Clay, Bill."

"Yes, and congratulations. The trouble about Meadows is that Dan Caine won't forget it."

"Why the hell not? He was old and he was sick, and he was worthless."

"Caine set store by the old man. He said Meadows saved his life when he was just a youngster and then he raised him."

"He didn't have any gold stashed away," Roche said.

"I know. Me, I think he spread that rumor himself," Pete Clay said. "If he did, it was a stupid thing to do. Got him killed for it."

"How the hell did we know the old coot's heart would give out?" Decker said.

"You shouldn't have tried to rob him in the first place," Barton Clay said.

"It was just a fun thing we done, Pa," Decker said. "Call it a good joke that went bad."

"Listen up, Dan Caine is no joke," Roche said.

"He's not? So, tell us why, Bill."

"As I said, old man Meadows raised him, and Caine is beholden to him. He's a problem that needs to be solved, but I don't want another killing. He says he plans to talk with Luther Wheeler and . . . you ain't gonna believe this . . . Toby Reynolds."

"Toby Reynolds!" Barton Clay said. "Why does he want to talk with him?"

"Reynolds wrote Caine a letter, blaming your sons for the murder of Meadows. I saw it and read it. I didn't like it then, and I don't like it now."

"Reynolds is a damn snake in the grass and a rustler to boot. I should've hung him years ago."

"Don't do it now," Roche said. "Or at least wait until the Caine business is taken care of."

"We can solve it without killing," Barton Clay said.

Decker smiled. "You always find a way, Pa."

"Because no matter the problem there's always a way to solve it."

"So let's hear it, Mr. Clay," Roche said.

"All right, Bill, on your way back to town stop at Wheeler's Crossing and talk with Luther. Tell him this, now listen carefully, when Caine comes out to talk to him, he's to put a whore on a hoss and have her come here to tell us about it. Then double quick, we'll ride for the Crossing and catch up with Caine there."

"And do what?" Roche said. "Not another killing."

"Nothing so crude, Bill. No, what we'll do is beat Dan Caine until he can no longer stand or talk or remember the name his mama gave him. What's left of him will go back to Texas in a gunnysack, and he'll never come back this way again."

"Caine has a big Apache breed with him, calls him his deputy," Roche said.

"Good," Clay said. "The breed can carry him back to . . . where the hell is it again?"

"Broken Back," Roche said.

"Yeah, he can take what's left of Dan Caine to Broken Back."

"Roche, tell Wheeler to put the whore on his fastest horse." Ruben Webb spoke for the first time. Medium height, medium build, brown hair and eyes, he looked ordinary, but was almighty sudden and a stone-cold killer. "We don't want to ride to the Crossing only to find the bird has flown."

"I don't know when that might be," Roche said. "I mean I don't know when Caine will be at the Crossing."

"Whenever it is, we'll be waiting," Barton Clay said.

"A whore on a hoss," Decker Clay giggled. "That's funny."

Barton Clay was not amused. He stood up from his leather easy chair and looked out the parlor window. His land. As far as the eye could see and then farther into hazy distance, mile after mile of shaggy green grass crossed by underground streams and fat cattle. It was the foundation of an empire that would one day spread over all the Arizona Territory south of the Mogollon Rim. Barton smiled. His land. The birthplace of his empire. His destiny. Without turning, he said, "Ruben, Toby Reynolds could become a problem. Take care of it."

"Sure thing, boss," Webb said.

So, now it was old Toby Reynolds. Bill Roche's hands trembled. Once again, he'd be forced to plunge headlong into the scorching flames of Barton Clay's lake of fire.

Chapter Eight

Mary Jane Hillman was a whore by necessity, not choice.

The alternative was grim, a return to the Virginia cotton mills where young girls grew old in a year and regularly died of smallpox, typhoid, typhus, or overwork, spending sixteen hours a day, six days a week serving dangerous spinning machines. In a noisy working environment, the air saturated with cotton dust, women caught mill fever, or brown lung disease, that left them gasping, struggling for breath and ensured a long, lingering, and terrible death. Her mother contracted the illness and Mary Jane entered the mill when she was twelve to help support a family of eight, including a sickly father, working day and night, subject to harsh discipline and abuse. At sixteen, after both her parents died and her brothers and sisters were forced into workhouses, she left the mill and became a street-walker in Richmond. Ten years later she moved west and ended up in Tucson where she was soon recruited by Luther Wheeler who promised her the world and delivered only degradation and occasional violence. When City Marshal Bill Roche visited the Crossing after a talk with the rancher Barton Clay, Mary Jane looked much older than her years and was no longer in great demand by high-rolling clients.

Wheeler spoke at length with Roche behind closed doors and when the lawman left, he called his five ladies together in his parlor for a talk.

"First things first," Wheeler said. "Can any of you ride a horse? What about you, Daisy? You were a farmer's daughter."

Daisy Tweed, a hard-faced blonde who had a talent for playing the piano said, "Among other things, Luther. Yeah, I was a farmer's daughter, and yeah, I can ride a horse."

"Anyone else?" Wheeler said.

"I can ride," Mary Jane said. "But I haven't done it for years."

"How did you manage that? You were a street whore," Daisy said.

"A smiling man took time to teach me and he also taught me to shoot."

"What happened to him?"

"I don't know. I woke up one morning and he was gone."

"All right, that's two," Wheeler said, disturbed by whores' talk. "Anyone else? No? Then Daisy you're my first choice and Mary Jane, I'll use you if Daisy isn't available for any reason."

"I'll be available," Daisy said. "Where am I riding?"

"When the time comes, to the Clay ranch."

Daisy made a face. "That's not far."

"I know, but I want you there fast."

"How much for my time?" Daisy said.

Wheeler's apparent good humor evaporated instantly,

and he scowled, "You'll do as you're told, and no backtalk or you'll be out in the street with a pair of black eyes right quick."

Daisy was alarmed. "I was only joking."

"Then don't. Joking doesn't become whores."

Mary Jane took the pressure off Daisy. "Why the sudden need to ride to the Clay ranch, Luther? We can do that any time." She smiled, a rare event. "In fact, some nights it seems that the whole ranch comes here."

"A man, two men, one of them a breed, will visit the Crossing sometime soon to talk with me about the death of Dick Meadows," Wheeler said.

"The Clay riders found the murderer and shot him," Rose Richards said. She was very young, a petite brunette with large, permanently startled brown eyes. The story is that by 1907 she ended up a widow with a small ranch and a hundred head of Herefords.

"And that shooting is what the white man wants to talk about," Wheeler said. "His name is Dan Caine and he was raised by old man Meadows. He's looking into the circumstances of Meadows' death, and Barton Clay wants to help him. Marshal Roche told him Caine wants to talk to me, so Mr. Clay decided to meet him here and save Caine the ride."

"I don't think Meadows ever came here?" Rose said.

"He didn't. He was too old for whoring, I guess."

Another woman, blond and wearing a black corset and red split skirt, laughed and said, "I thought men were never too old for whoring."

"Meadows was. He was about a hundred," Wheeler said, grinning. "Hell, he was half-dead even before he was murdered."

That last brought a ripple of feminine laughter and when it stopped, Mary Jane Hillman said, "I can't help but feel sorry for the old man. He didn't deserve to be murdered."

Wheeler said, "Men who didn't deserve it are killed every day. This is the frontier where the weak die and the strong survive."

"It's a law of nature," Daisy said.

"It's a law of the West," Wheeler said.

"True," Daisy said.

"Thanks to me, you women have it easy," Wheeler said.

"Whoring ain't easy," Daisy said. "Some drunks are violent, some stink and some are just insane."

"That's why Luther is our protector," Rose Richards said.

"Do we need protecting?" Mary Jane said.

"All women need protecting, especially whores," Wheeler said.

"I thought the British Bulldog .44 in my purse was all the protection I needed," Mary Jane said.

"Maybe it is, if you can hit with it," Wheeler said.

"I can hit with it," Mary Jane said. "Across a bedroom."

"Anybody tell you about Tess O'Reilly?" Wheeler said. "She's the only whore that shot a man in one of my rooms. Your room in fact, Mary Jane."

"Since my room is only nine feet across, she didn't have to be much of a shot."

"And that is so," Wheeler said. "But Tess emptied all six barrels of a .36 pepperpot at a drunk teamster who wanted to whip her with a riding crop and she didn't miss with any of them. Tess could shoot."

"Did the teamster die?" Rose said.

"He surely did, but it took him all night and most of the

next day. We buried him out back with his riding crop. That was Tess's idea."

"Where is Tess O'Reilly now?" Mary Jane said.

"She married a peg-legged man by the name of Sam Berrycloth and then I lost track of her," Wheeler said. "She was a good whore, was Tess. I reckoned she'd dress out around three hundred pounds, but still, a good whore." He rose to his feet. "All right, ladies, get yourselves ready and let me see those smiles. It's Friday night, and you know how busy you'll be."

Mary Jane Hillman forced a smile. And died another little death.

CHAPTER NINE

After Dan Caine and Crow left the courthouse, delicious odors wafting from the O.K. Restaurant at the corner of Church Plaza and Mesilla Street convinced them that they were hungry and that hungry men don't make good decisions.

To their surprise the grinning proprietor was Chinese, as were his staff of waiters, dressed in white shirts, black pants, and white aprons.

Dan and Crow were ushered to a table in a room with yellow walls and paper lanterns hung from the ceiling. The interior smelled spicy, like cinnamon, and when the kitchen door opened Dan saw a pair of cooks almost invisible behind billows of steam.

Even sitting, Dan was taller than the waiter who stood beside the table, his head cocked to one side like an inquisitive sparrow. "Beef stew?" Dan said.

As he half expected, the waiter shook his head. "No beef stew. Twenty-five cent special lunch today . . . pork ball soup and sliced pork with melon fried rice. Tea to drink." The waiter smiled. "You like."

"Want to try it, Crow?" Dan said.

"Sounds good to me."

"Everything sounds good to you, so long as it's food."

"You're picky, Dan. Peck, peck, peck, you eat like a bird."

"All right, we'll have the special," Dan said.

"Good choice," the waiter said. "You wait and see. You like."

The food was good, the first Chinese dishes Dan had ever tasted, and its delicate flavors suited his finicky appetite. Crow also enjoyed it, finishing off the last of his pork and rice with a satisfied grunt.

To Dan's delight, the tea was served in tiny porcelain cups and as he enjoyed it, he built a cigarette and from behind a cloud of blue smoke said, "We're not going to get any help from City Marshal Roche. He knows more than he's saying but we'll never drag it out of him so long as he's taking Barton Clay's money'"

"He's a coyote," Crow said. "The Apaches call the coyote a trickster."

"He's all of that," Dan said. "A trickster who helped the Clays concoct their confession story." He picked up his tiny teacup between his thumb and forefinger and drank, then, "We'll head out to Wheeler's Crossing tomorrow right after breakfast."

"Wheeler must know who confessed to Dick Meadows' murder," Crow said.

"And how the so-called killer died. I believe he was a nameless drifter who didn't attack Barton Clay's men like they say but was shot down in cold blood."

"What about Toby Reynolds, the rancher who wrote the letter? When do we talk to him?"

"Tomorrow, before I meet Luther Wheeler. I remember Toby as a friendly, peaceable feller, and I don't want to get him involved unless I have to," Dan said. "Besides, he must be pushing seventy by now, a bit too old to be taking on the Clays. But Toby knows this town, and all I expect from him is advice. He'll tell me who's on the side of the law and wants to see justice done."

"Could be Toby Reynolds will help, but maybe not. What's more certain is that Luther Wheeler will offer no help at all."

"I must talk to him because he could lay another murder at the Clay doorstep, the man who was killed to spring Barton's sons."

"Dan, the Clay punchers keep Wheeler in business," Crow said. "He's gonna keep his mouth shut, depend on it."

"All I'll probably get is shut doors, I know, but this thing's got to be done legally."

"And if it legally doesn't pan out?"

"I've been studying on that and the answer is, I don't know."

"You can't take on a big cattleman like Barton Clay with a gun. He can throw twenty hard cases against you, maybe more. And he's got Ruben Webb."

"Crow, don't you think I know that?"

"The law won't help us, Wheeler won't help us, so why are we still in Tucson?"

"Because if you give me some time, I'll figure a way. Maybe I can get the attention and support for a new trial from the country sheriff and some of the more respectable citizens of the town."

"And if that don't work and you're standing here in Tucson like a bride left at the altar, what then?"

Dan smiled. "Shouldn't that be bridegroom?"

"Bride, groom, the question is the same."

"Crow, I feel strongly about this," Dan said. "For all his

faults and they were many, Dick Meadows didn't deserve to die the way he did."

"We know all that," Crow said. "And we know that he saved your life and then took you roaming all over the frontier and now you feel obligated to punish his killers. But you still haven't answered the question."

"If I have to go it alone?"

"Yes, but with me to keep you away from bad company."

"I'll wage war on the Clays, and that includes their pa. One way or another the murder of Dick Meadows will come back to haunt them."

Crow lifted his porcelain teacup and drank. It looked like a thimble in his huge hand. "There will be no prisoners taken in that lopsided war," he said.

"Nope, there won't. The living will have won the battles and the losers will all be dead."

Crow's eyes were bleak. "Dan, do you really think Dick Meadows, by all accounts a miserable human being, is worth risking your life for?"

"Worth dying for, you mean?"

"Yeah, I'm dancing to that tune."

"Helen asked me that same question . . . is Dick Meadows worth dying for? And my answer was the same . . . of course he isn't. He was a mean, nasty and blasphemous old man, but he saved my life and I owe him. As I see it, it's a responsibility I can't just shrug my shoulders and walk away from."

"I understand," Crow said. "I guess."

"There has to be a reckoning, Crow," Dan said. "I have no other choice and that's the truth of it."

CHAPTER TEN

Ruben Webb was an assassin of infinite patience and expertise. But he had a code he lived by . . . and others died by . . . he would not gun a man unless someone else paid for the bullet. And Barton Clay was paying for the cartridge in the chamber of Webb's .44-40 Winchester.

It was dark, under a gibbous moon, when Webb ground-tied his horse and made his way to Toby Reynolds' modest ranch house. No oil lamps glowed inside, and the two front windows were black rectangles and that touched a smile to Webb's thin lips. Like sodbusters, it seemed that Reynolds and his missus believed in early to bed, early to rise.

Level grassy ground, with many dusty bald patches, stretched away from the house for fifty yards before rising to a shallow escarpment crested with live oak and mesquite. Webb found a hiding place in the brush around the trees and lay flat, his rifle pushed out in front of him. Judging by the moon, he put the time at just after midnight. It would be at least six and a half hours to first light and now all he could do was wait.

Long, dark, dreary hours dragged past as Webb kept up his vigil. A man who could go days without sleep, staying awake presented no hardship. A faint breeze rustled in the oaks, in the distance a pair of hunting coyotes yelped back and forth and once a frightened jackrabbit bounded through the brush close enough that it gave Webb a start.

Finally, the long night shaded into morning and washed away the shadows around the ranch house. The breeze had picked up, and the oaks rustled restlessly above Webb's still form. Both windows were now showing a yellowish orange tint, and the stone chimney smoked as more wood was thrown into the stove. Webb consulted his watch, its thin gold hands now visible. It was six-thirty, high time Toby Reynolds was up and about and doing his chores. Unlike Barton Clay he could not afford year-round hands, and it was his practice to hire a couple at roundup.

Damn it, where was the man?

Ruben Webb shouldered his rifle and sighted in on the ranch house. Unless the rancher was in bed sick, any time now he would head for the barn or gather breakfast eggs from the nearby chicken coop.

Ruben Webb waited. There was no hurry. Like the Grim Reaper, he observed closely and bided his time.

The ranch house door opened and Toby Reynolds, a tough, knotty little banty rooster, his iron-gray hair turning white as he aged, stepped outside. The man had an egg basket in one hand, a rifle in the other.

Webb smiled and laid the sights on him.

Reynolds stood at the door for a few moments and looked up, staring at the red-streaked sky. He wore white long johns, a battered hat, and scuffed boots and he scratched his belly before he walked on, showing his back to Webb.

The killer placed the sights between Reynolds' shoulder blades. His finger took up some slack on the trigger, and he let out some breath and . . .

Toby Reynolds turned quickly, and his far-seeing gaze went directly to Webb's position on the rise. The assassin was stunned. The old coot had the instincts of a lobo wolf.

The rancher dropped the basket and started to bring up his rifle, but he was too slow and too late.

Webb fired. Fired again. And again.

Three shots, all of them hits, formed a cloverleaf on Reynolds' chest. The old man was scrawny, thin from front to back, and all three of Webb's bullets went right through him and exited his back. Six wounds in total and when Toby Reynolds thudded into the dirt, he was already a dead man.

Even historians hostile to guns and gunmen agree that Ruben Webb's shooting at a distance of some sixty yards was superb. Three hits in as many seconds found their target, all of them deadly shots, and the kill was clean. By any standards, it was efficient, professional work.

As Dan Caine was destined to discover, Ruben Webb was a force to be reckoned with.

Webb saw Mrs. Reynolds, a plump matron with gray hair, leave the house and run screaming to her dead husband. But his work was done, the order obeyed, and he melted into the glowing morning, found his horse, and headed back to the Clay ranch.

CHAPTER ELEVEN

After an early breakfast of bacon sandwiches and coffee, Dan Caine and Crow walked to the livery stable, saddled their horses, and were on their way west to the Reynolds spread just after sunup.

At noon, under a hot sun that blackened their shirts with sweat, the Reynolds ranch house came into view in the distance.

"Crow, Ma Reynolds bakes the best peach pie you ever tasted," Dan said. "And her apple pie is nothing to turn your nose up at either."

"I'll settle for one or t'other," Crow said. "And a cup of coffee to go with it."

"Toby always has a Havana cigar for visitors, and he keeps a jug of busthead handy as well."

Crow smiled. "My kind of man."

"You'll like them. Toby and Ellie are real nice people and over the years they've worked hard to make their place pay. When I visited here as a child even Dick Meadows liked the Reynolds and that's saying something. I reckon they were the only people he ever cottoned to in his life." Dan grinned. "A word of warning though, Toby loves to sing, but he doesn't do it very well."

"What does he sing?"

"His favorite is, 'She's More to Be Pitied Than Censured,' but he's got scores of others. Ellie plays the piano for him."

Crow, a farseeing man, suddenly stood in the stirrups. "Hello, what's this?"

Dan peered into the distance. "What do you see?"

"There's something wrong. A man lying on the ground and a woman kneeling beside him."

Dan didn't wait to hear more. He kicked his horse into a gallop, Crow right behind him.

Dan Caine drew rein, and his horse stopped on a dime, throwing up an exclamation of dust. He jumped out of the saddle and three quick strides brought him to Ellie Reynolds' side.

He husband lay on his back, his white long johns scarlet with blood. Ellie turned her face to Dan. She was pale, tearless, stricken, a woman who'd stepped beyond the threshold of grief. "I can't move him," she said. And then, sounding like a question, "You're here. After all these years."

"I was hoping for a happier reunion, Ellie," Dan said.

He took a knee beside the dead man. Toby Reynolds was a small man and his killer's bullets had mangled him. Crow's shadow fell across him. "The shooter was up on the rise, hidden in brush," he said. He opened his fisted hand and revealed three brass cartridge cases. "Forty-four-forty."

Dan nodded. Then, "Ellie we'll take Toby inside. I'll lift him."

"He was such a small man," the woman said.

"Yes, he was," Dan said. "But he had a big heart and he had sand."

He picked up Reynolds' body as though he lifted a child and followed Ellie into the house and then laid out the body in the bedroom, on top of a patchwork quilt that the woman had made herself. Dan noticed that one of the patches was red, in the shape of a heart, and had embroidered on it in blue yarn, TOBY & ELLIE 1830. He guessed, correctly, that it was the year of their marriage.

Ellie pulled off Toby's boots and laid them by the bed where he always kept them. She then got a folded white sheet from a closet and spread it over him.

"Ellie," Dan said, "do you want me to get a preacher from town?"

The old woman shook her head. "Toby didn't have much time for preachers when he was alive. I won't force one on him now he's dead."

Dan hesitated, framing his words, and then said, "Ellie, we need to lay Toby to rest."

The woman's stare was penetrating. "Who killed him, Dan?"

"A man with a rifle," Crow said. "That's all we know." He was trying desperately to shield Dan from what he knew was to come and failed.

"Who killed my husband, Dan?" Ellie said. Her voice sounded strange, hollow, like a whisper in a sepulcher "And why are you here?"

"Toby sent me a letter, Ellie," Dan said.

"What kind of letter?"

"He told me that Dick Meadows had been murdered by the Clay boys and that they walked free to boast of it."

"And why are you here?"

"I'm here to see justice done."

"Who else read this letter?"

"I showed it to City Marshal Roche."

Ellie absorbed that without a change in her facial expression. "I have coffee on the stove," she said. She led the way out of the bedroom into a spacious living room with a large stone fireplace and a dining table and chairs. The kitchen was at the far end of the building dominated by a large stove and shelves filled with crockery and an assortment of pots and pans. There were framed prints on the walls, ornaments on the mantel, and a shelf holding books, all revealing the kind of people who lived there.

Ellie seated Dan and Crow at the table, laid cups and saucers in front of them and then poured coffee. She left and returned with a pie, plates, and forks. "Peach," she said. "It's Toby's favorite."

Ellie placed a generous wedge of pie on each plate and said, "I do hope you enjoy it."

Crow was the first to comment. "Excellent pie, Mrs. Reynolds," he said.

Dan with little appetite, nodded agreement.

Ellie had been holding herself together, but the strain was too much and she broke. She sprang off her chair, knocking it over in her haste, and yelled, "Damn you to hell, Dan Caine! Why did you come here?"

Dan was suddenly at a loss for words. "Ellie . . ."

"If you hadn't come to the territory, my husband would still be alive."

"It's . . . it's something I have to do," Dan said. "Dick Meadows saved my life and I owe him."

"And how many more people have to die until you get your revenge? You know and I know that Dick wasn't worth that kind of devotion. He probably saved your life, but he gave you no childhood, no love. To him you were just another orphan to take on all the dirty or dangerous jobs he didn't want to do himself. I remember when he staked you out as bear bait and the number of times you were nearly stung to death gathering wild honey for his damned coffee. He believed that there was no God and that human beings were just animals like any other. He was a cursing, profane, soulless man, and I hope he burns in hell. You want justice for that kind of man, he who never gave it to anyone else? Now my husband lies cold and dead on our bed and you and Dick Meadows killed him."

Crow rose to his feet and put his arm around Ellie's shoulder. The distraught woman did not attempt to pull away.

"Mrs. Reynolds, Dan did not want to get your husband involved," Crow said. "But what he didn't count on was City Marshal Roche's treachery. Dan feels he owes Dick Meadows his life, and it's for him to figure out the right or the wrong of the thing. In the meantime, if blame has to be laid at someone's doorstep it's got to be Barton Clay's."

"Ellie, I reckon Roche told Clay about the letter Toby wrote me," Dan said. "The letter was your husband's death warrant and if I could go back in time, I would never have shown it to Bill Roche. I made a bad decision, and it cost Toby his life."

"Barton Clay always hated my husband. He tried to buy our range a dozen times, and Toby always refused. Then Clay accused him of rustling and tried to use the courts to take it, but Toby beat him every time and Barton never forgave or forgot that. He's a big, important man who wants to be bigger and more important, and he hates little people like Toby and me who stand in his way."

Ellie looked at Dan. "And now Toby is dead."

"I'm sorry, Ellie," Dan said. "Deeply sorry."

"Right now, Dan, sorry doesn't cut it," Ellie said. "I need time. I need time to think. Right now, I can't think, I can only feel. And I feel that I don't want you here and will never want you here."

The cabin had darkened, and outside the sky was black. Thunder rumbled in the distance, announcing its coming.

"Ellie, we have a burying to do," Dan said.

"No, not you, Dan, not you. Not today." Ellie stepped from under Crow's arm and said, "You're half white man, half something else, Comanche maybe."

"Half Apache and as you say, half white man," Crow said.

"Will you help me bury my husband? I can't do it alone."

"Of course," Crow said. Then, his voice plaintive, "Mrs. Reynolds. I think Dan . . ."

"Today . . . how do I feel?" Ellie said. "I feel the man who helped kill Toby should not bury him. Dan, I hope you understand."

A knife twisting in his belly, Dan nodded. "I understand."

"Listen to that clamor," Ellie said. She looked uneasy, haunted.

"It's only the thunderstorm," Crow said

"No, it's not. It's the terrible roar of damned souls," Ellie said.

"I'm wet because I was digging a grave," Crow said. "How come you're soaked, Dan? You should've stayed in the cabin."

"I figured if you and Ellie got drenched by the storm, then so should I," Dan said.

The sky had cleared, the afternoon sun shone, and a breeze rippled the prairie grass.

"We'll be dry by the time we reach Tucson," Crow said.

"Uh-huh."

"Don't feel like talking, do you?"

"Not much."

"Mrs. Reynolds concerns me," Crow said. "Her dead husband will sleep on her pillow for the rest of her life and she just ain't thinking right."

"Her husband was murdered this morning. She hasn't had time to think."

"I understand that. But I don't think she'll ever get over it. You know what she said to me? She said she'll never stand over a hot stove ever again on account of how she's got nobody to cook for."

"It's worrisome," Dan said.

"Over where we buried Mr. Reynolds, I saw another grave, it was real small. Looked like a child's grave."

"That was from a time ago after Ellie delivered a baby girl that was born dead. She was getting up in years then, and she and Toby never had another. Maybe right now, up in heaven, Toby's bouncing that babe on his knee and they're both laughing and having themselves a time."

"It's good to think that way," Crow said.

"It helps the hurt," Dan said.

CHAPTER TWELVE

"Did you take care of business?" Barton Clay said. He looked huge, a hulking giant beside the much smaller Ruben Webb.

"He's as dead as three rifle bullets in the chest can make him, boss," Webb said. "Who's next? The rube?"

"No, Caine is lawman and I've always shied clear of killing a man who wears a star," Clay said. "There are too many questions asked. Texas Rangers stick their noses in, and there's always a danger that folks will come looking for their sheriff or marshal or whatever. I want rid of him, beat him so badly he'll never want to come back to Tucson. Are you catching my drift?"

An abstemious man, Webb drank coffee from a thin china cup and glanced out the parlor window. Half a dozen hooting and hollering hands sat on the corral fence and watched another put a pretty, two-year-old paint mare through her paces. Above the ranch, the sky was blue with just a few cottony clouds, all traces of the recent thunderstorm gone except for some patches of rapidly drying mud.

Webb gingerly settled his cup on the saucer and then

looked over at Clay. "I understand, boss, but I'm not a pugilist. That's kind of out of my line."

"The hands and my sons will take care of that bit of business," Clay said. "I want that half-Indian of Caine's to load him onto the train piece by piece. When he reaches . . . what's the name of that damned burg?"

"Broken Back."

"Yeah, Broken Back. His rube pardners can put him together again."

Webb grinned. "Humpty Dumpty sat on a wall . . ."

Clay said, "Humpty Dumpty had a great fall . . ."

"All the king's horses and all the king's men . . ."

"Couldn't put Humpty together again."

Barton Clay laughed. "Why the hell do we remember that?"

"Anybody who had a mother remembers that," Webb said.

"Well, Humpty Dumpty is in for a great fall," Clay said. "At Wheeler's Crossing." He picked up an envelope from the side table next to him and passed it to Webb. "Five-hundred-dollar bonus for the kill and another five hundred because it was Toby Reynolds who died. I plan to move cattle onto his range tomorrow."

"What about the old lady?" Webb said.

"Old ladies have accidents and sometimes they even shoot themselves out of grief. Too bad, I remember Ellie made a powerful good peach pie."

Webb shoved the envelope inside his shirt and said, "Do you want me at Wheeler's Crossing?"

Clay shook his head. "No, I don't want you there. I have an empire to build, and I'll need your gun beside me every step of the way. You're fast on the draw, Ruben, and as a shootist you're way too valuable for me to risk damage to your gun hand. Leave the roughhousing to the punchers and my sons." The big rancher's smile was unpleasant. "They've all kicked the tar out of men and left them crippled before."

"A bullet's neater," Webb said.

"Maybe. But not for Humpty Dumpty," Barton Clay said, grinning.

Webb held up the tall, china coffeepot and said, "Boss?"

Clay shook his head.

Webb poured himself a cup and said, "Do you mind if I give you some advice?"

The big rancher was wary. "It depends on the advice. I don't want to hear anything personal, mind."

"Not personal. It's business."

"Then advise away. I'm listening."

"We're spending too much time talking about a no-account lawman from a hick town and what he's gonna say and what he's gonna do. The truth is that he ain't that important. I understand the need to blow out Toby Reynolds' candle since he could've become a nuisance . . ."

"And I needed his range," Clay said.

"Yeah, now that's important and worth talking about. But this Dan Caine . . . well, we're making a timber wolf out of a maiden aunt's lapdog."

"So what do you suggest?" Clay said, a half-smile on his lips.

"I suggest I meet Caine at Wheeler's place, gun him, and then bury his carcass out back under a hackberry tree." Webb grinned. "Somebody comes looking for him, we say the sheriff left and we don't know where he's gone and we hope he's all right because he was a right nice feller. Problem solved."

"It's a way and a good way," Clay said. "But I still don't

want to take any chances. You'd also have to gun the breed and then things get a tad complicated. No, I'll send a broken man to Broken Back. No bodies to bury, and Caine will never dare show his face in Tucson again. The rube will spend the rest of his days rocking on the porch under a blanket, relearning his ABCs and thanking God that he's still alive."

Webb nodded. "And if he ever did come back . . ."

"He'll have to take on the biggest, richest rancher in the Arizona Territory. Barton Clay, a man Territorial Governor Wolfley calls 'Sir' will hardly be asked to answer for the death of one crazy old man."

"I'm with you, boss," Webb said. "After you take over the Reynolds' spread, where do we go?"

"North, all the way to the Mogollon Rim. I have a list of ranches in my safe and some of those I'll buy, the others I'll take by force. That's when you'll use your gun, Ruben, you and the other revolver hands."

"I've seen them shoot and I reckon we have an even half-dozen gun-handy punchers who have killed their man, and the rest ain't so good."

"When the time comes, and it will be soon, we'll weed out the weaker hands and hire more guns."

"Plenty of those looking for work in Texas," Webb said. "I know John Selman and young Jim Miller are on the market and the last I heard Shotgun John Collins is in Fort Worth. He was a gun in the Lincoln County war in the New Mexico Territory and ran wild with that Bill Bonney kid. He wrote to me a month ago and said he wants a good, high-paying situation."

"Keep those boys in mind and in the meantime get the word out," Clay said. "I'll start recruiting in a month or so."

Webb smiled. "Times as big as Texas coming down, boss."

"Yeah, and that's only the beginning," Barton Clay said. "With a bit of luck and a sight of speechifying I plan to be the next territorial governor."

CHAPTER THIRTEEN

Amitola is the Sioux word for "rainbow" and it was the name of a ghost town two miles north of Wheeler's Crossing and Mary Jane Hillman's favorite place. As far as she was aware, no one ever visited the slowly vanishing burg but her. In its heyday, when the population numbered one-hundred-eighty-nine men and two women, a dozen tents with timber false fronts, and some ramshackle cabins once lined an optimistically called First Street. There never was a Second Street. The tents were long gone and only the false fronts remained, stark monuments to a town that was, then wasn't. A few nuggets of gold found in a nearby stream had triggered a small rush that lasted for a year and then petered out. The tinpans moved away from Amitola and the Sonoran Desert and headed for Tombstone and the Chihuahuan Desert and left their town to curl up and die under the relentless sun.

As often as she could, Mary Jane borrowed one of Luther Wheeler's horses and rode to Amitola to enjoy the solitude and silence. She'd found a chair in the debris of what had been the Hundred Dollar Saloon and sat in the shade of a live oak that was regularly visited by scrub jays, and she read and listened to the silence of the surrounding desert.

The rickety cabins that had once housed the tinpans had fallen down, all except one, a slightly sturdier timber building with a wood shingle roof and planed door that was decorated with a horseshoe. Mary Jane called it the "tea lady's cabin" because a woman had lived there, judging by the fragments of china teacups, saucers, and plates that littered the dirt floor. A small fireplace substituted for a stove, and there was still a rusty, blackened pot hanging from a hook.

The day after the death of Toby Reynolds, Mary Jane had taken advantage of Luther Wheeler's rare, good mood and borrowed a horse, promising to be back in time for the Saturday night sporting crowd.

Now she sat under her oak reading *Twenty Thousand Leagues Under the Sea,* arguably Mr. Jules Verne's masterpiece. Soon she was immersed in the soggy adventures of Ned Land, Captain Nemo, and Dr. Aronnax, and the ghost town slowly receded away from her as she became lost in the vast wastes of the blue Pacific Ocean . . .

Mary Jane wore an off-the-shoulder white blouse, embroidered along the neckline, and a dark red skirt over a snowfall of petticoats. Her fair hair was brushed back in a bun tied with a red ribbon, and she wore a silver signet ring on her left hand, the gift of a satisfied customer.

What the drifter who watched her from a tangle of mesquite noticed most of all was that the woman had hiked up her skirt to let her legs catch some sun, and they were very shapely. He wanted her and he planned to take her by force.

There were drifters of all kinds on the frontier, cowboys seeking work, gamblers looking to outrun an unlucky streak, gunmen for hire, outlaws on the scout, itinerant

preachers, bounty hunters and assorted riffraff, petty
thieves, con artists, young men on the make and worst of
all, the violent element, murderers, highway robbers, and
rapists, cowards most of them, and a dangerous breed.

One such was Jack Carver, age thirty-six, five-foot-
eleven inches tall with lank, dirty, shoulder length yellow
hair. Despite the heat, he wore an old Union army greatcoat and a fur cap with earflaps, and belted around his
middle was a Colt revolver and a bowie knife in a beaded
Indian sheath. Carver had murdered, robbed, and raped his
way from the Texas and Mexican border country and had
slithered into the Arizona Territory just a week before.
Drifting, he stumbled on the ghost town and the woman in
the red skirt and high-heeled ankle boots by accident.
Some say Carver, known and feared in Mexico, could've
murdered as many as twenty people and that may be true.

The man dismounted and led his mustang out of the
mesquite. The wind was blowing from the west and Mary
Jane Hillman smelled the rank sweat of the man before she
saw him. An urgent alarm bell rang in her head and she
picked up the purse that lay at her feet and opened it.

Carver stopped and the reins dangled from his hand. He
grinned, showing black teeth under his thick beard, and
said, "What you doing in a ghost town, girlie? You like
being around ha'ants and stuff?"

"I'm reading," Mary Jane said. Her hand was in her
beaded red purse. "I like it here. It's quiet."

The noonday sun was unrelenting, and out in its glare
Carver sweated and stank.

"So, what are you reading?" he said. "If I might in-
quire?"

"A book," Mary Jane said. She pushed her skirt down,

her gun hand still inside the purse. "Have you ever heard of them?"

"You're sassy. What kind of book?"

"About sailors."

"What do they do?"

"Nothing much."

Carver hawked and spat and said, "I can't read no books and women shouldn't read them either, gives them airs above their station and they get uppity. I can't abide an uppity woman and never could."

"I'm uppity. Now ride on."

"You're a whore, girlie."

"No, I'm not."

"Whores lie and you're lying. You got the look of the whore about you and I want a taste. It's been weeks since last I lay with a woman."

Mary Jane shook her head. "You come right to the point, don't you, mister? You want me, then take a bath first. From here you smell like you fell off a manure wagon."

Mary Jane knew she was talking tough, but inside her belly was tied in knots. The man was big and he'd be strong.

"Stand up," Carver said.

"No."

"Stand up and shuck yourself. I want to see what I'm getting."

"You're getting nothing," Mary Jane said. "Ride on."

Carver grinned and pulled his huge bowie. "Shuck yourself or I'll cut them corsets right off'n you, lady."

"Why don't you just ride on?" the woman said. "There's a cathouse just a couple of miles south of here."

"I don't want no cathouse, I want you," Carver said. "And when I leave, you're coming with me. I'll soon beat the sass right out of you."

"I feel sick," Mary Jane said.

Carver stepped toward her, and his rank breath scuttled across her face. "What do you mean you're sick?"

"I mean unwell."

The man grinned. "You look well enough to me."

"It must be something I ate. Come here, feel my forehead and tell me if I have a fever."

The man stopped and Mary Jane died a little.

No, please don't stop. Come closer. Keep walking toward me.

"Here, you ain't got nothing catching, do you?" Carver said.

"I've been around this town. I think it was wiped out by the cholera."

Carver looked alarmed, then slowly rearranged his face into a snarl. "You're a whore and whores lie all the time. Now I'm gonna cut them duds off'n you."

He took a step forward.

It was close enough.

Mary Jane pulled her .320 caliber, five-shot British Bulldog revolver from her purse and fired.

Carver shrieked, dropped his knife and did a little jig of pain as his hand went to his bloody right ear. "You shot me," he wailed, disbelief writ large on his face.

"Damn right, I did," Mary Jane said. "Now unbuckle the gunbelt with your left hand and let it drop or I'll shoot off the other ear."

"I got shot by a whore," Carver said. "I don't believe it."

"Believe it, tramp. You were about to abuse a poor,

helpless woman and she bit you up the ass. Now drop the gunbelt."

Carver hesitated. His eyes shifty.

Call it woman's intuition, but Mary Jane just knew he was about to make a play. The Bulldog barked again. Left ear, shot through and through, and the man howled and danced some more.

From behind a haze of gunsmoke, the woman said, "I have three bullets left for you, you damned lowlife, and I was taught to shoot good and have a prayerful aim. I reckon left eye, right eye and then one in the mouth. You care to try me?"

His hands trembling, Carver unbuckled his cartridge belt and let it drop to the ground. Blood ran down both sides of his face, turning his yellow hair red. "You got me beat," he said. "I'll ride on."

"Not yet," Mary Jane said. "Treat me like a two-dollar whore and that's what I'll be. Now shuck yourself."

"Whaaat?" Carver said.

"You heard me, shuck yourself. It's what you wanted me to do."

"Damn you, I ain't doing it. My ears are punched and you ain't no lady."

"Look on the bright side, you can wear earrings." Mary Jane got to her feet and sighed. "All right, then let's try a different tack." The muzzle of the revolver lowered and she said, "Right ball, left ball and one shot in the middle. Care to try me?"

Alarmed, Jack Carver peeled off the greatcoat and then shucked his filthy clothes until he stood naked except for his mule-eared boots and shapeless hat.

Mary Jane looked him over, shook her head and said,

"Mister, you sure ain't much. Now back away. Stand over there where I can see you."

She stepped to the gray, slid a Winchester out of the boot and stripped off the saddle and let it fall to the ground. Then she said to Carver, "Where's your poke?"

"I ain't got any money," the man said.

"My guess it's in the pocket of your coat. Let's find out, huh?"

Mary Jane's guess was right. There was a new-looking brown wallet, obviously stolen, in the right-hand pocket of the coat. She searched its contents and said, "Twenty-three dollars. Well, that's about enough to recompense me for a spoiled day." She motioned with her revolver. "Now on your horse and git and count yourself lucky that I didn't put a bullet in your brisket."

"I'm nekkid," Carver said.

"Unfortunately, I can see that."

"And I got no saddle."

"I can see that too."

"You're the meanest damn whore I ever met."

"Others have told me that. Now, get on the horse."

"Whore! And if I don't?"

The Bulldog's muzzle lowered again.

"All right, all right, I'm riding!" Carver yelled. "I'm sorry I ever set eyes on you. Why does stuff like this always happen to me?"

"I don't know, but maybe the next time you'll think twice about abusing a poor little ol' whore like me."

"Damn it, I got no saddle. I've got sensitive skin and I'll get chafed."

"If you don't get on the horse, you'll get shot. Seems like you got a choice to make, mister, so make it fast."

Carver scrambled onto the back of the gray. Not a pretty sight, Mary Jane decided.

The man sat upright and said, "When we meet again, I'll get even for this."

Mary Jane smiled. "The nearest town is Tucson, nekkid man. I'm sure they'll welcome you with open arms."

After the man was gone, Mary Jane Hillman did a strange thing that surprised even her. Knowing that Luther Wheeler would confiscate Carver's guns and keep them for himself, she planned to hide the rifle and holstered revolver somewhere close to the mercantile and sell them later. But without really knowing why, a woman's intuition perhaps, as one female writer claimed in a 1935 edition of *McCall's* magazine, she obeyed the insistent, whispering voice in her head and stashed the firearms in the tea lady's cabin and felt better after she did.

But the why of the thing she did not know . . . or could even begin to guess.

CHAPTER FOURTEEN

The murder of Toby Reynolds had shaken Dan Caine to the core, and for the first time his resolve began to waver. Toby had been an honorable man, a fine man, and he had died because of Dan's obsession to deliver justice for a disreputable old scoundrel who couldn't hold a candle to him.

How many more corpses would he stack up before this was over?"

Maybe Ellie Reynolds had been right . . . her husband's murderer was not fit to bury him.

After Mrs. Dale's supper of chicken and dumplings that he barely touched, Dan walked out to the porch and sat in one of two rockers. He carried his cartridge belt and holstered Colt over his left shoulder. Bookending the deck on both sides were small gardens of blooming butterfly weed and daylilies that even in the shadows put on a flower display. But Dan didn't notice. Nor did he pay any attention to the moon climbing in the sky as round and shiny as a newly minted silver dollar, putting the stars to shame. Only his brain was busy, and tormenting pictures flickered through his mind like a magic lantern show.

Dan heard boot heels behind him and said, "Speak."

"It's me, Crow."

"Advance, friend, and be recognized and take a seat."

Crow sat in the other rocker and said, "You seem to be in a better frame of mind. I'd say you're downright neighborly."

"You're wrong, I'm not. The death of Toby Reynolds keeps punishing me like a toothache. I remember his face, gray, so lifeless and his small, dead body sprawled in the dirt. And I remember the tears that ran down Ellie's cheeks and how they liked to break my heart."

"And now you have a mind to avenge him as well as Meadows?"

Dan sought Crow's face in the gloom. "No, I reckon I'm out of the revenge business. Being a vigilante on the vengeance trail sure doesn't cock my pistol." Crow made no answer, and Dan said, "I can tell you're sorry to hear that. Well, are you?"

"Not sorry. Surprised maybe, but not sorry."

"That sums up the whole story right there. We're surprised, but not sorry, and now we can head home like a pair of whipped dogs, huh?"

"Sure thing, Dan. Meadows and Reynolds, two useless old men. Who gives a damn about them?"

"Toby fit Comanches and Apaches and he was a Texas Ranger for a spell, at least a couple of years, and that was after he married Ellie. He wasn't a useless young man and he wasn't useless when he was old. To sum it up, I do give a damn."

Crow's grin was white in the gloom. "Hell, I just tested you and no matter what you say, you ain't ready to give it up."

"Then test me again and after you've done that tell me what to do next."

"No more tests," Crow said. "But I tell you this much . . ."

"For what it's worth?"

"Yeah, for what it's worth."

"Go ahead."

"If we can get Luther Wheeler to identify the man the Clay boys murdered to provide their alibi, then even a gutless wonder like City Marshal Roche has to act."

"To get all that to work, Wheeler would have to tell Roche face-to-face what he knows. And getting him to talk might not be easy. Wheeler's bound to be terrified of Barton Clay and his boys."

"I can get him to talk," Crow said.

"How, for God's sake? I reckon the man will shut up tighter than a clam."

"I can make him talk. I watched Geronimo's young wife, Zi-yeh, torture a teamster who'd raped a Bedonkohe girl. He was a big, strong, heavyset man and he lasted four days." Crow closed his eyes as though shutting out a vision, and then opened them again. "Zi-yeh was a skilled girl and she taught me a lot."

"She taught you how to make a man scream?" Dan said, smiling.

"Yeah, that . . . and also how to make a man like Wheeler talk."

"It's thin," Dan said.

"What's thin?"

"The whole damned plan is thin. In fact, it stinks."

"Well, right now it's all we've got."

Dan sighed. "You ever think that maybe Tucson just ain't the kind of town to have trouble in?"

"No, Tombstone is. And Deadwood. Yes sir, it's a bad idea to make trouble in either of them burgs."

"You ever been in Tombstone?"

"No."

"Deadwood?"

"No."

"Then how do you know they're such unforgiving towns?"

"From what I've heard."

"What have you heard about Broken Back?" Dan said.

"I wouldn't cause trouble in that town. I hear they got a tough sheriff and a mean Apache deputy."

Dan smiled and began to build a cigarette. Without looking up from the makings, he said, "All right, we'll give Luther Wheeler a whirl. Then, when I walk away from it, I can convince myself that I tried everything I could. How does that set with you, Crow?"

"It sets fine with me, but what do I know? I'm just a poor Indian boy off the reservation."

"So was Geronimo," Dan said.

"So when do we try Wheeler?"

"Tomorrow after first light we'll head out that way. Just don't get your hopes up, Crow. I don't think he's going to help us."

"Neither do I," Crow said. "But there's one alternative to your problem we haven't discussed yet."

"And here I thought we'd discussed them all. What's on your mind?"

"It ain't easy and it might take time."

"So tell me," Dan said, his patience fraying.

"We seek them out, and I'm talking about the Clay brothers, and we gun them one by one. Make them pay for what they done to Reynolds."

"And Dick Meadows." Dan's smile was faint. "So we stand in the street and call out the three brothers and Ruben Webb and Pa Clay and his army of gun hands? How's your draw, Crow? No, don't tell me, I've seen it. You're a man who believes in taking his time, and we'd be up against drawfighters. Without a posse behind us, how long do you think we'd last."

"I don't know."

"But I do. We'd be lying dead in the street quicker'n scat."

Crow looked solemn, like a medicine man about to impart great wisdom. "Dan, beggin' your pardon, but what I had more in mind was to bushwhack them boys, blow them right out of the saddle. They'll never know what hit them."

"No, I won't do it. And I want the Clays to know what hit them, why they're being punished. Besides bushwhacking is a helluva way to kill a white man."

"The Clays did it to Toby Reynolds, gunned him at a distance," Crow said.

"I know, but that don't make it right."

"Then we're back to making big medicine talk with Wheeler."

"Seems like," Dan said. He smiled. "Maybe he'll surprise us, huh?"

But Crow's attention was elsewhere. His gaze was fixed somewhere in the surrounding darkness, and he closed his eyes and for long moments made no answer.

"Crow, what do you see?" Dan said finally.

After a while Crow said, "I saw muh."

"I'm not catching your drift," Dan said.

"In Apache, muh means owl. The owl is a night traveler and a bird of ill-omen and it brought me a vision."

"What kind of vision?"

"I saw a man, bloody and near to death and wolves surrounded him on all sides and I could not drive them away. Then, a woman came and talked to the wolves and she brought the lightning with her and they went away."

Dan smiled and said, "What does it mean? Who is the man?"

"I don't know what it means," Crow said. "If I'd dreamed of an owl, it would mean that it was bringing death. But I was not dreaming. I had a vision."

"Who was the man, Crow?"

"I don't know."

"Was it me?"

"I don't know."

"Who was the woman?"

"I saw her face, but I don't know her."

Crow rose to his feet. "I feel tired. Time to seek my blankets."

He stepped to the door and then turned and said, "To the Apache, the owl is the most feared of all the animals and it visited us tonight with bad tidings. We must take care."

Before Dan could comment, Crow opened the door and went inside, closing it after him.

The owl was an ill-omened bird, and the vision disturbed Crow more than anyone who was not Apache could ever understand. And he'd lied to Dan . . . the face of the bloody man surrounded by ravening wolves was his.

CHAPTER FIFTEEN

Dan Caine and Crow sat their horses and studied Luther Wheeler's mercantile, partially hidden behind a torn lace curtain of morning mist. Two intersecting wagon roads met near the east gable of the structure and gave the place its name. The building itself was two story, eight narrow windows on the upper level suggesting small bedrooms that were not intended for sleeping and a slate-covered gable roof. There was no porch, but three wooden steps led up to the door of the mercantile and a few yards away another flight led to what Dan guessed was the saloon. From time to time impoverished blanket Indians, mostly Navajo, came to the mercantile steps to beg for food. Wheeler, a contrary man, always fed the starving people and gave them gifts of coffee, sugar, and salt. The women sometimes asked for the crates that once held the sacks of Arbuckle since they were the right size to bury their dead babies. No one ever discovered why Wheeler had such a soft spot for Indians, though in 1910 Rose Richards told a reporter that it was because the man was part Navajo himself. Whatever the reason, he took his secret with him to the grave.

This early in the morning the place looked deserted.

There were no horses tied to the hitching rails outside the mercantile or the saloon and Dan would've thought the Crossing abandoned but for the rectangle of hazy light that was the store's front window.

"Someone is stirring. I guess Wheeler has the coffee on," Crow said.

"I could use a cup," Dan said. "Mrs. Dale's coffee is muddy swamp water."

"Well, let's see if Mr. Wheeler will oblige us with coffee and information," Crow said. "Though I don't think either will be very forthcoming." He looked around him. "The mist is lifting."

Remembering the owl, Dan smiled and said, "Is that a good sign?"

"It means we can see better," Crow said, smiling. "That's all."

"I'm relieved to hear it," Dan said.

Dan Caine and Crow looped their reins to the hitching rail and stepped into the mercantile, a large, gloomy space surrounded by shelves crammed with all manner of goods. The floor was also crowded with boxes, barrels, crates, and tables holding clothing, shoes, and other merchandise. The front counter held cases for smaller goods like folding knives, cheap rings, and nickel watches, and there was also a coffee grinder, scales, and a cash register. The surrounding shelves were stacked with canned meat and peaches, coffee beans, spices, baking powder, oatmeal, flour and sugar, hard candy in jars, eggs, milk, butter, jugs of honey and molasses, crackers, cheese, syrup, dried beans and cigars and tobacco. To the left of the entrance a sign hanging from the ceiling said APOTHECARY and displayed shelves of patent medicines, soaps, and toiletries, and another handwritten sign tacked to the front of a shelf proclaimed, *Dr. Dean's Female Remedy at Cost*. The dry goods section of the store offered bolts of calico cloth, pins and needles, thread, ribbons, buttons, collars, undergarments for both sexes, suspenders, dungarees, hats, and shoes. There were also rifles, revolvers, ammunition, lantern lamps, rope, crockery, pots and pans, cooking utensils, and dishes. A cast iron stove in one corner that burned all day every day produced soot that covered everything, and families of rats had made the place their home.

When Dan and Crow stepped to the counter, a tall, gaunt man with graying black hair on the sides of his head and none on top, emerged from the shadows of the store and said, "Good morning, gents. What can I do you for?"

"Coffee," Dan said.

Looking a little disappointed that his greeting drew no smiles, Luther Wheeler said, "Coffee's on the stove and there's cups hanging on hooks over there. Help yourself." Before Dan could turn away, the man said, "I've got biscuits and bacon for breakfast." He smiled. "If you've a mind to try something else this early, I can go wake the girls."

"Coffee will suit us just fine," Dan said.

Again, Wheeler looked dejected. "Suit yourselves," he said.

Dan said, "However, I'm in the market for some information."

"What kind of information?" Wheeler said. Suspicious, his eyes narrowed

"The kind that tells me about the man who was killed right here in your store a while back."

That last closed Wheeler down fast. The man flushed and he said, "Drink your coffee. I'll be right back."

He knew the tall man who looked as though he was born to the gun he wore had to be Dan Caine, the nosy hick lawman prying into the death of Dick Meadows, the piece of trash and faceless nonentity the Clay boys had done for. It seemed that Caine was a born troublemaker and now he was Barton Clay's problem to solve.

Wheeler stepped through the door to a staircase that marked the division between the mercantile and the saloon and climbed the rickety steps that led to the top floor. Daisy Tweed's room was the closest one on the upstairs hallway and two long steps took him to the door. He pushed it open and the girl didn't wake. Wheeler shook her roughly and whispered urgently, "Get up."

"Wha . . ." Daisy said. Drowsy.

The man grabbed clothes from the hook on the wall and threw them on the bed. "Get dressed, hurry."

Now the woman was wide awake. "Why?"

"Dan Caine is here. Ride to the Clay ranch and bring Ben and his brothers. Tell them Caine is getting ready to ask questions that he shouldn't be asking. Now go, quick as you can."

Within minutes Daisy Tweed used the chamber pot, dressed, saddled a horse and galloped away from the Crossing.

As he stood with Crow drinking coffee, Dan didn't hear the girl leave, and if he had, he'd have paid little heed. But unbeknownst to him fate was closing around him . . . soon to change him from the man he was into a man he never wanted to be.

* * *

Luther Wheeler played for time.

Yes, he'd heard that a drifter had confessed to murdering old Dick Meadows but he'd never met either of those men before. He thought that a couple of Clay's riders triggered the man, his name was Bowman or something like that, after he drew down on them. There were witnesses willing to swear that they heard Bowman's confession, including myself, so the Clay boys were off the hook for the Meadows killing.

"Do you think justice was served?" Dan said.

"Sure, it was," Wheeler said. "The drifter got drunk and said he'd killed the old miner. He told me right here in my saloon that it was the dirtiest trick he'd ever played. Everybody heard him."

"Who was everybody?"

"Well, me, the ranch hands, the whores and, oh yeah, there were a couple of others, but I don't remember who they were, traveling men passing through, I guess."

"Did you know a rancher by the name of Toby Reynolds?" Dan said.

"Can't say that I did. There are all kind of spreads to the east and north of Tucson and ranchers come and go. A bad winter or low cattle prices sees them off."

Wheeler looked uncomfortable and Dan pressed him.

"Toby Reynolds ranched east of Tucson for years," he said. "Strange that you wouldn't know him."

"I can't be expected to know everybody in Pima County."

"Toby sent me a letter. He said the Clay brothers murdered Dick Meadows."

"Then he was wrong."

"Toby was murdered a couple of days ago, so somebody thought he was telling the truth," Dan said. "He said the Clay brothers laughed about how they tortured the old man, trying to discover the whereabouts of his hidden gold."

Wheeler shook his head. "Folks make up all kinds of stories. Certainly, the Clay brothers are kinda wild, but they're straight shooters and not into killing an old man for his gold." The man smiled. "Now, how about some bacon and biscuits hot out of the oven? On the house, seeing as this is your first visit to Wheeler's Crossing. The first of many I hope."

"Serve them up," Crow said. "I reckon that's all we're going to get here."

"Now, now, let's be fair," Wheeler said. "I've told you all I know."

"Yeah, sure you did," Dan said.

Wheeler smiled. "Good. Now if you boys would care to step into the saloon and choose a table, I'll serve you there."

CHAPTER SIXTEEN

The saloon was about a third of the size as the mercantile and consisted of an abbreviated mahogany bar with a French mirror behind it and four shiny brass spittoons in front. A scattering of tables and chairs surrounding a small dance floor. A sign above the bar asked the question, *Have You Written to Mother?* and several smoke-darkened oil paintings of rural landscapes hung on the walls. The place smelled of cigars, spilled beer, sweat, and cheap perfume.

Dan Caine and Crow sat at a table near the bar and Luther Wheeler was a long time in bringing their food. "Sorry, gents," he said. "I burned the first batch of biscuits, but these are just fine." He laid a platter on the table piled high with soda biscuits and slices of fried bacon. "Bon appétit."

Wheeler's eyes moved to the saloon door.

Where the hell were the Clay boys?

He needn't have worried. The three Clay brothers and four tough hands were on their way to the Crossing at a distance-eating gallop . . . and they had already made their plans.

Dan and Crow talked little as they ate. They'd just suffered another crushing defeat. Closemouthed Luther

Wheeler had told them nothing, yet another brick wall of lies, half-truths, and silence. There was nowhere to go from where they were, nowhere to turn.

Then Crow put into words what Dan was thinking. "I guess now we head for Broken Back," he said. He pretended enthusiasm he didn't feel. "Hey, Dan, maybe we can get the Rangers interested."

Dan shook his head. "The Rangers don't give a damn about what happened to an old man in the Arizona Territory. And right now, they've got their hands full with renegade Apaches and their own home-grown Texas outlaws. You might say they're a tad preoccupied."

"Still, it might be worth a try," Crow said.

"Yeah, it might be worth a try. I'll study on it."

Crow picked up a biscuit crumb with the tip of his finger and shoved it into his mouth and then said, "It's funny when you think about it, but by this time tomorrow we'll be at the train station, homeward bound."

"I know. And we'll look around at Tucson and say, 'Why the hell did we ever come here?' At least I will."

"You're feeling a might low right now, ain't you, Dan?"

"I don't know how I feel. It could be I've lost my wife and all for nothing. It doesn't make a man feel anything. It just makes him numb."

"Helen will be waiting for you," Crow said.

Dan's smile was thin. "I'm not counting on it." He saw Crow stiffen as the man stared over his shoulder, his face rapidly draining of all expression, and said, "Now what are you thinking?"

"Men just came in," Crow said. He got to his feet, his hand lowering to his gun.

"I wouldn't, breed," a man said from behind Dan. "I can cut you in half with this here scattergun."

Dan Caine rose, slowly turned and looked into the cold, dark eyes of the shotgun. The man holding the weapon was tall, broad-shouldered, his mouth wide and cruel under a cavalry mustache. The knuckles of his hands were scarred, the thick nails of his thumbs filed into points, the fists of a bar brawler. "Unbuckle the gunbelt and let it drop to the floor," Ben Clay said.

The man was flanked by two others, mustached peas in a pod, the younger one grinning, his face alight, enjoying this. He wore his gun drawfighter low and he had the icy, hazel eyes of a poisonous reptile.

Dan hesitated and failed to anticipate the shotgun stock that slammed into the right side of his face that sent him staggering backward, his cartwheeling legs collapsing under him. Dan's back slammed so hard onto the timber floor that Mary Jane Hillman, watching with the other women from the mercantile door, would later say the building shook.

The odds were three to one, but the warrior in Crow rose white hot to the surface and he might have made a play. But the muzzle of a Colt screwed into his left ear quickly dissuaded him. "I'll blow your brains out," a man said. "Now drop the iron."

Out of the corner of his eye Crow saw that four men, punchers by the look of them, had come in the front door of the saloon. The three that he guessed by their similar looks were the Clay brothers had entered from the mercantile. The odds were suddenly a lot steeper and then someone snaked Crow's Colt from his holster and he gave up all thought of resisting. Guns prodded him into a corner where he was made to sit and a man with a Winchester rifle stood behind him.

Groggy, his head spinning, Dan struggled into a sitting

position. He felt blood trickle from a cut on the side of his head, and scarlet droplets fell on the floor.

Grinning, Ben Clay handed the shotgun to one of the cowboys . . . and then the boots went in.

Ben aimed a vicious kick at Dan's head that connected with a thud and sent him sprawling. His body totally unprotected, Pete Clay and his younger brother Decker, joined Ben in kicking Dan in the ribs, face, and everywhere else the toes of their boots could do damage. He groaned as three strong men pounded him like a bloody rag doll, the thump . . . thump . . . thump . . . of the savage kicks as loud as the beating of a bass drum.

Then Ben Clay got bored with it.

To the men around him, he said, "Form a circle, boys. Let's have at it."

Ben Clay dragged Dan to his feet, held him upright and then slammed a fist into his jaw. Dan staggered back on rubbery legs, only for another man to slam a fist into his face and push him toward Pete Clay, who punched Dan away from him and sent him staggering to someone else. The Clays and their hands were having themselves a time, yelling, laughing, making a punching bag of the bloody, battered Dan Caine, reducing his once handsome face to a scarlet pulp, like a raspberry tart dropped on a bakery floor.

Mary Jane Hillman saved Dan Caine's life.

"Stop it! Stop it!" she yelled, running into the circle. She grabbed Dan but couldn't hold him upright and dropped him to the floor. "You're killing him."

Ben Clay backhanded the woman, who was staggered by the blow, a red welt livid on her cheek. "Keep out of this, whore."

"No! She's right." This from Pete Clay, the ranch bookkeeper and a smarter man than his brothers. "Ben, we don't want to kill him, remember? All we want is to beat him within an inch of his life. Well, he's within an inch of his life." Pete smiled. "If he survives this beating it will be a goddamned miracle."

"Yeah, you're right. We don't want to kill him."

"He's had enough," Pete said. "As it is, you'll have to get him off the floor with a sponge."

"Where's the breed?" Ben said. "Bring him over here."

A couple of cowboys pushed Crow toward Ben Clay, but he broke away from them and kneeled beside Dan. But he didn't speak. Dan was unconscious and couldn't hear. But Crow raised his face to Ben and said, "You're a dirty, low-life piece of trash."

As he'd done to Mary Jane Hillman Ben Clay aimed a vicious, backhanded blow at Crow's face. But the slap never landed. Showing the speed of a striking rattler, Crow's big, muscular hand grabbed Ben by the wrist . . . and squeezed.

His wrist caught in a clamp of iron, Ben yelped in pain and astonishment. He tried to pull back his arm but it was caught in a vise of bone, tendons as strong as steel cables and muscle.

Crow squeezed harder, and Ben shrieked. "Shoot him off me," he screamed. "He'll break my wrist."

"No! No shooting," Pete Clay said. "Pa says to keep him alive."

Crow smiled at Ben. "I can break it like a dry twig." He squeezed. "Snap!"

At that Ben squealed again, his face twisted in pain.

Pete Clay shoved the muzzle of his gun into Crow's temple. "All right, breed, let him go," he said. "Pick up your friend and get him out of here and the hell out of the Arizona Territory. And never come back."

"Hey, breed, you might need a sponge to pick him up," one of the cowboys said. And except for Ben Clay, who was in pain, the others laughed.

Crow pointed at two of the hands. "You and you, carry him outside to his horse."

One of the punchers, a towheaded youngster with a tough face, said, "The hell I will."

Crow's strong fingers clamped tighter and Ben Clay yelled, "Do as he says! He's killing me here!"

"Dave, Floyd, do as the breed wants," Pete said.

"Go to hell," the towhead named Floyd said. "I ain't taking orders from a breed."

"You're taking orders from me," Pete said. "Now get the rube out of here."

Floyd cursed under his breath, but he and Dave, a lanky puncher with hound dog eyes, carried Dan outside and Crow followed, dragging the whimpering Ben Clay with him. "Put Sheriff Caine across his saddle," he said. "And do it gently."

When Dan had been loaded onto his horse, Pete Clay said, "Breed . . . what do they call you?"

"Crow."

"Then, Crow, take this man to the station and you and him get on a train to Texas."

"What's left of him," Decker Clay said. But this time no one laughed.

"Tell Sheriff Caine if he ever shows his face in Tucson again, we'll kill him," Pete said. Then, "Floyd, take the Winchesters from their saddles." He looked at Crow. "Where you're going you won't need a rifle."

Floyd removed the rifles from the boots, and Pete Clay said, "Now let go of my brother's arm or I'll drop you right where you stand and your pardner can find his own way home to Texas."

"You're trash, mister," Crow said. "All of you, just a bunch of cowardly, no-good trash."

"Let go of my brother's arm and get on your horse," Pete said, his face stiffening. "And think yourself lucky that you're still alive."

Crow let go of Ben Clay's wrist, and the man immediately grabbed it and tried to massage the pain away. He flexed his fingers, grimaced, and went for his gun, his eyes on Crow.

But he never completed the draw. Pete pushed his arm down and Ben triggered a shot into the dirt. "Damn you, Ben," he said. "The rube is still a lawman and we don't want to take any chances. After the beating he took he'll run for Texas with his tail between his legs and never show his face back to the Territory. He's learned his lesson . . . don't ever mess with the Clay brothers." Pete looked at Crow. "Now ride on out of here." He slapped the side of Dan's bloody head and said, "And take that with you."

The sun was high, the day was hot, and men sweated. As Crow rode away, the reins of Dan's mount in his hand, his horse kicked up little eruptions of dust.

"He's gonna die anyway," Ben Clay said.

"Pa's making too much of this," Pete said. "If the law comes looking for him, and that ain't likely, we just say that we never met the man."

"What about the breed?"

"The breed? Who's gonna take the word of a half-Apache for anything? Would you?"

"Hell, no," Ben said.

"The white man hasn't been born yet that would believe an Indian over his own kind," Pete said.

"You should've told that to Pa," Ben said.

"Pa already knows. But a man who plans to run for high political office can't be too careful. Besides, when Caine gets back to his hick town what's he gonna tell the folks? Will he say that he tried to pin the murder of an old tramp on the sons of a respected rancher and got beat up for his trouble?"

"I reckon not," Ben said, grinning.

"Not if he wants to stay a sheriff he won't," Pete said.

Ben laughed. "He won't ever be a sheriff ever again. He'll be lucky if he can walk."

CHAPTER SEVENTEEN

Crow was two miles west of Wheeler's Crossing when he saw the dust column rising behind him. At first, he thought it might be the Clay brothers looking for more fun, but then the dust told him that it was caused by only one rider. He had no gun but still had his knife and he determined to sell his life dearly. But to his surprise the rider was a woman, by the look of her the whore who'd tried to stop Dan Caine's beating and had gotten a backhand to the face for her trouble. Mary Jane Hillman's cheek was still red from the blow Ben Clay had dealt her.

She drew rein and stepped from the saddle, pushed her red skirt over her naked thighs and quickly stepped to Dan's unconscious body.

She glared at Crow. "Get him down from there. Now!"

"Lady, we're headed for the Tucson train station," Crow said. "We'll take the rails to San Antone and from there ride for Broken Back, Texas."

"Ride? Mister, he'd be dead before you got him there. Now bring him down and let him breathe."

Crow swung out of the saddle and took Dan by the shoulders.

"Gently," Mary Jane said. "He's in a world of hurt."

Crow eased Dan's limp body to the ground and the girl pressed her ear to his chest. "His heart is strong," she said. She put her arm around Dan's shoulders and raised him a little higher. "Give me your canteen."

"I don't have one and neither does Dan."

Mary Jane shook her head. "Damn rubes."

"Is he going to make it?" Crow said.

"Maybe. But in his present state he won't survive the journey back to Texas."

Crow looked both confused and scared. "There are doctors in Tucson."

"If he's still breathing when you get there. I think he's got broken ribs and that means at least six weeks of healing, maybe more."

"Then Tucson is my best bet."

"Not if you want to keep him alive. A man in your friend's condition will be noticed and talked about and pretty soon City Marshal Bill Roche will tell the Clay boys that they have to finish the job."

"The Clays don't want him dead," Crow said.

"Well, they succeeded. Now he's only half-dead. You know something, mister, doctors are curious, and they'll want to know who did this to him and why. And if your friend dies, well then it becomes a case of murder. That would sure inconvenience Barton Clay and his spawn."

"So what would he do?"

"Money talks and doctors can be bribed. A death certificate can say anything Barton Clay wants it to say. That your friend . . ."

"His name is Dan Caine."

"That Mr. Caine died of heart failure is the most likely."

"I told you, the Clays don't want Dan dead."

"That was then, this is now. Do you really think anyone from . . . what's the name of that hick town again?"

"Broken Back."

"Will come all the way to the Arizona Territory to hunt all over creation for their beloved sheriff?"

"I don't know."

"Think about it . . . who would come?"

"Well, there's John Taylor who owns the mercantile."

"A family man, huh?"

"Yeah, a bit of a blowhard who has a brood of young-'uns."

"Who else?"

"Well . . . there's Frank Lawson the gambler."

"He'll soon figure the odds and decide that finding a hayseed lawman south of the Mogollon Rim is such a long shot he won't take cards in the game. Who else?"

Crow thought hard and said, "Well, there's the Reverend Oscar Bottle, the preacher . . ." He saw the look in the woman's eyes and said, "All right, all right, I catch your drift."

"I'm so glad you understand, finally. No one is coming to find Dan Caine, and if you take him to Tucson, he'll never leave the town alive, and neither will you," Mary Jane said. "Barton Clay and Bill Roche will see to that."

"Then where do I take Dan?"

Mary Jane laid her hand on Dan's forehead and said, "He's running a fever. He needs rest, a lot of rest."

"Woman, where can we go?" Crow said. For such a big man he suddenly looked helpless and hopeless and more than a little panicked.

Mary Jane caught the alarm in the man's voice and said, "There's a ghost town a mile north of us. When it was alive, its name was Amitola. We can take him there."

"Ghost town?" Now Crow sounded even more alarmed.

"There was a gold rush there a while back, but the gold played out quickly and the town was abandoned. Now nobody lives there and no one goes near the place since a story went around that cholera killed all the miners." Mary Jane smiled. "But I go there. It's my secret place."

She saw Crow's doubt and said, "There's a stream nearby and I'll bring you grub when I can. Now get your friend . . ."

"His name's Dan Caine."

"I know. You told me that already."

The woman stepped to her horse, hiked up her skirt, and swung into the saddle. "Bring him here, Crow, in front of me. I'll hold him."

"He's a sizable man and heavy," Crow said.

"I'll hold him," Mary Jane said. "Just hoist him up here."

Crow was a strong man, big in the arms and shoulders, and he picked Dan up like a rag doll and heaved him onto the front of Mary Jane's saddle. Dan's eyes were open in his bloody face, but unfocused, staring at nothing, a man who'd no idea who he was or where he was. He slumped, unconscious, and the woman cradled him in her arms.

"You ready?" she said to Crow.

The man nodded, mounted his horse and gathered the reins of Dan's mount. "How far did you say?"

"Not far. Just a mile or two." Crow drew rein beside Mary Jane and looked into Dan's battered face and said, "They sure cleaned his plow, didn't they?"

"Yes, they did, and your friend may not make it. If he dies the Clay boys will have chalked up yet another murder."

"Why are you doing this, ma'am?" Crow said.

"Call me Mary Jane for heaven's sake. "I'm a whore not a ma'am."

"Why are you doing this, Mary Jane?"

The woman kicked her horse into motion. "Let's ride." Then after a while, riding through the oppressive day's tunnel of heat, "I don't really know why I'm helping you. Maybe it's because I have no regard for the Clay brothers. Barton allowed those boys to grow up wild and mean and do whatever they pleased to whomever they please. No matter the crime, they knew their pa's money would always bail them out."

Mary Jane adjusted Dan's position on her saddle, his head lolled and a string of bloody saliva hung from his mouth. From somewhere, the woman produced a scrap of handkerchief and wiped it away.

"Dick Meadows wasn't the Clays' first killing, not by a long shot," she said. "The murder of Melissa Mayes was covered up by City Marshal Roche, and Ben Clay wasn't arrested even though he was the last person to see the girl alive. According to Ben, him and Melissa went out riding together and quarreled about another woman he was seeing. Ben said that the girl, she was only fourteen, threw a tantrum and rode away and he never saw her again. But everybody knew Ben had raped and then killed her. Certainly, her father, a Tucson blacksmith, did and he went after Ben with a shotgun and vowed to kill him."

"And Ben Clay shot him." Crow said.

"Ben hid behind the striped pole of a barbershop and after Barnabas Mayes passed by, he shot him in the back. Since Mayes had threatened to kill Ben on sight, the shooting was dismissed as a clear case of self-defense."

A jackrabbit jumped up from under Crow's horse and bounced away like a rubber ball. He settled his spooked mount and said, "It seems that Ben Clay has much to answer for."

Mary Jane nodded and said, "He sure does and there's more to come. Three days after her father was killed, Melissa's body was found hidden in brush under a mesquite. She'd been stripped naked, strangled and violated. It so happened that some Navajo were camped close to a nearby stream. Ben and his brothers, a dozen of their hands and City Marshal Roche accused three men, one of them only a boy, of the rape and murder of Melissa Mayes. They hung all three from a cottonwood while Barton Clay looked on." The woman turned her face to Crow and said, "It seems that everybody in Tucson, including Bill Roche, knew Ben Clay had murdered the girl but they kept their mouths shut about that and the dead Navajos. Barton Clay made for a powerful enemy and still does."

"When did all this happen?" Crow said.

"Two years ago. I know because it all came down when I first arrived at Wheeler's Crossing."

Then suddenly Crow said, "What's that sound?"

"You hear Dan struggling to draw breath," Mary Jane said. "Broken ribs will do that to a person."

Crow, steeped in Apache spiritual beliefs, was upset enough to invoke his father's stern Scottish deity. "May the Lord help him," he said.

"And us," Mary Jane Hillman said, crossing herself.

CHAPTER EIGHTEEN

When Crow and Mary Jane Hillman rode into Amitola, the ghost town that still clung to its name, the wind had risen. It blustered hard from the east and set up a strange symphony of clacking boards and sighs and whispers, as though the old tinpans had all returned.

Mary Jane drew rein outside what she'd begun to think of as the teacup cabin and told Crow to lift Dan Caine from her horse.

"Then carry him in here," she said. "At least it's got four walls and a roof."

Crow eased the unconscious Dan Caine from the horse and held him effortlessly like he carried a sleeping child. He laid Dan carefully on the dirt floor and said to Mary Jane who'd just joined him, "He doesn't look good."

"We've got to get him off the dirt," the woman said. "I'll strip your horses and bring the saddle blankets. In the meantime, just stay with him."

"I wasn't planning on going anywhere," Crow said.

Mary Jane returned a short while later lugging a saddle and the blankets. "Put him on these," she said, "and use your saddle as a place to lay his head. And get those bloodstained clothes off him."

Crow was horrified. "You mean naked?"

"That's what I mean."

"But you'll see his . . . his . . ."

The woman's exasperation showed on her face. "I'm a whore, remember? I've seen one before. While you're doing that, I'll fill my canteen at the stream."

"Maybe you'll find some gold," Crow said, smiling, trying to lighten the mood.

"And maybe pigs will fly," Mary Jane said, frowning.

Crow's attempt to inject levity into a devastating day had failed badly.

When the woman returned with the water, Dan Caine was on his back, naked on the horse blankets. Mary Jane took one look at his bruised, hammered body and said, "Up Colorado way, I once saw what was left of a puncher whose pony threw him in front of a stampeding herd. He looked better than your friend does."

Mary Jane kneeled beside Dan and raised his head. She wiped blood from his face with his shirt, and then held the canteen to his split lips. But he choked and the water ran into his mouth and dribbled out again.

"Crow, try to get him to drink," the woman said. "If I can make it, I'll be here first thing in the morning. I'll bring some grub and a bottle of whiskey. Do you need anything else?"

"Some shag tobacco for my pipe. If Wheeler has any."

"He'll have it. Wheeler has everything."

Mary Jane gently laid Dan's head back on the saddle and rose to her feet. She stepped to the corner where she'd stashed Jack Carver's rifle and gunbelt and handed them to Crow. "I hope you won't need these," she said.

The Winchester and Colt were chambered for the same .44-40 caliber round, and the heft of the rifle told Crow that all fifteen cartridges were loaded. The revolver held five and there were another twelve rounds in the cartridge belt.

"Now you're not defenseless," Mary Jane said.

"If the Winchester is fully loaded as I figure it is, then I have thirty-two rounds. I can do some damage with that."

"If it comes to it, say a prayer and aim straight."

Mary Jane stepped out of the ruined cabin and mounted her horse. The reins in her hand, she looked down at Crow and said, "Keep him alive, half-Apache man." The rude wind slapped at her skirt and teased her hair into dancing strands.

"I'll stay with him," Crow said.

"See you do. Don't let the Clays win yet another round."

The woman kneed her horse into a canter and rode into the still bright day.

CHAPTER NINETEEN

Crow staked the horses out on a patch of good grass. He brought his saddlebags into the cabin and removed several small, deerskin pouches that contained powdered face paint. Using some of the shards of china that were scattered about the floor as containers, he mixed several colors with a little water and then laid them beside Dan Caine.

He then sat cross-legged on the floor and chanted a prayer to the great supernatural power that existed throughout the universe and controlled every facet of Apache life. As he sang his song, Crow asked for another vision of the future and that he might be given the gift of healing to save Dan Caine's life.

He then used his thumb to paint green stripes on Dan's cheek. Next to those he applied black. Green had great healing ability, and black was a living color of tremendous power that brought strength to the wearer. Crow's chant rose and fell for the next hour, unnaturally loud and eerie amid a ghost town as silent as a sepulcher.

The moon had risen, and the first stars appeared when Dan Caine stirred and his eyes opened. He muttered something that Crow didn't hear. Crow leaned his head closer to Dan's mouth and this time caught his whispered words . . .

"It's you, Crow. Then I must be in hell."

"Close enough," Crow said. "You're still in the Arizona Territory."

Looking surprised, Dan gasped and said, "It punishes me when I breathe."

"That's because a couple of your ribs are broke. Later I'll see if I can find you something for the pain."

"What happened to me?"

"Don't you recollect? You took a terrible beating."

That last silenced Dan for long seconds, then he said, "The Clay brothers."

"Them and a few others."

"The Clay brothers," Dan said again, slowly, as though branding those three words into his brain. Crow had lit a fire in the middle of the cabin's dirt floor, and he stared at the man in the crimson-streaked gloom. "At Wheeler's Crossing . . . they kicked me . . . kicked me . . ."

"And bust your ribs. Your face ain't looking too good either, but your nose ain't broke. At least I don't think it is."

"What did I do to the Clays?" Dan clutched Crow's shirt, his fevered eyes on fire. "Did I get my work in?"

"Dan, you need to rest. Not talk. You're very weak and Mary Jane . . ."

"Did I draw down on them? Did I get my licks in?"

"No. You were buffaloed by Ben Clay and didn't get the chance."

"Who's Mary Jane?"

"One of Wheeler's whores. She helped us."

"The Clay brothers walked away without a scratch?"

"Yeah, that's how it played out. They walked away

mighty pleased with themselves, and I had to carry you from your horse."

"Help me to my feet," he said.

Crow shook his head. "You're going nowhere, pardner."

"There has to be a reckoning," Dan said. "They tried to kill me."

"No, they tried not to kill you. All they wanted was to cripple you, send you back to Texas a broken man, and it seems to me they damned near succeeded. Dan, you're sure hurt, so hurt that if you hope to get better you'll need to ride the bed wagon for weeks, if not months."

"Damn you, Crow, help me up or stand aside. I'm going after those Clays."

"That's the fever talking," Crow said. "You ain't fit to stand, never mind ride a bronc. Hell, you're as weak as a two-day old kittlin."

The fire in the middle of the room snapped and cracked, and black smoke from burning dry wood rose to the roof and escaped through its many gaps. In the distance Crow heard a coyote, a notorious trickster, yelp its hunger, hunting close to the ghost town where there could be rats.

Dan tried to sit up, but the pain from his broken ribs stabbed at him, and he was glad to immediately lie flat again. He found it was painful to breathe and it seemed that his many cuts and bruises had conspired to hurt like hell and keep him abed. He wasn't as weak as a kitten, he was even weaker. He had come to terms with his frailty, but now for the first time Dan discovered his nakedness, and he suddenly felt powerless and vulnerable.

"Crow," he whispered, "where am I?"

"In a ghost town north of Wheeler's Crossing."

"And where are the Clay brothers?"

"Far from here."

Crow lifted Dan's head and put the canteen to his lips. He drank a little and then the soaring fever took him and he whispered, "I feel like I'm being drug headfirst across hot coals."

Crow took the bandanna from around his neck, wet it down and laid it on Dan's forehead. "Close your eyes and try to sleep now," he said.

Dan grabbed Crow's arm in a weak hand and murmured, "Where are the Clays?"

"Not here," Crow said. "Far away."

"I'm scared."

"Don't be. No one can harm you here."

"I'm scared of the Clays. They might be close."

"They're not."

"Crow, am I going to die?" Dan said. His lips were pale, white.

"I don't know."

"I'll make peace with my Maker."

"Sleep now, Dan," Crow said. "All your pain will sleep with you."

But Dan Caine was already asleep and didn't hear.

Throughout the long night, Crow chanted his songs again and asked the spirits for a vision.

But the night slowly turned from black to misty gray, and he saw nothing.

CHAPTER TWENTY

"You think I see nothing, but I see everything," Luther Wheeler said. "Where are you going with all those supplies?"

"I'll pay for them," Mary Jane Hillman said. "Take it out of my mattress time."

The two stood in the mercantile where the guttering oil lamps had not yet banished the gloom of night. Wheeler looked at the woman from her ankle boots, upward to a gray skirt then to her homespun shirt and finally to the battered hat on her head. Whores always had a collection of men's hats, and Wheeler wondered why that was. He admitted to himself that Mary Jane, despite a little hardness to her mouth and eyes, looked very pretty that morning. He was not tempted. He never put hands on his ladies, scrupulously keeping their relationship on a business foundation.

"I asked you before, I'll ask you again . . . where are you taking those supplies?" Wheeler said.

"To the Amitola ghost town," Mary Jane said. "I don't advise you to go there."

"Why not?"

"You'd walk into the lion's mouth."

Suspicion dawned on Wheeler. He visibly paled, his face aghast. His voice fracturing, he said, "No . . . don't tell me . . ."

"Don't tell you what?"

"That instead of on a train to Texas, Dan Caine and his Injun are in the ghost town."

Mary Jane smiled. "That's what I'm telling you."

A moment of stunned silence, then, "Oh my God . . . if the Clays find out, we're all dead . . . Caine . . . you . . . me . . ."

"Why would they kill you? I'm the one that's trying to keep Caine alive."

"Guilt by association. Have you heard of that?"

"No, but I understand what you're saying."

"How is Caine?"

"Still alive, the last time I saw him. Don't worry about it, Luther."

"You don't listen, do you? If Ben Clay finds out what you're doing, he'll kill us all."

"He won't find out, unless you tell him."

"I don't need this," Wheeler said. He wrung his hands. "What can I do?"

Suddenly he brightened. "I know . . . just leave them there. Don't go back, and if the Clays find them, well, we can deny all knowledge."

"No, I won't let them starve, and I won't stand aside and let Dan Caine die. That . . . that would be inhumane."

"You'd rather we all get killed?"

"We're in no danger. The Clays won't even know they're in Amitola."

Cranky now, Wheeler said, "Amitola . . . Amitola . . . ghost towns don't have names."

"This one does," Mary Jane said. Then, "Now look on the bright side, Luther. If Caine and his Apache are bent on revenge, they won't start with you because I'll tell them you've been such a big help."

Wheeler shook his head. "You're a whore to try a man. The worst whore I ever had." He sighed. "What have you got in your poke?"

Mary Jane opened the canvas sack and said, "It's heavy. A slab of bacon, coffee, lard, sugar, baking powder and flour for biscuits, canned peaches, a small skillet and a coffeepot. Oh, and a hand towel and a pouch of shag tobacco for Crow."

"Crow's the Indian?"

"Yes, he is. He's half-Apache."

"And a scalp hunter."

"That would be my guess."

Wheeler sighed again. "All right. Take them the grub, and that's about ten dollars out of my profits for the month." He took the sack. "I'll carry this to your horse. Correction, my horse. Which one?"

"The grulla mare."

"That's a fifty-dollar hoss."

"I'll take good care of her."

"See you do."

Mary Jane and Wheeler walked outside into the new morning. Sunlight already filtered through the tree canopies and birds sang in the branches and the air was crisp and smelled of sage and of the damp earth around the well.

Wheeler helped Mary Jane into the saddle and said, "Be back soon. I have a feeling we're going to be busy today. I think it's something to do with this time of the year, heading into fall."

"Cooler weather makes men friskier, especially the

married ones. Don't ask me why that should be, I don't know. I'll be back soon."

Wheeler laid his hand on the saddle horn. "If Ben Clay discovers you out there with Caine, we're all dead. You know that, don't you?"

"He won't discover us. Relax, Luther."

"Easy for you to say," Wheeler said.

He watched the woman ride away and shook his head.

This business with Dan Caine didn't bode well. It gave him a queer, twisty feeling in his gut, always a bad sign.

CHAPTER TWENTY-ONE

Crow took the sack of supplies from Mary Jane Hillman, and she stepped out of the saddle. "How is he?"

"Sleeping. He talked some, or raved some, last night, but he's still very weak."

"Did he drink water?"

"A little. Early this morning I made a salve from the chaparral that grows around here and spread it on the worst of his cuts and bruises. It may help with the pain. But I can do nothing for broken ribs."

Mary Jane said, "Let him sleep. We can't let him move around. His broken ribs need time to mend."

Crow's smile was fleeting. "Don't fret about that. Dan ain't going anywhere."

The woman dipped into the sack and handed Crow his pouch of tobacco. "I thought you might want this."

Now Crow's smile grew. "I sure do."

He found his pipe and was soon lost behind a cloud of smoke.

Mary Jane filled the coffee pot at the creek, threw in a handful of Arbuckle and then added more broken slats of wood to the fire before setting the pot on the coals to boil.

She then kneeled beside Dan and wiped off his face with the hand towel she'd brought. "I don't like this, he's still very hot," she said. "We have to break his fever or it will kill him."

Crow laid his pipe aside. "What's he saying?"

"It's the fever talking. He keeps calling for Helen."

"Helen is his wife."

"Soon to be his widow if we don't do something."

"If I can find a moringa tree . . ."

"Apache man, in this part of the Arizona Territory you could search for days to find that tree, whatever it is. Dan's fever must be broken and soon." Mary Jane thought for a while and then said, "Pick him up and follow me."

"Where are we going?"

"The creek," the woman said.

The creek water came from an underground source and wasn't icy, but cold enough to cool down a fevered man, or so Mary Jane hoped.

Crow had Dan Caine's naked body in his arms, and he said, "What do I do with him?"

"Put him down right there, in the deep water by the bank."

"Lady, he'll get wet."

"Of course, he will. Wet and cold, I hope. Now, put him in the water but hold up his head. He has to breathe."

Crow did as he was told, and the water cascaded over Dan Caine's naked body while he held his head. "How long do we do this?" he said.

Mary Jane shook her head. "I have no idea. As long as it takes."

"How will we know if his fever breaks?"

"I have no idea."

Crow glanced up at the blue bowl of the sky where a few white clouds drifted like lilies on a lake and said, "Then we might be here for a while."

"Not too long, I hope. I don't want the coffee to boil dry."

Crow smiled. "You're a strange lady."

"I'm a whore. How can I be otherwise?"

In later years, Crow said that he had no idea how long Dan Caine was in the creek. Judging by the sun, maybe two hours, maybe longer, long enough for Mary Jane to bring him coffee and his pipe and hold Dan's head while Crow smoked and drank and watched her lay her cheek on the unconscious man's forehead now and again to test the heat of his skin. Some historians speculate that the cold creek water didn't save Dan Caine's life that day, suggesting that the fever more likely broke naturally. But Crow said otherwise, and he was there.

As it happened, Dan Caine's eyes suddenly fluttered open, saw Mary Jane bent over him and said, "Are you trying to drown me?"

Excited, the woman didn't answer but called out to Crow, "He's awake!"

Crow, who'd wandered off looking for a moringa tree, came running back. He saw Dan glare at him and, as excited as Mary Jane, exclaimed, "He is, by God!"

"I'm freezing to death," Dan said. "You damned assassins . . . get me out of here."

"Hold on, we'll lift you out," the woman said. "But slowly, on account of how you're all broken up." Then, "Crow, get his shoulders and I'll grab his feet. Lay him on the bank in the sun. Are you ready? Gently, remember."

"Ready," Crow said.

It turned out to be a lot harder to get Dan out of the

creek than it was getting him in, and he cried out in pain a few times before they got him onto the bank.

Mary Jane kneeled beside him and said, "How do you feel?"

"Cold."

The woman stretched out next to Dan and held him close but was careful not to hurt his ribs. "Just lie still," she said. "I'll warm you up."

"I'm a married man," Dan said, shivering.

"And I'm a whore," Mary Jane said. "When you see your wife again, you'll have a story to tell, huh?"

"I'm warming up."

"I figured you would."

"But I'm very tired and weak and I hurt all over."

"Then I'll have Crow carry you back to the cabin."

"Fine, but first warm me up some more."

Mary Jane smiled. "I believe you're starting to feel better, married man."

CHAPTER TWENTY-TWO

Around the same time Mary Jane Hillman rode back to Wheeler's Crossing, one of the Clays killed again, this time in the Old No. 9 saloon in Tucson near the train depot. The place was a gambling den that didn't allow women on the premises and was famous for its single barrel bourbon and fine Cuban cigars. The proprietor was three-hundred-pound Eden Cooke, a genial rogue who'd made his fortune shanghaiing sailors for the New York hell ships.

Cooke would later tell City Marshal Bill Roche that the shooting of bartender Shane Battle was, "entirely justified, by God." It seemed that Cooke was the only person in the saloon who thought so.

According to the *Arizona Daily Citizen,* Battle had not shown up for work on the day of his death, having just received a five-hundred-dollar legacy from a distant relative in Philadelphia. He was quarrelsome in his cups and had been drinking steadily since eight o'clock that morning. Around noon, Battle was playing poker with two others when Decker Clay and a cowhand named Sam Bradshaw, or some say Bradford, entered the saloon and the youngest Clay took a hand at the poker table. The *Citizen* pointed out that "Mr. Clay was heeled, carrying a revolver of the largest kind in a leather scabbard at his hip. It is not known at this time whether or not Mr. Battle was armed, though City Marshal Roche said he was, and showed this reporter a small Smith & Wesson revolver he said fell from Battle's pocket."

The newspaper account said that Battle began to lose heavily, "disposing of his inheritance at a breakneck pace," and then angrily accused Decker Clay of cheating.

The *Citizen* said, "To a man, the denizens of the saloon declare that they heard Mr. Clay say to Mr. Battle, 'Shut up, and play cards.' At this juncture, Mr. Battle was seen to calm down and for a while he played poker without directing any further recriminations at Mr. Clay."

But the peace was soon shattered.

And again the *Citizen* had it covered.

"To the surprise of those present, Mr. Battle sprang to his feet a second time and declared in a loud voice, 'Return my money and be damned to ye for a cheating hound.' Following this accusation, Mr. Clay drew his revolver, pointed it at Mr. Battle, and said, 'Take that back or pull your pistol and get to your work.' Mr. Battle then opened his coat and said, 'I have no weapon.' Witnesses say that at this juncture, Mr. Eden Cooke, the proprietor of the Old No. 9 establishment, called out, 'Here, that won't do!' It was then that Mr. Clay said, 'If you're going to accuse a man of cheating, you should have armed yourself.' He then discharged a ball into Mr. Battle's chest and the mortally wounded man cried out, 'Boys, he has killed me!' before falling to the floor where he expired, cursing Mr. Clay. Mr. Battle was twenty-three years old and is believed to have relatives in Philadelphia. City Marshal Roche says no charges will be filed against Mr. Clay since the shooting was in self-defense.

"Mr. Clay, the son of rancher Mr. Barton Clay, is described by some Tucson citizens as a desperate character who has killed his man in the past. At the time of this writing, the *Arizona Daily Citizen* cannot confirm that statement."

"How much, boss?" the puncher said.

"I'll count it," Decker Clay said. He stood in the stirrups, took a wad of notes from his pants pocket and thumbed through them. After a while he said, "Three hundred and forty. The other gents won some pots. Here, Sam, take this," Clay handed the puncher forty dollars. "You brought me luck today."

The puncher thanked Clay and shoved the money into his shirt pocket.

Decker Clay grinned his merriment and said, "Hey, did you see the expression on his mug when my bullet hit him? It was like, 'This isn't really happening to me.' I almost laughed out loud."

"That's how the cow ate the cabbage all right. He looked as surprised as hell," the puncher said.

"A .45 bullet hitting his chest can surprise a man all right. Maybe he thought I wouldn't shoot."

"He said he wasn't heeled."

"He wasn't. Roche must've had the stingy gun in his pocket and dropped it beside Battle's body, about the only thing he's ever done right."

"I didn't know that feller before today, did you?"

"Battle? Yeah, I knew him slightly. He was the bartender at the Calico saloon and I spoke to him a few times and I'm sure he shortchanged me the last time I was in there."

"Then he deserved to be shot. Serves him right for shortchanging a man."

"I don't know for sure if he shortchanged me. He might have." Decker Clay shrugged. "What the hell does it matter?" He glanced up at the fading blue sky and said, "We should be back at the ranch in time for supper. Killing a man always gives me an appetite."

Clay grinned, tilted his head back and sang . . .

"Cheyenne, Cheyenne, I'm a-leavin' Cheyenne."

The man called Sam took up the song . . .

"Goodbye, old Paint, I'm a-leavin' Cheyenne."

Decker Clay sang . . .

"My foot's in the stirrup, my rein in my hand."

Then Sam . . .

"I'm a-leaving Cheyenne, I'm off to Montan'."

Clay, grinning . . .

"Goodbye, old Paint, I'm a-leavin' Cheyenne."

And so it went, Decker Clay and his puncher singing until the song was sung.

They sang "My Dearest Heart" and "Sweet Mary Ann," and they were still singing songs as the day shaded into evening and they rode onto the Clay range.

Later Decker told his father and brothers that he'd killed a man in Tucson. City Marshal Roche had ruled the shooting self-defense, so no one was overly concerned, though Barton Clay asked how many shots were fired. When Decker replied, "Just one," his father smiled and nodded his approval.

CHAPTER TWENTY-THREE

Time passes slowly in a ghost town.

As the days grew into weeks Dan Caine, a tough, robust man, began to heal and regain his strength. Mary Jane Hillman brought grub when she could, but it was barely enough to keep him and Crow fed. The problem was partially solved when Crow shot a couple of white tail deer and fed Dan hearty meat broths that helped bolster him, but coffee, flour, lard, and smoking tobacco were always scarce.

It was on an afternoon at the end of the third week that Crow told Mary Jane about Old Moses, their regular nocturnal visitor.

The woman was alarmed. "Who is he?"

Crow shook his head. "I don't know who he is or what he is. I think he comes because I have strong medicine."

Dan said, "I've never believed in ghosts and ha'ants and sich, but Old Moses leaves me wondering."

Mary Jane looked at them both in silence, drawing a blank.

They were outside, sitting on two salvaged chairs and a stool, enjoying the sun. Mary Jane had washed Dan's clothes by throwing them in the creek and agitating the duds with a wooden paddle, finishing them off with a bar of yellow lye soap. Dan said they were clean and Mary Jane said they were half-clean.

Crow asked the woman, "Do you see what's left of the false fronted building at the end of the street?"

"Not much street and not much building," Mary Jane said. "But yes, I see it. Didn't you kill a deer down there?"

"I surely did, and maybe that's what made Old Moses restless, because every night for the past week he's walked down the road toward us under a moon as big as a silver plate."

"What does he want?" Mary Jane said. She had her gray skirt hiked up, getting sun on her pale legs.

"We don't know what he wants because he never speaks," Dan said.

"Then how do you know his name?"

"We don't. I just made that handle up," Crow said. "He's an old black man with white hair and I thought Old Moses suited him."

"How is he dressed?" Mary Jane said. "In a white sheet, like a shroud?"

"No, he's all dressed up like a tinpan, plug hat, plaid shirt, canvas pants, and mule-eared boots. I reckon he must've turned up his toes here during the gold rush."

Mary Jane said, "Dan, you say he never speaks, but he could've been polite enough to ask after your health."

"I guess being healthy never enters a dead man's thinking," Dan said.

"I must make his acquaintance before you and Crow leave."

"Leave where?" Dan said.

"The Territory. I meant before you head back to Texas."

Dan shook his head, and his chin took a stubborn set. "I'm not going anywhere."

The woman stood, sunlight tangled in her hair, settled her skirt and said, "Dan, your ribs are healing faster than I thought."

"Because he's as tough as a sow's snout," Crow said.

"Another week or so, you'll be hale and hearty enough to go home to the loving arms of your wife where you can live your life away from the Clays and whores like me."

Dan said, "Mary Jane you're . . .

"I know, a whore with a heart of gold. Well, here's a surprise, I don't have a heart of gold, and I don't even know why I helped you."

"You helped him because your heart is good, woman," Crow said. "You helped him because you couldn't bear to see another human being suffer. To deny this truth is to tell a lie."

"Then I won't lie to you," Mary Jane said. "Dan Caine, I want you out of the Territory. I want you far from here where the Clays can't reach you and harm you. Why? Because I think . . . God help me . . . that over the past weeks I've fallen in love with you." She managed a slight smile. "A whore in love with a married lawman. Don't that beat all?"

"I'm sorry," Dan said.

"Don't be sorry," Mary Jane said. "The fault is mine, not yours. I know that being close to you all this time is as good as it's gonna get. It's a great big world, Dan, and how I feel doesn't matter a damn. I'm only a tiny speck of dirt that gets trodden underfoot every day of the week."

"Mary Jane, you're a fine woman," Dan said.

"I'll pretend I didn't hear that. Now, when are you leaving for Broken Back, Texas?"

"When will I leave? I'll leave when the reckoning is over and done."

"I don't understand," Mary Jane said. "Crow, do you understand?"

"Let the man talk, woman."

"The Clay brothers treated me badly," Dan said. "They kicked me when I was down, beat me mercilessly as though I meant nothing to them, a cur maybe, but not a human being. They did it because it amused them, and in the end they hoped I was crippled. I can't let that go unpunished."

"Dan, don't let yourself fall to their level. The Clays are trash."

Dan's face hardened. "They murdered Dick Meadows, and I vowed to square things with them. Well, I failed, and I considered walking the whole thing back and returning to Texas with my tail between my legs. But then the Clays added another wrong when they murdered Toby Reynolds, and then the beating I took at Wheeler's Crossing changed my way of thinking. If Dick Meadows taught me anything it was that if somebody does you wrong, there has to be a reckoning."

Mary Jane said, "Dan, you're one man . . ."

"Two men," Crow said.

"All right, two men. What can you do against Barton Clay and his sons and his gunmen masquerading as cowboys? And what about Ruben Webb, the shootist? Ask anyone about him, or don't. I can tell you he's pure evil. His mind is filled with darkness and crawling things. He once asked Luther Wheeler how much to use me all night and then whip me in the morning. Wheeler was afraid of him, but to his credit he told him that no one abuses his girls. Webb pistol-whipped him, and Luther had to lay abed for three days. Now do you see what you're up against?"

"I've faced long odds before," Dan said.

"Then there's nothing I can say that will make you change your mind, is there?"

"Nothing. And my decision isn't up for a vote."

"I'll grieve for you, Dan Caine," Mary Jane said. "And your widow back in Texas will do the same. Does she work?"

"She's a schoolteacher."

"Then a whore and a schoolteacher will shed tears over you. How does that make you feel?"

Dan managed a smile. "Honored. Proud even. But don't write me off so soon. Rough vigilante justice is headed Barton Clay's way and he's not going to like it. There is something you can do for me."

"A lot of men have told me that."

Dan let that pass and said, "Tell Luther Wheeler to return our pistols and gunbelts."

"If he's got them."

"He's got them," Crow said. "The Clay boys didn't bother to take our guns."

"I'll see what I can do."

"Crow, how much money do we have?" Dan said.

"About five dollars, I reckon."

The woman looked suspicious. "What do you need money for?"

"We'll need a couple of boxes of .45 cartridges and a box of .44-40s if he's got them. Crow, give Mary Jane the money."

"I'll see what Wheeler's got and you can pay me later. I have a feeling you boys are going to need all the dollars you have. It takes a lot of money to fight a war."

"Not if it's over quickly, and that's what I plan," Dan said.

Mary Jane shook her head and walked through the bright sunlight and gathered up the reins of her horse. She mounted and looked down at Dan. "Did you ever read the Bible?"

"Now and again," Dan said. "I'm not a Bible-reading man."

"Do you know the tale of David and Goliath?"

"Sure. Everybody knows that story."

"Against all odds David slew Goliath, right?"

"Yes, that's right. But I'm not catching your drift."

"You're David going up against the Clay Goliath, only this time it will turn out different."

"You mean this time Goliath wins?"

Mary Jane nodded, no joy in her face. "That's exactly what I mean," she said.

CHAPTER TWENTY-FOUR

"I told her what you told me to say, Pa," Ben Clay said. "And I even offered her a little extra."

"What else did you offer the old hag?" Barton Clay said.

"A carriage drive to the station in Tucson and a train ticket to anywhere she chooses. And then I added five hundred dollars for her expenses."

"Hell, we can't say fairer than that, can we?" Barton said.

He and his son and a few hands now stood their horses around a buckboard on what had been Toby Reynolds' shaggy acres but would soon belong to the Clay Land and Cattle Company. Below them the sun-dappled grassland swept away on a gradual slope for about a quarter mile before it leveled out around the Reynolds ranch house.

"What did she say?" Barton Clay said.

"She said it's her house and she refuses to leave," Ben said. "She says we're a bunch of no-good . . ."

"I don't care what she says we are," Barton said. "I want Ellie Reynolds out of there and the shack she calls a ranch house off my land."

"You want me to shoot her, Pa?" Ben said.

Barton Clay saw a look of dismay exchange among the punchers. Obviously shooting the old lady didn't set well with them. But dealing with an obstinate woman was no part of his plans, and he had to get rid of her.

"All right, like I told you, we'll burn the place down around Ellie Reynolds' ears," Barton said. "That will drive her out fast enough and maybe then she'll see reason and take what I'm offering."

This time there was no reaction from the hands. Burn the old hag. Just don't shoot her. Sometimes Barton Clay wondered about the thinking of people.

"Ben, take Steve and Andy and burn the place," he said. "When she comes out, we'll come down and grab her and put her on the first train to anywhere."

The puncher named Steve swung out of the saddle and climbed onto the buckboard seat beside Andy, the driver.

"Ben, secure the kerosene," Barton said.

Ben dismounted and pushed the kerosene cans behind the seat and then jumped onto the rear of the wagon. "Let's go, Andy," he said.

Ben Clay and the two punchers poured kerosene liberally around the base of the ranch house, a timber structure, and then what was left on the barn and other outbuildings. The sunbaked wood was tinder dry and would flare into flame like a struck lucifer.

"What are you doing out there?" Ellie's voice from inside.

"Come out, you old witch, or we'll burn you out!" Ben Clay yelled.

"Scum! Vermin!" Ellie yelled.

A bullet from the old woman's Winchester shattered a window close to Ben's head, spattered him with sharp shards of glass and he yelped in alarm. "Burn it!" he screamed.

Fagots of brushwood were lit and thrown at the house. In a matter of minutes, the building was ablaze from end to end, a scarlet inferno belching a column of smoke that blackened the blue sky. The barn and outbuildings joined the conflagration, and soon the Reynolds home gasped its last smoky breaths and collapsed into ashes.

Ben watched the place burn and it surprised the hell out of him that Ellie Reynolds had hardly screamed. He figured she must've burned up quick like a roman candle. Then it dawned on him . . . the old woman was dead and what would his pa say?

As it turned out, he said very little.

Barton Clay watched the latter stages of the fire when the ranch house quickly became a pile of ash and blackened spars. He called Ben over to him.

"Pa, I didn't mean for her to die," Ben said. "She burned up real fast."

"No harm done," Barton Clay said, the smoke smell acrid in his nose. "The old lady must've knocked over an oil lamp and was then trapped in her burning home. What a terrible tragedy. Heartbreaking, just heartbreaking. I'll ask City Marshal Roche to see if dear Ellie has any living relatives so I may offer them my condolences."

Father's and son's eyes met, and they both burst into laughter.

"Pa, you've got style," Ben said. "You're gonna be president someday."

"Someday," Barton Clay said. "In the meantime, I've got other fish to fry. Send the hands back to the ranch, we have to talk."

After the punchers left with the buckboard and empty kerosene cans, Barton said, "We'll talk in the grove of trees over yonder, get away from the stink of the fire."

"It's still smoldering," Ben said. "But I don't see any sign of the old lady."

"The place burned like an empty shuck, so she's probably just ashes."

"No body, no prying eyes, and no questions."

"Bill Roche will square it with the county sheriff, so there will be no questions." He swung his horse in the direction of the stand of wild oaks and mesquite. "Follow me," he said.

The two men sat their mounts in the shade of the trees. Ben waited until his father lit a cheroot and then said, "You want to talk, Pa?"

"Yeah, better here than back at the ranch," Barton said through a cloud of blue smoke. "No curious eyes and ears."

"I'm listening, Pa."

"Then listen good. There's a two-by-twice ranch to the north of us, they call it the Rafter-T, and I want it. It's only five hundred acres, stocked with longhorns and a few dozen American horses. The spread is worked by the rancher, a widower called Silas Lee, his daughter and a couple of hands. Ruben Webb already scouted the place, and he says it ain't much, a timber cabin, a barn, a sizable corral, a smokehouse, and other outbuildings. But the grass is good, and near the cabin a spring runs through a grove of apple trees. The trees I'll keep, the rest we'll burn and let the ashes blow away in the wind."

"How do we play it, Pa?" Ben said. He was the least intelligent of the brothers and Barton spelled it out for him.

"Drive a few of our cows onto Lee's land and then later I'll have Bill Roche check the Rafter-T brands. Now Roche is the city marshal but the Pima County sheriff will believe anything Bill tells him. They go back a ways and still have their thieving fingers in a few pies together."

"Bill Roche will say Lee's rustling our stock. Is that it, Pa?"

"Good boy, you're learning. We arrange a meeting with Silas Lee but our only representative in attendance will be Ruben Webb." Barton Clay changed into a wheedling tone, mimicking Webb. "City Marshal Roche, Lee grew angry when I accused him of rustling, and the next thing I knew, he drew down on me. I was plumb sorry that I had to kill him. It was self-defense."

Ben clapped his hands and yelled, "Huzzah!" Then, "You got that down pat, Pa. When do I start hazing our cattle onto Rafter-T range?"

"In a week or two. We'll let any speculation about the old lady's death simmer down first."

Ben looked away to the smoldering ruin that had been the Reynolds ranch house. "I can't help but feel sorry for her."

"And that's why you're an idiot. What was she?"

"A rancher's wife?"

"Ellie Reynolds was a useless, no-account old harridan whose only claim to fame was that she made a good peach pie. Who cares that she's dead? I sure as hell don't."

"You're right, Pa. Who cares?"

"Don't go soft on me, Ben, not now. We have an empire to build, and the strong killing off the weak must be a part of it."

"I'll stand strong, Pa. When it comes to killing, no one has a percentage over me."

Barton Clay's wide, hard-lipped mouth widened in a grin. "That's the kind of talk I want to hear from my sons. Damn it, boy, when all this is over and I'm in Washington, you'll already be a rich man. How does that set with you?"

"That sets with me just fine, Pa," Ben Clay said, matching his father's grin. "Just point me in the right direction and tell me who to kill."

CHAPTER TWENTY-FIVE

Their names were Calvin Owen and Jasper Shaw, a pair of Barton Clay's gun hands, fast-drawing lowlifes who'd built their reps shooting down ham-fisted, backcountry hicks caught nesting on the wrong range and big-talking wannabes who should never have picked up a Colt's gun in the first place. What the two gentlemen had in mind that day was not gunfighting but Mary Jane Hillman. They planned to run her and then jump her and then, being sporting gents, have themselves some fun.

Owen and Shaw saw the woman ride away from Wheeler's Crossing with a sack tied to her saddle horn. She headed north, into open range country where there was nothing but grass and the prairie wind.

Owen looked at Shaw and they both grinned. They didn't have to say anything. Hunting a whore was a lot more fun than facing the chores that waited for them back at the ranch. Driven by the tobacco hunger, they'd come in for tobacco and papers and had told Luther Wheeler that they couldn't linger. But Mary Jane Hillman, Luther's priciest girl, was too good an opportunity to miss.

The woman's dust hadn't yet settled when the punchers

took up the chase. But it was a good ten minutes before Mary Jane turned and saw them on her back trail. It was unusual for cowboys to ride this way, though the word was out that Barton Clay had claimed all the open range north of Wheeler's Crossing. This must be a couple of his riders and as yet she was not alarmed and the possibility of forceable rape didn't enter her mind. But as the grinning riders drew closer their intent became obvious as they yelled at her to draw rein and become sociable. Now Mary Jane knew exactly what was on their mind and it wasn't to sit down together and play pat-a-cake. She kicked her mare into a gallop, but her pursuers were gaining on her, the manes of their horses flying.

The ghost town was a mile ahead.

If she could make it in time.

"Riders coming in," Crow said. "Looks like Mary Jane and two fellers."

Dan Caine had been checking a sore on his horse's left foreleg and now he straightened up. His eyes scanning into the distance, he said, "Give me the gunbelt. And grab the Winchester."

"Trouble?"

"Something tells me it could be."

Dan had just buckled the gun rig around his hips when Mary Jane came in at a gallop, reined her horse in a cloud of dust and yelled, "I'm being followed."

The two riders were more cautious. Seeing two men where they expected none, they came on at a walk, their eyes wary.

They reined up and Jasper Shaw, slower on the draw and shoot than Owen but a sight meaner, looked Dan up and down and then Crow and said, "What the hell are you?"

Dan ignored that and said, "It seems to me your face is familiar."

"Oh yeah, well your mug ain't. Now we're taking back our woman."

"No, you're not," Dan said. "I've took to liking her."

"You look half-dead, mister. A man as downright puny as you should keep his trap shut."

And Jasper Shaw was right.

The beating from the Clays had taken its toll on Dan Caine. He'd lost weight and muscle with it, his face was skeletally thin, his shabby clothes hanging on him like a fat man's ditto suit on a scarecrow. He was pale, not from lack of sun but from pain and sickness, and he'd not regained his strength.

Shaw was a stocky, robust man, big in the arms and shoulders, and he sat his saddle straight. He had a spade-shaped beard, heavy black eyebrows and he was tanned a deep mahogany color from the sun. Calvin Owen was smaller, leaner, with hard blue eyes, now amused as he stared at Dan, and a shock of blond hair showed under his pushed-back hat. He was as mean and sudden as a Louisiana alligator and he'd killed more than his share. His malevolent, dark presence made strong men walk around him and at that moment, sitting his horse under a burning noon sun, he planned to shoot Dan Caine. He knew the gray-faced skeleton was no match for him, but even so, from horseback it would be a challenging kill.

To Owen's surprise it was Dan who spoke next, the tone of his voice challenging. To Shaw, he said, "Two things. Miss Hillman stays with us. The second is . . . have you seen me before, at Wheeler's Crossing maybe?"

Shaw's grin was unpleasant. "Two things. We'll do whatever we want to Miss Hillman when you're dead. The second . . . why would I remember a skinny stick like you?"

"The man on the floor that you and the Clay brothers almost kicked to death? If you don't recollect me, you have a bad memory. I remember you just fine, and I still hear the sound of those fancy jingle bob spurs of yours when your boots came at my ribs."

Jasper Shaw's face lightened, and under his beard his mouth widened in a grin. "Yeah . . . yeah, now I remember you. I thought you'd be in Texas by now . . . or dead."

"Seems like you thought wrong," Dan said.

"I'll soon fix that, Mary Jane," Shaw said.

He went for his gun, worn high, horseman style.

That day, Dan Caine put a lot of faith in Crow, trusting to the man's intelligence and fast reaction to danger. He drew, but shot at Webb, the man he judged to be the more dangerous of the pair. He left Crow to handle Shaw and his gamble paid off.

Taken by surprise at the speed of Dan's draw, Calvin Owen was a fraction of a second too slow. A bullet crashed into his right shoulder, a clean in-and-out wound that missed bones and arteries but took the fight out of Owen, a born killer but not the bravest of men. Dan was aware that Crow had fired. At close range, a .44-40 rifle round will punch clean through a human body and do terrible damage as it travels. Crow, good with a Winchester rifle, slammed three bullets into the center of Shaw's chest, destroying the man's heart, making his survival impossible. Gamer than Owen, but having to choose between two opponents, Shaw had hesitated, fatal in a gunfight, before he got off a shot that went inches wide of Dan's head.

Shaw toppled from the saddle as Owen yelled. "I'm out of it!" He let his Colt drop from his numb gun hand.

"Damn you, you're in it up to your ears," Dan said. "What's your name?"

"Owen, Calvin Owen, and I'm hurting here."

"The dead man?"

"Jasper Shaw. He was fast on the draw, but you confused him."

"He was easily confused and not fast enough," Dan said.

"Your name is Dan Caine and before Wheeler's Crossing, I'd never heard of you. Where did you learn the draw and shoot?"

"I was taught by the best in Huntsville. Using a wooden gun and a canvas holster John Wesley Hardin taught me the ways of the draw."

"Jasper could've shaded you if you hadn't muddled him."

"Jasper couldn't have shaded my maiden aunt. And if you survive the wound I gave you, I suggest you get out of the gunfighting business your ownself."

Mary Jane Hillman stepped next to Dan and raised her British Bulldog revolver and yelled, "Owen, you were fixing to rape me and now I'm gonna blow your brains out."

"No!" Dan said. He lowered the woman's arm. "I need him alive. He's my messenger."

"I ain't carrying no messages for you, mister," Owen said. "You've shot my shoulder all to pieces."

"You'll carry my message to Barton Clay and Jasper Shaw's body will send him another."

"And what's your message?"

"I'll tell you by and by. I don't want you to go forgetting it, Calvin."

"What kind of man is called Calvin?" Mary Jane said.

"His kind, I guess," Dan said. Then, "Crow, help me get Jasper on his horse. Poor feller can't do it by himself."

Crow, with little help from Dan, manhandled the dead man across his saddle and then Dan handed the reins to Owen and said, "Let the Clays bury him."

Owen's shoulder felt like it had been hit by shrapnel, every shard of it spinning around like a flaming Catherine wheel. He bared his teeth and said, "Barton Clay will kill you for this."

"Then give him my message, will you?"

"Damn your eyes, Caine, what message?"

"Tell Barton Clay that the war has started," Dan said.

CHAPTER TWENTY-SIX

"Dan, the first thing Barton Clay will do is burn this place," Mary Jane Hillman said. You'll have to ride out at first light tomorrow." She looked around her. "I'll miss Amitola and its ghosts."

"I'm sorry, Mary Jane," Dan said.

"I enjoyed the peace and the solitude. Perhaps I can find those things somewhere else."

Then, an impulsive gesture, Dan said, "When the war is over, why don't you come to Texas with Crow and me?"

Mary Jane smiled. "Two women in love with the same man in the same little jerkwater town? I don't think it would work, do you?"

"No, I guess not," Dan said.

Crow said, "Pity you can't have two wives, Dan. It's the Apache way."

"And soon we could be two widows," the woman said. She shook her head. "I don't want to think about that."

Mary Jane untied her bulging sack from the saddle and tilted its contents on the ground. "Your gunbelts and re-volvers," she said. "Tobacco and a pint of whiskey. How are you going to live when you're waging war on Barton

Clay? It's a war you can't possibly win, but you'll need grub and a place to spread your blankets."

"We'll manage," Dan said.

"No, you won't," Mary Jane said.

Crow said, "Ma'am. you know this country better than we do, so tell me, where do we hide out?"

"We're not hiding from Barton Clay," Dan said. "We're going after him."

"Hiding out as just a manner of speaking," Crow said. "But Miss Hillman is right, we need a safe place to camp."

"To the east the Rincon Mountains are less than a day's ride away," Mary Jane said. "Luther Wheeler told me that men on the scout often lose themselves among the pine and ponderosa forests on the slopes. But just to the north of Tucson are the Santa Catalina Mountains and they might be your best bet. An army officer told me he once chased Apaches that way. He said the mountains are full of canyons with water running through them and stands of pine and oak everywhere. You could establish a camp and stay hidden from Clay and his boys forever if you wanted."

Dan shook his head. "No, Crow and me aren't going to huddle in the trees like a couple of maiden aunts expecting to see Barton Clay behind every bush."

"Where then? I've told you the two best places to hide . . . I mean go."

Crow smiled and said, "Dan, you're a white man who sure makes a lot of plans for this poor Indian boy."

"So we're vigilantes, but you're my deputy and that hasn't changed."

"As you say, Sheriff," Crow said.

"Do you have a plan and are you going to tell us about it?" Mary Jane said.

"Yes, we'll be in the last place Barton Clay will think to look."

"Where is that?"

"Mrs. Gertrude Dale's Boarding House for Christian Gentlemen."

Mary Jane said, shocked, "Where is that?"

"Tucson, the fairest city in the Arizona Territory."

"You're mad," the woman said.

"I don't think so," Crow said. "I think Dan's as crazy as a fox, because Barton Clay will never think to look for us in Tucson. But there's only one problem."

"What's that?" Dan said.

"We're not just borderline broke, we're full broke . . . as in we ain't got a tail feather left between us and Mrs. Dale wants cash on the barrelhead from her Christian gentlemen."

"She might take tick," Dan said.

"Getting the nice lady to take tick would be like trying to broom sunshine off the front porch."

"Oh, my Lord, I don't know why I'm saying this, catering to your insanity, but I'll lend you the money and you can pay me when you're in funds."

"I can't take money from a woman," Dan said.

"Mister, who do you think paid Luther Wheeler for the groceries you've been eating?"

"Miss Hillman has a point," Crow said. "She's telling it like it is, Dan."

"I'll pay you back, every penny," Dan said. He smiled. "With interest."

A random wind tossed a question mark of hair across Mary Jane's forehead, and sweat beaded between her breasts. The day was hot, and the sunlight had taken a harsh edge. Nearby, a goldfinch warbled, note after note popping in the air like soap bubbles.

Mary Jane, a whore with a strange mix of kindness, courage, and sadness, opened her purse and withdrew two twenties that she passed to Dan.

"That will keep you going for a while," she said.

"Can you afford this?" Dan said.

"It's my life savings."

"I can't . . ."

"Take it. Don't make things worse than they are."

Dan searched his mind for words, couldn't find them and remained silent.

"I was in love with another man once," Mary Jane said. "His name was Alan and we got married when I was sixteen and then after two years he died of consumption. That was in Louisville. We'd bought a little house with a garden front and back. I planted sweet corn and tomatoes, and Alan said I had a green thumb." She smiled at Dan. "Maybe I fall in love too easily." The woman mounted her horse, gathered up the reins, and said, "Dan, the Clays are primitive, barbaric people and you're dealing with the devil." Tears welled in her eyes, and she said, "Take care."

Dan Caine watched Mary Jane Hillman ride away and when Crow stepped close to him, he said, "Don't say a word, Crow. Later, but not now."

CHAPTER TWENTY-SEVEN

"You're wounded, you've brought back a dead man, and you're bleeding all over my rug," Barton Clay said. "What the hell happened?"

"Me and Jasper gun-fought Dan Caine and his breed," Calvin Owen said.

"And now Caine is dead, right?"

Owen grimaced at the pain in his shoulder and said, "No, he's alive."

"He shaded you on the draw and shoot?"

"He's fast, boss. I didn't reckon him to be that fast."

"Maybe he ain't fast, Owen," Ruben Webb said, his eyes malevolent. "Maybe you're slow or you were on the grog."

Owen was stubborn. "I wasn't drunk. Caine surprised us was all and the breed is all kinds of hell with the rifle."

"How did all this happen?" Barton Clay said.

Owen hesitated, then, "Me and Jasper ran a whore."

"You what?" Barton said, more of a yell. His Chinese cook pressed a bloody towel against Owen's shoulder, and Barton waved the little man away.

"Me and Jasper, we seen one of Wheeler's whores leaving the Crossing and we figured to run her."

"You ran her where?" Barton Clay said. His voice was even, slow, ominous.

"To a ghost town north of the Crossing . . ."

"I know the place. They called it Amitola," Barton said.

Pain making him testy, Owen said, "I don't know what they call it, but that's where Dan Caine and his breed were."

"Who was the whore?" Pete Clay said.

"Mary Jane Hillman," Owen said.

"I know her," Pete said. "Why did she fog it to the ghost town?"

"I don't know. I guess that's the way we run her. She knew what was going to happen when we caught her and she wouldn't draw rein."

"Maybe she knew Caine and the breed were waiting for her in the ghost town," Pete said.

"Could be. I don't know," Owen said.

"What do you think, Pete?" Barton Clay said. "Could she have been supplying Caine with grub?"

"It's possible," Pete said. "But who knows how a whore thinks?"

"If she did, she'll regret it," Barton said.

"I'll ask Luther Wheeler," Pete said. "He'll know."

His face vicious, Barton Clay moved his attention back to Owen.

"You said Caine sent me a message," he said.

"He sent two messages, the dead man was one and the other was that the war has started."

Fury burned in Barton Clay's face. "That no-account hick, that . . . that nonentity has the bald-faced impertinence to declare war on me?"

Owen nodded. "That's what he said."

Barton turned his head and glared at Ruben Webb and

his sons Pete and Decker. "I want Caine dead," he said. "I want him deader than dead. I want him destroyed, annihilated, wiped off the face of the earth. When Ben comes back, I'll tell him to take as many hands as he needs to hunt Caine down. Burn him or use a razor and cut him into a thousand pieces but let him know he's dying. At first light tomorrow we'll set that damned ghost town on fire, raze it to the ground. Caine won't use the place as a hideout again."

"Boss, this man need doctor. Shoulder shot up very bad," the Chinese said. His name was Quan Wen, and he was small and slight with a long pigtail. Dressed in a black tunic and white pants, he was a veteran of the savage San Francisco Chinatown Tong wars and in 1930 a former Clay cowboy remembered him as "a good cook but a vicious little whoreson."

"I'm in pain," Owen said. "And I've lost blood." He was ashen under his deeply tanned skin.

"A wound like that, blood poisoning is always a danger," Pete Clay said. "I once saw a man die that way. He wasn't even shot, cut himself with a log saw."

"Boss, send for a doctor," Owen said, grimacing. "I'm all shot to pieces here."

Barton Clay shook his head, his face like rough-hewn granite. "Hell no. You let Caine put the crawl on you and as far as I'm concerned you ain't worth doctoring. I want you out of my house and off my range."

The Chinaman scowled. "You hear Mr. Barton. Get out of his domicile."

"Pete, Decker, take him to his horse," Barton said.

"No, boss! You can't do this to me," Owen wailed. "I'll bleed to death before I make Tucson."

"Ruben, I want you on Ben's posse," Barton said, ignoring the man. "Find Caine and kill him."

"You can depend on me, boss," Webb said. "We'll run him down."

Owen, cursing Barton, was half-pushed, half-carried out of the parlor by Pete and Decker, helped on his way by a kick from the Chinese cook.

"Bad man," he said. "Upset Mr. Clay."

The story of Calvin Owen's fate gets murky. It's known that his horse, with bloodstains on the saddle, returned to the Clay ranch sometime after midnight. Owen's body was never found. But according to some accounts, on Christmas Eve 1892 a man named Cal Owens was shot and killed by a lawman in a Fort Worth saloon. Was it Calvin Owen? We'll probably never know.

CHAPTER TWENTY-EIGHT

The morning Barton Clay burned down the Amitola ghost town and banished the spirits, in Tucson Dan Caine and Crow were back in Mrs. Gertrude Dale's good graces, having paid what they owed her and reserved two rooms for an indefinite stay.

After a celebratory breakfast of flapjacks and bacon, they mounted their horses at the livery on Cemetery Street and rode west. A war not of Dan's making had started and he wanted to make sure that Ellie Reynolds would not be harmed by it.

When they rode onto the Reynolds' range, they saw a lot of cows with the Lazy C brand and only a few with Ellie's Flying R. It looked like Barton Clay had moved cattle onto the old lady's range, but was she unharmed? Had he paid her off? That seemed unlikely. A tightness in his belly, riding under an ominous sky with gray clouds piled one on another like gigantic boulders, in the distance Dan expected to see a trim little ranch house. What he did see was a pile of black ashes and an old black man with white hair leading away a stubborn, overloaded burro.

When he saw Dan and Crow, the old man stopped and watched them come.

Dan drew rein and said, "Howdy."

The man nodded. "And you."

He was tall, skinny as a rail with mahogany-colored skin and a face networked by wrinkles. He was dressed much like the ghostly Amitola tinpan with the addition of a huge dragoon Colt that hung on his right hip, and a Sharps big .50 was in a scabbard strapped to the burro's pack.

Dan looked beyond the man to the ashes of the Reynolds house.

"Miss Ellie ain't here no more," the man said.

"Where is she?" Dan said.

The black man turned and pointed. She's over there. I buried her, but there wasn't much of her left to bury. Didn't put up a marker for her because the cows would just knock it over."

"How did this happen?" Dan said.

"I don't know."

"How did she die?"

"Looks like she burned up wit' the house."

"Who would do this?"

"I don't know."

Dan glanced at the threatening sky, then said, "How did you know Ellie?"

"I used to come by. She'd give me pie and coffee . . . coffee with cream and sugar. I sure was partial to that."

"You're a tinpan." Dan said.

"Yup, that's what I am. I tried hard rock when I was younger. Never struck paydirt though."

"Have you seen any riders around here?"

"Nope. Just you. My name is Joe Lark. And I'm eighty

years old, and Sophie, my burro, is about the same in donkey years. Now we're looking fo' a porch with rocking chairs and hanging water ollas, Sophie and me."

Dan smiled. "Then howdy again, Joe. Name's Dan Caine and I've got a calico cat named Sophie."

"Me and cats never did get along," the old man said. "Seems that every time I get close to one, I start into sneezing. Strange that." He let his eyes wander to Crow. "Seems to me them bear claws around your neck are Apache."

"I'm half Mescalero, old-timer," Crow said.

"I've had trouble with white men, but never had my biscuits burned by Mescalero. Now Utes are different. They're as mean as curly wolves and one time a bunch of them gave me a scare up in the Green River country. There was about two dozen of them, and I was sure they were after my scalp, but they rode right past this old black man like he wasn't there. It seems that when a Ute aims to war on the Navajo and steal women and horses that's all they think about and ignore all the rest like nothing else exists."

Joe Lark tugged on Sophie's lead rope and said, "Now I got to go, have some grieving to do. I'm a man as likes to grieve alone so's not to burden other folks."

"You won't burden us," Dan said. "We're all grieving for Ellie. She was a fine woman."

"And Mr. Reynolds," Joe Lark said. "He must've died unexpected like."

"He was murdered," Dan said. "Shot down at his door. He didn't expect that."

The old man looked stricken. "But . . . but who would do such a terrible thing?"

"I think I know and I'll see they're punished for it," Dan said. "But go on your way, Joe, I don't want to make our troubles yours."

"I hope you find them," Lark said. "Now me and Sophie are headed for Tucson."

"I hope you find your porch with the ollas to keep you cool," Dan said.

Joe Lark nodded and tugged on the burro. "In Tucson, I'll go to the place where the black folks live. I reckon I'll find a porch there."

"Good luck, Joe," Dan said.

As he walked away, Lark waved a hand. "Good luck."

CHAPTER TWENTY-NINE

Ben Clay lowered the brass ship's telescope from his eyes and handed it to the recently hired gunman sitting his horse beside him, a drawfighter named Jess Gentry who'd run with Sam Bass and Seaborne Barnes and them and in his time had killed more than a few. "What do you see down there?" Ben said.

Gentry put the telescope to his eye and after a while, his face perplexed, he said, "I see two men standing looking down at the ground. They have their hats off. Is it a grave of some kind?"

"Describe them," Ben said.

"A big man with yellow hair to his shoulders and a smaller man who looks like he ain't been eating reg'lar."

Ben nodded. "It looks like Dan Caine and his breed. But it can't be. I beat Caine so badly I figured he'd never get over it."

"When was that?"

"A few weeks ago."

"Well, if that's the Caine you're talking about, he's over it."

Ben Clay thought for a spell and then said, "It would

make sense that he'd come looking for Ellie Reynolds. Caine was friends with her and her husband. Caine must've buried what was left of the old lady, a handful of bone and ashes, I reckon."

"You got a problem with Caine, Mr. Clay?" Gentry asked. He had a seven-kill gun rep and didn't come cheap.

"Yeah, he's a troublemaker."

"I guess I know how to deal with troublemakers."

"He's trespassing on our range, Jess. I'd say he's fixing to rustle our cattle."

"Well, when you come right down to it, rustling is a shooting matter."

"And a hanging matter."

"Except there ain't a good hanging tree around these parts."

"You want to take them fellers?"

"Who's the gun?"

"Caine probably. I don't know about the breed."

"We gonna mosey on down this slope and make some war talk? I have to be close when the jawing is done."

"Yeah," Ben Clay said, "that's what we'll do. We ride down there at a walk. I don't want to alarm them into grabbing rifles." He kneed his horse into motion. "Let's go."

Under a sullen sky, the long-blowing west wind carrying the musky scent of cattle, Dan Caine and Crow watched the riders come.

"Ben Clay," Crow, a far-sighted man, said.

"Seems like."

Flashy, even in the gloom of the scowling day, Clay's silver saddle gleamed as did his cartridge belt and holster, both decorated with polished brass tacks. He was tall, well-built, and handsome, but not yet thirty. His face sagged, already showing the effects of alcohol and a dissipated lifestyle. Like all the Clay brothers he wore a huge cavalry mústache and sat a horse well, straight in the saddle, giving him the appearance of a particularly arrogant Civil War general. The man with him rode a beautiful sorrel, a chestnut horse with a light color mane, tail, legs, and belly. He affected the look of a frontier gambler, even to the silver ring on the little finger of his left hand, but he had an air of danger about him, a hired gunman who was prospering.

There was nothing Dan liked about this situation.

His health was far from recovered and he was uncertain about Ben Clay. The man had a rep as a fast draw, but on his best day Dan figured he could shade him. Unfortunately, this wasn't his best day. He'd gotten lucky with Jasper Shaw and Calvin Owen, but bracing Ben Clay was another box of worms entirely. The beautifully dressed gun with him was an unknown quantity, but he'd be sudden, there was no doubt about that.

But Dan Caine made up his mind right there and then. The war had started, and now there was a reckoning close. Ben Clay had helped murder Dick Meadows and he'd almost kicked Dan to death and there was no walking away from that.

The day and hour of the gun had come unexpected and unwelcome, and now he could only see it through.

Ben Clay would not put the crawl on him, not today, not any day.

He turned his head and said to Crow, "This isn't your fight."

The big man's expression didn't change. "Dan," he said, "shut the hell up."

Dan smiled. "Crow, you'll do to ride the river with."

"I'm a stander, not a runner. You should know that by now."

"If I didn't know it before, I know it now," Dan said.

"About time," Crow said.

Ben Clay and his gunman dismounted and walked their horses, left hand holding the reins, gun hand clear. As rain ticked on the grass around them, they looked like a formidable pair. And Ben was smiling, a sign of confidence.

Jess Gentry wanted it close, so Ben didn't halt until only six feet of ground separated them from Dan and Crow.

Four men stood in rain and looked at each other for long moments.

Dan looked into Clay's eyes and knew the man wasn't going to parley. There was no bragging to be done, no threats. All four knew why they were there and that the time had come.

"Let's open the ball," Clay said. "Get to your work."

He drew. Fast and smooth but a fraction of a second slower than Dan Caine.

Years later Bat Masterton wrote about Dan in his column for the *New York Morning Telegraph*. He said, "Dan Caine was one of the premier gunfighters in the West, up there with Hardin and Longley, but he didn't know it. He never sought a gun reputation, never boasted of the men he'd killed and so bad men always underestimated him. Texas bred some dangerous men, but I say Caine was the deadliest of them, and the most modest."

In 1928, Wyatt Earp, then living at 4004 W 17th Street in Los Angeles, said Masterson didn't know Dan Caine, had never met him, and was just repeating what he'd heard. That may be so, but on that late summer day, sick and not at his best, Dan outdrew and killed Ben Clay, a braggart and a bully who was a mite slower on the draw than he thought he was.

Dan's shot to the chest staggered Ben, and he took a step back, lowering his gun hand. He knew he was a dead man and as the darkness closed in on him, he saw Dan Caine at the end of a tunnel. With the last of his strength, screaming his rage, he raised his Colt and fired.

In the split second he had to make a decision, Jess Gentry ignored Dan, figuring Ben was taking care of him, and drew and fired at Crow. The big man took the hit and assumed the duelist's stance, gun arm held straight out, left foot behind the right heel. A second shot tugged at the left side of his chest as he laid the front sight on Gentry and deliberately fired. A hit. A bullet crashed into the gunman under the man's ribs on the left side. Gentry knew unless he could find a doctor it was a killing wound and he was out of it. He'd kill for Barton Clay, but he was sure as hell not going to die for him.

He dropped his gun and yelled, "I'm out of it."

He was appealing to two entities in one man . . . the Apache not overly inclined to spare a defeated enemy, and the white man who would, at least now and then, heed a plea for mercy. That day Gentry was lucky, his cry fell on the ears of the white man. Crow held his fire and was witness to the last exchange between Ben Clay and Dan.

Ben Clay's final bullet went nowhere, and Dan advanced on him, firing as he walked. Four paces, four shots, each one a hit. When Ben finally collapsed, he was already a dead man. Through a haze of gunsmoke, Dan eyed Jess Gentry who was still on his feet.

"I'm out of it!" he yelled. "Don't shoot."

Dan raised his Colt and thumbed back the hammer.

Gentry's terror-filled eyes were as round as coins.

Dan squeezed the trigger and the gunman yelped.

CLICK!

The sound of the hammer striking an empty chamber.

"Damn," Dan said, "I'm out of cartridges." He shook his head. "I was sure I'd loaded all six chambers."

Weak, scared, and losing blood, Gentry sank to the ground, rain falling around him, and hung his head.

"Crow! Where are you hit?" Dan said.

The right side of Crow's shirt was red with blood.

"Bullet burned across my ribs," Crow said. "It hurts like hell, but I'm all right. He shot too fast." Crow stepped to the wounded man and stood over him. "You hear that?" he yelled. "You shot too fast! It's fine to hurry but take your time."

Regaining some of his sand, Gentry said, "Go to hell." Then, "Ben told me you were a pair of hicks."

"He told you wrong, drawfighter, didn't he?" Dan said.

Gentry nodded. "I should've known better. You look like a couple of saddle bums, but not rubes. You sure as hell don't shoot like rubes."

"Go to the Tennessee hills one day," Dan said, "You'll find all kinds of rubes who shoot a sight better than you. What's your name?"

"Jess Gentry."

"Mister, that's a ten-dollar name," Crow said, smiling. "It makes a feller proud to get plugged by a man with a fancy handle like that."

"Go to hell," Gentry said for a second time. He stared at Dan with pain-filled eyes. "Mister, you've killed Barton Clay's son and he'll hunt you down and slaughter you like you're a wild animal."

Dan said, "There's only one thing wrong with that speech."

"There's nothing wrong with that speech. It's the truth."

Dan shook his head. "No, the truth is that I'm the one doing the hunting. My name is Dan Caine, and I want you to remember it."

"You're leaving me here?"

"Seems like. I can't take you where we're going. Maybe one of the Clay hands will come this way by and by." Dan looked casually over his shoulder. "Back there, is Ellie Reynolds' grave. Maybe you should visit and say a prayer."

"I didn't kill her," Gentry said.

"No, but your boss did. I heard a judge once call that collective guilt, a monkey dancing to the tune of the same organ grinder. Do you smoke?"

"Yeah."

"Have you the makings?"

"I had, but by now I reckon they're covered in blood."

Dan built a cigarette, stuck it in Gentry's mouth and thumbed a lucifer into flame that was promptly extinguished by the rain.

"This isn't going to work," Dan said. He took the soggy quirly from Gentry's mouth and threw it away. "Sorry."

Shadows had gathered in the hollows of the gunman's cheeks, and the skin of his face looked like candle wax.

Dan read the signs and said, "Mister, best you make peace with your Maker. I think your time is short."

"I don't want to go this way, bleeding to death in the rain."

"A man can't choose the time and manner of his death. You're in a dangerous and mighty uncertain profession and you took your chances."

The light in Gentry's eyes faded, and he said, "I was

born and bred in New Orleans, you know. You ever been there?"

"Can't say as I have."

"When I visited the city, do you know when I always realized I was home?"

"No," Dan said. "I don't want to hear it but tell me if it makes you feel better."

"The smell, a wonderful smell, rich and sweet, the scent of jasmine and roses growing in old courtyards and of the fish shoaling out in the bay. It's a fragrance like no other." He smiled faintly and said slowly, "Caine, I would've killed you if I could."

"I know that."

"You and the white Indian."

"I know that too."

"Now I'm dying, you've done right by me. You didn't let me die alone."

"I don't want your thanks, Gentry, and save your breath, don't make your peace with me, make it with your God."

The gunman shook his head. "I think not. The Deity and me have never been on what you might call speaking terms. But take off my boots and let me die like a Southern gentleman."

"You're a paid killer, and never lived like a Southern gentleman," Dan said. "Taking off your boots won't change that. Mister, you're way too late."

To Dan's surprise, Crow brushed past him and, steel needles of rain falling around him, quickly removed Gentry's boots. He said nothing and returned to Dan's side.

"Thank you, thank you kindly," Gentry said.

He closed his eyes and died.

"Why?" Dan said, frowning.

"A small kindness for a dying man."

"He didn't deserve it. He wasn't with those who tried to kick me to death, but he was a part of it and he would've killed us both if he could."

"Sometimes the best revenge is to be unlike those who carried out the injury," Crow said.

"Don't worry about that. No matter the reckoning, I'll never be like the Clays," Dan said.

"Don't change on me, Dan," Crow said. "Don't become hard and uncaring, someone I don't know. Revenge is sweet, but it can leave a taste in the mouth that's as bitter as wormwood."

"Who told you that, a preacher?"

"No, old Geronimo told me that, and he knew a thing or two about an eye for an eye."

"I didn't think Gentry was going to turn up his toes," Dan said. "He surprised me."

"But you wanted him dead."

"Yeah, but only after he told Barton Clay about his son's death and who killed him."

Crow said, "This could get out of hand mighty quick. Like a runaway train there might be no way of stopping it."

"Until?"

"Until we're all dead. Barton Clay, his sons, you, me, all of us."

"Crow, you don't have to stick."

"I'll see it played out to the end."

"Who knows, we might come out on top."

"How many dead bodies will we have to pile up to reach the top?"

"As many as it takes."

"You're changing, Dan. After what happened at

Wheeler's Crossing, you changed, not all of it for the better."

"I'll try to be nicer," Dan said. "Look at us, we're soaked to the skin."

"Mrs. Dale isn't going to like us dripping all over her floors."

Dan glanced at the sky. "Clouds are clearing. Maybe we'll dry out before we get to Tucson. Bring the horses, Crow, I've got something to do."

"Do what?"

"Take another look at Ben Clay and make sure he's staying dead."

Crow walked away, shaking his head, then turned and said, "You're fast on the draw and shoot, Dan. Maybe the best there is."

"I don't think so."

"I've never seen faster."

"I doubt that."

"I don't lie. You surprised the hell out of Ben Clay."

"I got lucky."

"You're not fast, just lucky."

"That's it."

"And that a bunch of crap. You're fast."

"In Broken Back you never said I was fast."

"I never saw you draw in Broken Back."

"Seems to me, I wasn't fast back then."

"I know, but something happened to you after Wheeler's Crossing, and I don't know what is was."

"Was it good or bad?"

"Both."

Dan stepped to Ben Clay's body. "Look at him, he tried to kill me twice, and now he's as dead as a rotten stump."

"You shot him all to pieces," Crow said.

"It's another message for Barton Clay, closer to home this time."

"When it comes to messages, I think Barton Clay is as deaf as a cow skull. He'll raise all kinds of hell to find you and set the whole Arizona Territory afire if he has to."

"Let him come, I'll be waiting," Dan said. "I'm not running."

"No, you'll wait for the devil on horseback," Crow said. "May the Great Spirit help us all."

CHAPTER THIRTY

Barton Clay sat his horse and watched stone-faced as the ghost town blazed from end to end, destroying the ruined buildings and exorcising the spirits that haunted the place. When the rain came, it tamped down the ashes and extinguished the remaining flames that clung to the blackened spars like crimson butterflies, but the damage was done and Amitola was no more.

Beside Barton, Ruben Webb's slicker glistened wetly and rainwater dripped from the brim of his hat. "Boss, Caine won't use this place as a hideout any longer," he said, stating the obvious.

"He'll find another," Clay said. "We must hound him, corner him like a rat and kill him."

"He might head for the rim, try to draw us there," Webb said.

Barton shook his head. "He won't. He'll stay here where he's got people to help him."

"Like the whore Calvin Owen told us about?"

"Yeah, her and others, maybe Luther Wheeler himself."

"He wouldn't cross you, boss. He knows you butter his bread."

"Wheeler is an idiot."

Webb nodded. "He's all of that. But he handles the whores well."

Barton looked around him at slanting rain and a few tendrils of lingering black smoke. "We're done here," he said. "Go round up the boys."

"Then where to?"

"Back to the ranch. We got some planning to do. And I want Ben with us."

"I'll send one of the punchers to bring him in," Webb said. "He's moving a herd onto the old Reynolds' place, ain't he?"

"Wrong," Clay said, irritated. "He's moving a herd onto my eastern range is all. It's got nothing to do with the Reynolds, so forget they even existed."

"As you say, boss," Webb said. "I'll go round up the boys and send somebody for Ben."

"Mister Ben. I'd rather you call him that on account he's my son and will own the ranch one day."

"Mr. Ben it is," Webb said. He kneed his horse into motion and started calling in the punchers.

Barton Clay was uncomfortable, breathing harder, his closed face holding something back. It was nothing to do with the rain that trickled down the nape of his neck or his wet saddle, but a discomfort that he knew was a lot more serious. A few times in the recent past he'd experienced the same alarming symptoms, a sudden numbness in his arm and the left side of his face and trouble seeing out of his left eye. Clay knew what all that portended, doctors had told him so, but he refused to accept it. He had too much at stake, a cattle empire to build, then the territorial governorship and finally Washington and power and politics for him to hustle and bustle and get rich in. He rubbed his left arm with a gloved hand. It was high time to consult Paola Gaudet again. She was a voodoo priestess who lived and worked her wonders from a tiny storefront on Court Street in Tucson. Her herbal remedies and voodoo spells for all kinds of illnesses were famous and she'd kept his threatening apoplexy at bay for years. He'd visit her soon.

Clay blinked and realized that Ruben Webb was talking to him. "Huh?" he said.

Webb looked closely at him. "Are you all right, boss?"

Clay nodded. "Yeah, I'm just fine."

"The hands are headed back to the ranch and I sent Bob Harvey for Ben . . . Mr. Ben."

Clay swung his horse around and by the power of his will the reins were in his benumbed left hand. "Let's get the hell out of here," he said.

It took young Bob Harvey an hour to find Ben Clay and Jess Gentry, fifteen minutes to round up their horses, and another ten minutes of struggle to get the heavy bodies draped over the saddles. Under a scarlet-streaked sky, the day was slowly giving way to evening when he stopped in front of the ranch house with his silent, unmoving burdens.

Hands came running when they saw Harvey ride in and then Barton Clay stood in his doorway, his face stricken. But wait, his numbness was gone but he still wasn't seeing too well, only vague shapes. Could it be that Dan Caine and his Indian were dead?

"Who is dead this night?" he said.

"Boss, it's Ben," a puncher said. "Him and Jess Gentry."

Barton Clay almost screamed his anguish. "Oh, my God, no! Can it be?"

Ruben Webb stepped out of the parlor, brushed past Clay and quickly walked to the dead men.

"It's Mr. Ben all right," he said. He and Harvey hauled the body off the horse's back, carried it to the porch and laid it out. "Look, he's been shot through and through four or five times," Harvey said. He looked at Barton's racked face, the tremble of his lower lip, and beat a hasty retreat. "Bring Gentry," Webb said. "And then stay close. We want to know what happened."

"Hell, you see what happened," Harvey said. He'd seen dead men before, three of them of his own making. "Him and Gentry were shot, all their wounds to the front. Looks to me like they lost a gunfight."

Webb ignored that as Barton sank to his knees beside his son's body. He palmed Ben's hair off his forehead and whispered over and over, "My son . . . my son . . . oh, my beloved son . . ."

Then he tilted his head back and a terrible sound burst from his throat that men would later say sounded like the scream of a cougar or the scared shriek of a woman. A moment later Barton Clay collapsed over his son's body and lay still.

"Get him into the house," Webb said to the stunned, gawking hands who had gathered around the scene. "Lay him on his bed." Then, "Damn it, be gentle, you damned churnheads. The boss is already hurting."

Barton Clay was lowered gently onto his bed and Quan Wen removed his spurred boots. "Master sleep now," he said.

But Barton Clay was awake.

"Get me out of this bed," he said. His speech was slurred and he seemed to have a problem with his sight, looking blindly around the room. "Pete, Decker, are you there?"

Pete stepped to the bed and leaned over his father. "I'm here, Pa," he said. "And so is Decker. I'm sending to Tucson for a doctor."

"No doctor," Barton said. "Get the carriage out. Take me to Tucson."

Pete said, "But Pa, I can get the doc here and let you rest."

"Help me up," Barton Clay said. "And bring the carriage around. God damn you, boy, do as I say."

Pete hesitated, and then said, "You want to visit Paola Gaudet."

"Yes, I do. Now help me up, the left side of me feels weak."

"Pa, she's not a doctor," Decker Clay said. "She's no better than a snake oil salesman."

"A doctor can't help me, but Princess Paola can. She has ways."

"Then, we'll bring her and a doctor," Pete Clay said.

"No, I said. Get the carriage, take me there. Princess Paola doesn't go to people, they come to her."

"Pa, like I told you, she's selling snake oil," Pete said. "You need a real doctor."

"Princess Paola is a real doctor."

"A witch doctor, you mean," Decker said.

"Maybe she is, maybe she isn't, but she can restore me to health. Now bring the carriage around. I won't tell you again."

Pete turned to Decker and said, "Do as Pa says, harness

up the gray mare and tell Buff Grant to bring the surrey around."

With one last, lingering look at his pa, Decker left the bedroom.

Pete helped his father sit on the edge of the bed, and Barton Clay said, "Quan Wen, be damned to you for a heathen Chinaman, bring me my boots."

His words were still slurred, his voice weak, and the left side of his face was strangely immobile. As Quan Wen brought his boots, he said, "We'll bury my son at first light tomorrow morning." Then, the laboring words coming out as slow as molasses in January, "When I find Dan Caine, he'll curse the day he was born and the mother who bore him."

"Pa, we'll all see to that," Pete said.

Barton Clay was on his feet, unsteady, but nonetheless standing.

"Decker, I want you to drive me, not Buff," he said. "I trust your gun."

"I hope we run into Caine," the younger man said.

"So do I," Barton said. His bloodshot eyes turned skyward. "Dear God, let this be the day I kill him."

CHAPTER THIRTY-ONE

Princess Paola Gaudet's voodoo shop was a narrow timber building wedged between a pair of towering, corrugated iron warehouses. Her small front window was lit by candles against the coming dark and was crammed with voodoo dolls, spells and love potions, blessed chicken feet, mojo bags, gris-gris charm necklaces, and varieties of oils, herbs, and incense. A painted sign in the middle of the window read . . .

RITUALS, READINGS
AND CONSULTATIONS
BY APPOINTMENT

But Barton Clay did not need an appointment. He was a regular customer who was not above using voodoo to further his political aims. When he was a young mariner, still in his teens, his ship docked in New Orleans for repairs and he wandered into the shop of voodoo queen Marie Laveau. Just for the fun of it, he had the priestess read his future in her crystal ball and it was she who advised him to move to the Arizona Territory where he would become a rich and powerful man. What Marie didn't see in her crystal ball, or decided not to tell the young sailor, was that his heart was bad and he would not live long enough to scratch a gray head. Young Barton Clay did not return to his ship but left New Orleans for Arizona where he first worked as a puncher and then bought his first hundred-acre ranch that soon, by the way of the gun and the hemp noose, became one of the largest spreads in the Territory. He married and his wife gave him three sons before she died of nothing more serious than a summer cold. Her name was Cora but try as he might, Barton could never bring her face to mind.

Then his lofty ambitions took a backseat to his health.

A year after Cora died, when he turned forty, Barton had his first warning that his heart might betray him. A sudden weakness down his left side that spread to his arm and the side of his face and put him in bed for a week. The doctor told him he must take it easy, sit in a rocker on the porch drinking the odd mint julep and let his foreman run the ranch until Ben, his oldest son, came of age.

"That's all you can do for me?" Barton said. He was the picture of health, big and blond and strong as an ox. But his ticker was faltering.

"Unfortunately, yes," the doctor said.

"And if I don't sit on the porch?" Barton said.

"If you don't, you could die of a massive apoplexy," the doctor said.

Barton told the man to go to hell and cursed him for a quack.

Then he remembered voodoo queen Marie Laveau. In addition to being a seer she also had a reputation as a healer. Where modern medicine had failed, perhaps magic could help.

After a fourteen-hundred-mile trip by horse and train, Barton Clay was told by Marie Laveau's daughter that the voodoo queen had just died at the age of eighty. That was the bad news. The good news was that one of Marie's disciples, Princess Paola Gaudet, had fled the competition in New Orleans and opened her own voodoo practice in Tucson. Angry that he'd made the long, arduous trip for nothing and that there had been a voodoo priestess right on his doorstep, Barton Clay returned to the territory . . . and his relationship with Paola Gaudet began. He was convinced that the Princess's spells and potions had kept him alive and now she would work her magic again and restore him to good health.

Church Street in Tucson was a stretch of warehouses and office blocks lit by a few feeble gas street lamps that did little to lift the gloom. Only Paola Gaudet's candlelit shop window was a rectangle of light in the darkness, splashing on the sidewalk like spilled whitewash. The spicy fragrance of incense escaped from inside the shop, adding an exotic element to the dull night.

"Wait for me here, Decker," Barton Clay said after the surrey reined to a halt outside the shop. "I won't be long."

"Do you need some help getting down, Pa?" Decker said.

"I can manage," Barton said.

The surrey rocked as he climbed down and he stood on the sidewalk. He grabbed Decker by the arm and said,

"Son, we're not praying men. You, me, and Pete, we don't ever pray."

Decker looked at his father's wide, handsome face now grim, shadowed by the darkness. "I guess we can," he said. "You're thinking about Ben?"

"Yes, when we bury him tomorrow. Who will say the words?"

"I can read from the Bible, Pa."

"Would you read out the words and mean them?"

"No."

"Neither would I. It's a great pity."

"We'll miss Ben."

"Yes. We'll miss him. Maybe that's enough." Barton nodded. "I'll be back."

Decker Clay watched the moon rise, rolled and smoked five cigarettes and twice calmed the restive mare in the shafts before his father stepped out of the voodoo shop, a curling wave of blue incense smoke wafting after him.

After Barton settled himself in the seat, Decker said, "Well?"

"Princess Paola put her hands on my head and chanted and after a while she told me that she unblocked my chakras and I'll live for a hundred years," Barton said. "She's a wonderful woman." He showed his son a small red flannel bag tied with string. "This is called a gris-gris bag. It brings the person who carries it good health by healing the heart."

"What's in it, Pa?"

"Herbs, stones, roots, bones, and magic spells written on parchment and some other voodoo stuff. After she laid hands on me, Princess Paola said I must carry the bag in my pocket to bring on the healing. And listen to this, it's very important, the Princess says she'll send many protective spirits to Ben's funeral tomorrow and see him safely to the realms of the afterlife."

"I'm glad to hear that," Decker said.

He didn't believe a word of it, superstitious nonsense, but if old wives' tales helped his father feel better, that was all that mattered.

"I saved some mourning garments from your mother's funeral; see that the hands wear them tomorrow," Barton said.

Decker had seen those as a boy, black funeral robes that were worn over regular clothing and for a while had been popular on the frontier after the War Between the States. It was strange that his father, a forward-thinking man, clung to such things.

Barton Clay glanced at the rising moon that now spread an opalescent light over Church Street and made the rusty, eyesore buildings look as though they were sheathed in marble. From a distance away, a tinpanny piano played in a saloon and a woman's strident laugh was loud and long and false.

"Princess Paola wouldn't curse Dan Caine," Barton said.

"Why not?" Decker said. He slapped the mare's back with the reins, and, surprised, she lurched the surrey forward.

"She said cursing someone is not in her line of work."

"She a witch, for God's sake,"

"She said voodoo only works for good, not evil."

"It doesn't matter a hill of beans. A bullet will do the same thing to Caine as a curse."

Barton nodded. "I believe I'll hang him. I'd like that"

"If we can catch him alive, sure."

"If we don't, then I'll hang him when he's dead."

Decker grinned. "Kill him twice, huh, Pa?"

But Barton wasn't listening. His head was bent and his shoulders shook.

He was again mourning his dead son.

Ben Clay had been a monster, a murderer and rapist, but he'd been flesh of Barton's flesh, blood of his blood, and to his father that was all that mattered.

CHAPTER THIRTY-TWO

Under a rising moon, Dan Caine and Crow sat on rockers on Mrs. Dale's front porch and drank bottles of beer supplied by their landlady, perhaps to make up for a barely adequate beef stew at suppertime.

Crow turned his head to Dan, searched for the right words and finally said, "I feel a chill in the wind. Fall's coming down soon."

"If it's cool and sunny, it will be a grand day tomorrow," Dan said.

"Ben Clay won't see it," Crow said.

"No, he won't. Crow, he deserved what he got."

"He got dead, is what he got."

"Uh-huh."

"His death must've hit the Clays mighty hard."

"I'd say so."

"Dan, maybe Ben Clay was enough."

"What do you mean?"

"I mean maybe killing him was revenge enough."

"All three of the Clay brothers kicked me senseless and tried to cripple me. I won't let two of them walk away from it."

"Walk away from what?"

"The reckoning."

"Dan, you're obsessed. That's the word Geronimo used when he talked about white men. He said he was obsessed with killing whites wherever he found them. It was a sickness in him."

"I'm not Geronimo. I'm Dan Caine, sheriff of Broken Back, Texas, and I'm not making war on the white race, just a few of them, the Clays." Dan built a cigarette and then said from behind a smoke cloud, "Why do you find that so hard to understand?"

"I understood it this morning in the rain."

"Yes, you did. You stood your ground and got your work in and played a man's part. I couldn't have done it on my own, Crow. You saved me from the devil."

"But it isn't enough?"

"It will never be enough, not until all the Clays, seed, breed, and generation of them are dead."

"Then you will never stop. You'll fight them until you're the last man standing."

"If that's how it shakes out, yeah."

"Then I won't criticize a man for doing what he feels needs done. But I won't encourage him either."

"Then where do you stand?" Dan said. His eyes gleamed in the moonlight.

"I'll stand with you, Dan. I'll be there at the end, no matter what that end may be."

"Crow, you don't have to do that. As I tried to tell you in Broken Back, this is my fight not yours."

"I didn't listen to you in Broken Back, and now I'm in too deep and the water is closing over my head." Crow's smile flashed white in the gloom. "It's too damn late to quit." He studied Dan for long moments and then said,

"You have to draw the Clay boys to you. An attack on the ranch is a sure way to get us both killed."

"Killed mighty quick, I reckon."

"Then the Clays have to come out after you."

"That's my way of thinking, lure them into the open."

"I recollect my mother saying, 'desperate times, desperate measures.' I don't know who she learned that from. My Pa maybe. I just don't know."

"Your mother was right."

"I have a saying of my own," Crow said.

"Let's hear it."

"A rotten idea is a rotten idea."

Dan smiled. "You have anything better?"

"No."

"Me neither," Dan said.

A purple cloud drifted slowly across the bright face of the moon, and its edges were outlined in silver. A deeper darkness fell over the porch and brought a coolness to the night air, and Crow had a vision that sizzled in his mind like a lightning strike. He saw a huge tree, but only a single fruit hung from its branches, and the fruit swayed in the wind and dripped blood-red juice and did not fall. Then the strange vision was gone, leaving a throbbing headache in its wake. Crow looked across the porch at Dan Caine, but his head was again bent over the makings in his fingers, and he saw nothing. The cloud moved away from the moon, and the porch grew lighter again. But Crow felt a nameless fearful apprehension . . . as though his world was about to be turned on its head.

CHAPTER THIRTY-THREE

Was Barton Clay stark, raving mad?

Grotesquely violent events about to unfold would indeed seem to indicate that he was insane. But throughout the first decade of the twentieth century, doctors and historians argued the point and came to the conclusion that a series of relatively minor apoplexies had affected Clay's brain. A few apologists still claimed that after the death of his son and heir Ben in 1889, he was not responsible for his actions. But, despite the excuse of apoplexies, the consensus of opinion was that Barton Clay was a sadistic killer who knew exactly what he was doing. That is also the belief of the author of this volume.

Wrapped in a shroud, Ben Clay was buried beside his mother in a small graveyard situated on a knoll some distance from the ranch house.

The only prayer, haltingly read from the Bible by Quan Wen, was taken from Matthew 11:28-30 . . .

Come to me, all of you who are wearied and burdened, and I will give you rest. Take my yoke upon you and learn

*from me, for I am gentle and humble in heart, and you will
find rest for your souls. For my yoke is easy and my burden
is light.*

Barton Clay snapped at the Chinaman, "All right,
enough of that."

The prayer taken from Scripture annoyed him. A reader
of Norse mythology, he wanted his warrior son in Valhalla,
not Heaven.

Barton wore a black mourning garment as did his sons,
Ruben Webb, and a few of the punchers, but there was
little mourning at the graveside. The time for lamentation
was over and the time for vengeance was nigh. Barton
Clay, raving, his eyes popping out of his head, spoke to his
men of revenge, torture, killing and ravaging . . . of gut-
shooting, tearing to pieces, ripping a heart from its chest
cavity . . . and he promised his already decaying son that
he would place Dan Caine's skull on his grave, a trophy to
gift to Odin and his Valkyries.

A Christian burial it was not, and it was from this that
the question of Barton Clay's sanity first sprang. The cowboys and gun hands, even Ruben Webb, were uncomfortable with what was happening and finally Pete and Decker
hustled their father away from the grave.

The others followed to partake of the funeral feast that
Quan Wen had laid out on trestle tables in front of the
ranch house; pies, both sweet and savory, roasted meat,
biscuits, beans and potatoes, and syrup and molasses.
There was a barrel of beer, whiskey, and piglets turning
on a spit. On short notice, the little Chinese cook had done
most of the work himself, and all agreed that he was a
yellow-skinned wonder.

The eating and drinking lasted until nightfall and then

lanterns were lit and logs added to the fire. Then Barton Clay called his somewhat drunk crowd to order.

"Listen up, all of you," Pete said. "My father wants to address you."

Barton, not a big drinker, had a glass of beer in his hand.

"First of all, I want to thank everybody for seeing Ben off to the underworld," he said. "If he'd been here, boy, he would've enjoyed himself."

This brought a chorus of cheers and hear-hears and one rooster, drunker than the rest, pulled his gun and shot into the air.

"I know I work you to death on chores around the ranch . . ."

More cheers and damn rights.

"But I want you, now listen up, I want you to find Dan Caine. I want you to find him and bring him to me. I'll give the man who delivers Caine for my justice a thousand dollars in gold."

There were louder cheers, and a man yelled, "You can depend on us, boss," and the drunken rooster shot off his gun again.

"I know I can depend on you," Barton said. "Search, search, search and find him, boys, find him and bring him to me."

Decker Clay said, "Pa, the whore Calvin Owen told us about . . ."

"Mary Jane Hillman," Pete said.

"Yeah, her," Decker said. "She could know where Caine is hiding out."

"Then we'll talk with her tomorrow, find out what she knows," Barton said.

"That's all good and well, but can we trust what a whore tells us?" Pete said.

"Beat her enough, she'll talk truth," Barton said. "A whore never wants her pretty face pummeled."

That drew a laugh from the men within earshot, and one of them said, "Damn right, they don't."

"Pete, you, Decker, Ruben Webb, and six of the less hungover hands be ready to ride after breakfast."

"I've always wanted to beat an uppity whore like Mary Jane Hillman, beat her like a drum," Decker said. He grinned in the firelight, and his front teeth were as long and prominent as a rodent's.

"Never fear, you'll get your chance tomorrow," Barton Clay said.

He would've said more, but City Marshal Bill Roche jumped off his lathered horse with news that could not wait.

CHAPTER THIRTY-FOUR

"You can pick 'em," Daisy Tweed said.

"I know, I've fallen in love with a married man."

"What does Dan Caine's wife do?"

"She's a schoolmarm. And Crow told me she's pretty."

"A whore doesn't stand much of a chance with that particular gentleman."

"I'm well aware of that. I try not to think about it."

"Then don't look at me," Daisy said.

Mary Jane Hillman stood at her narrow window and gazed out at the moonlit night. "Why?" she said.

"Because you'll only get depressed."

"Again, why?"

"You'll see yourself in another ten years, a worn-out whore who has nowhere to go but down." Daisy touched her face. "I earned every one of these lines the hard way, first in the Dodge City cribs, then in Fort Smith, and after that I kept falling until I landed in Wheeler's Crossing. What age am I?"

"Daisy, don't . . ."

"What age am I?"

"I don't know."

"Give me your best guess."

"Forty? Forty-five?"

"Try again."

"Daisy, don't ask me that question."

"I'm twenty-eight years old and maybe I've got syphilis."

"Don't say that, Daisy."

"It's true. Why would I lie?"

"You have to see a doctor."

"In Tucson? A doctor who knows how to treat me with mercury? Don't make me laugh."

"Go somewhere else. A big city where you could play the piano in a saloon."

"I play badly."

"In a saloon nobody notices."

"I'll think about it."

"No, don't think about it, do it. Time is not your friend."

"Nor yours."

"I know that."

"Then I'll get out of the profession when you do," Daisy said.

"All right, we'll do it together. I'll help you."

"When?"

"Tomorrow or the next day. Soon."

"That soon?"

"You can't wait much longer."

"Mary Jane, why do you want to help me? I don't even like you very much."

"Because I look at you and see myself in ten years."

"And you don't want to be me."

"I never want to be you."

"That's good to hear."

"We'll both leave Wheeler's Crossing," Mary Jane said. "Start a new life, a new beginning."

"As whores?"

"No, as schoolmarms."

"Now that's a radical change of profession."

"And we'll find ourselves husbands."

"Only after I'm cured."

"Yes, only after you're cured. You may not even have syphilis."

"I have it."

"Daisy, if something happens to me, you still must get away from here."

"What could happen to you?"

"I feel strange, as if something is about to take place, like watching a thunderstorm gather on the horizon."

"Something bad?"

"I don't know."

"Then it might be something good."

"Like what?"

"Maybe Luther Wheeler will pension you off. Give you a hundred dollars and a horse and send you on your way."

Mary Jane smiled. "And maybe pigs will fly."

"Ah well, you can live in hope. I can see the moon from here. It looks like a big silver platter."

"Or a slice of cucumber. I need to beg a favor," Mary Jane said.

"I'm not much of a one for granting favors but ask it anyways."

"It's only if a bad thing happens to me."

"It won't. I've stopped looking at the moon, now what's the favor?"

"Tell Dan Caine what happened."

"Why?"

"I want him to know."

"Do you have a reason?"

"For the rest of his life, he might remember what became of me. In some strange way I'll always be with him."

Daisy looked into the other woman's eyes and saw a tangle of emotions. A whore with feelings, she told herself. Aloud she said, "Where is he?"

"You have to keep this secret."

"I'm good at keeping secrets. Do you know how many happily married men and preachers bedded me?"

"He's at Mrs. Gertrude Dale's Boarding House for Christian Gentlemen in Tucson."

"Mr. Caine went to West Point, huh?"

"No, he's the sheriff of Broken Back, Texas."

"An important man."

"Not hardly."

"Well, I saw what the Clay brothers did to him," Daisy said. "And all I can say is that it wasn't pretty."

"They plan to kill him. That's why Dan's location must be kept secret."

"The Clays won't hear it from me."

"And they won't from me," Mary Jane said.

It was a vow she would keep.

CHAPTER THIRTY-FIVE

The moon dropped and surrendered the sky to the rising sun. Birds sang, jays quarreled in the trees . . . and Barton Clay and his horsemen descended on Wheeler's Crossing like the wrath of God.

Luther Wheeler, barefooted, answered Barton Clay's rifle butt knock on the mercantile door and was then roughly shoved aside as a dozen men barged into the building.

"Open the bar, Wheeler," Barton roared. "I've got some men with Chinese gongs banging in their heads who need the hair of the dog."

"Damn right," Decker Clay said. "Wheeler, make it quick."

As ubiquitous as ever, Wheeler said, "Right away, gents."

He led the way into the next room, stood behind the bar and laid out whiskey bottles and shot glasses. Then, "You're early this morning, Mr. Clay."

"I'm here to talk with the whore Mary Jane Hillman," Barton said. "Get her out of bed now."

"It's early . . ." Wheeler said.

"I don't give a damn," Barton said. "Roust her, and if there's a man with her, throw him out of there. You two, Walt and Clark, guard the front door. I don't want her trying to escape."

"Hold on, Pa," Decker said. He downed a whiskey and said, "Let's pick ourselves up from the sawdust first."

Barton ignored that and said to Wheeler, "Go on, wake the whore, bring her here."

Wheeler looked into Barton's blazing eyes, glimpsed a chilling madness, and said, "Right away, Mr. Clay."

In fact, Barton Clay was in a splendid mood that morning.

The great news brought by Bill Roche was that a letter sent to Tucson's mayor Frederick Maish from a longtime friend in Washington stated that President Benjamin Harrison was seriously considering the appointment of rancher Barton Clay as governor of the Arizona Territory, pending the resignation of present governor Lewis Wolfley. The letter noted that recommendations from Mayor Maish, City Marshal Bill Roche, and Lewis Wolfley himself had helped the president reach his decision.

The five gold double eagles Barton counted into Roche's palm had thanked the lawman for his diligence in bringing such wonderful news. The governorship of the territory was a small step, certainly, but it could eventually open the door to the White House and President Barton Clay had a ring to it.

"Mary Jane is on her way, Mr. Clay," Wheeler said. "She's just getting dressed."

Barton grinned. "Hear that, boys, the whore is getting dressed? At one time or another haven't we all seen her buck nekkid?"

"Yeah," Decker said. "Wheeler, she ain't shy. Tell her to come just as she is."

Wheeler, trying to find his backbone, said, "Mary Jane will come down when she's ready."

Her hair brushed, face rouged, wearing her best dress, Mary Jane Hillman, head held high, walked into the saloon like a princess. There is no doubt that she knew she was going to her death.

"Where is Dan Caine?"

Barton Clay repeated that question time after time as Mary Jane went through her terrible ordeal. Historians have long agreed that what happened in the saloon was horrific and that Luther Wheeler and his prostitutes ran into the bright morning with their hands over their ears to block the sounds that came from the place. It would be gratuitous and serve no useful purpose to describe in detail what was done to Mary Jane Hillman. Years later, Wheeler said to a *British Woman's Temperance Journal* writer, "I have no comment. Some stories are better left untold."

Horror thrives on horror, but the question must be asked: Was Mary Jane Hillman still alive when Barton Clay hanged her? Mercifully, we'll never be able to answer that question. Dan Caine and Crow cut her down and buried her, but even they could not tell.

"The boys had fun but it was not a productive morning," Barton Clay said. "I still don't know where to find Dan Caine. I swear, that man is becoming the bane of my existence."

"Not all the boys had fun," Ruben Webb said, "Two guns, Vic Dane and Hoss Barnes and a few punchers rode out an hour ago. They said they'd had enough. I reckon they balked at hanging a woman, even a whore."

"Yes, I remember hiring Dane and Barnes," Barton said. "You handle the fighting men, Ruben. Are they a big loss?"

"They sold their guns in the Mason County War but didn't see much action and later Hoss did some Indian fighting. Dane knew Charlie Bowdre over in Lincoln County in the New Mexico Territory, but that's as far as it went. He never fought in the war over there."

"Could they stir up trouble?" Barton Clay said. "I don't want a pair of crybabies out there talking about what they saw this morning."

"I doubt it. They both have shady pasts and steer well clear of the law. Besides, what could a couple of low-ranked gunmen with no reps say that would trouble Governor Clay?"

Barton shook his head. "No, I'm uneasy. I don't care for their disloyalty and treachery, Ruben. It concerns me."

"All right, boss, if it troubles you, I'll take care of it."

"Be discreet, Ruben. Take care of the guns but not the cowhands. I don't want too much killing."

"Am I not always discreet?"

"Yes, you are, and now once again you've set my mind at rest."

Webb nodded. "Thank you. I'll saddle up and get after them."

"Dane and Barnes are snakes in the grass," Barton said. "Show them no mercy."

"You really want me to let the punchers go? They talk like anybody else."

Barton sighed. "Whatever you think is best, Ruben. I leave it in your capable hands."

* * *

Three days later, a peddler found two dead men on the wagon road he was traversing. He halted his wagon, climbed down and took a closer look. A pair of young men, each shot once at close range, probably by road agents. The peddler regained his seat and urged his nag into motion. After a couple of miles, he came across three more bodies, but this time he drove on. Dead men on a wagon road in the middle of a wilderness were no concern of his.

CHAPTER THIRTY-SIX

"Luther, come out from there and cut her down, damn you," Rose Richards said. She turned to another girl, a recent arrival by the name of Cloda Sullivan, an Irish lass fresh from the Bisbee cribs, and said, "Go get me Daisy Tweed."

"She's not here," Cloda said, her Irish accent strong.

Luther Wheeler's wails were so loud Rose Richards had to raise her voice. "Where is she?"

"I saw her ride out after Mary Jane was hung. I don't know where she was going." Cloda looked at the man in the cot. He sat upright and his head was covered by a pulled-up sheet and blanket, his big, long-toed feet bare. "Jesus, Mary, and Joseph and all the saints in Heaven, what ails him?" she said.

"What ails him is that he saw Mary Jane Hillman get hung, and he's still seeing her in his mind," Rose said. "And maybe he feels guilty because he didn't try to stop the lynching. He hid somewhere, shaking in his boots."

"But if he'd tried, the Clays would've shot him."

"Maybe, maybe not. I say he should've tried, but he didn't, and now he's got to live with it."

"I feel sorry for him," Cloda said.

"Don't."

"Why not?"

"He doesn't deserve it."

"No matter, I'll say a rosary for Mary Jane tonight and I'll say one for Luther, even though he bears a heretic's name."

"I guess we all need prayers about now," Rose said.

"It's a terrible thing to see the poor woman hanging there. Her tongue all sticking out," Cloda said. "I can't bear to look at her."

"Shut the hell up," Rose Richards said, her face bright red. Angrily, she tried to pull the covers off Wheeler's head but he held them fast and his sobs and lamentations grew louder. "Luther, get out of there," she said. "I can't climb out on a high tree limb to cut Mary Jane down. Heights scare me."

"No, go away," Wheeler said, his voice muffled by the blanket. "Did you see what they done to her?"

Tears welled in Rose's eyes. "I saw. Please, Luther, get up," she said.

"I'm trying to make my peace with my Creator. My mother once told me that God hates a coward, and I don't know if He's even listening to me." Wheeler's entire body trembled, and he whimpered, a grown man behaving like a frightened child.

"He's lost his mind," Cloda said.

"No, he hasn't. Right now, he's looking at himself in a mirror and he doesn't like what he sees."

"Poor man. May the Lord forgive him."

"Can you climb a tree?" Rose said.

"No."

"I'm afraid of high places." Rose shook her head. "I can't do it."

"I've never climbed a tree. Maybe some cowboys will pass by."

"You silly whore, it was cowboys who murdered her."

"Somebody else then."

"Who?"

"I don't know."

"I wish Daisy Tweed was here."

"Can she climb a tree?"

"Probably."

"Then maybe she'll come home soon."

"Home? You call Wheeler's Crossing home?"

"It's where I sleep at night."

"Irish, it's where you sell your body to men at night and it ain't home. And it will never be home, so get that out of your head."

"Then I won't say home. I'll just say that I sure hope Daisy gets here soon."

"Yeah, we're all waiting for Daisy," Rose said. "Daisy can climb trees. You bet." She slapped the back of Wheeler's head. "Luther, I always thought you were a poor excuse for a man and now you've proved it. You know what you are? You're a damned, yellow-bellied coward."

"Go away. Leave me alone," Wheeler said. "I'm in torment."

Five minutes later, as Rose Richards tried to coax Cloda Sullivan up the hanging tree, unable to live with himself a moment longer, Luther Wheeler blew his brains out.

CHAPTER THIRTY-SEVEN

Mrs. Gertrude Dale was unpredictable. It was not even noon and a frantic woman had just banged loudly on her door, demanding to see one of her guests. Mrs. Dale had an uncanny knack for nosing out other females and right away she pegged the hard-eyed, skinny blonde on her doorstep as a soiled dove on the loose. The horse standing head down behind her looked as though it had been ridden fast and far so she obviously lived a long way from Tucson.

"Mr. Caine is in his room," Mrs. Dale said. "He and his friend are riding out today."

"I must talk with him," Daisy Tweed said. "It's on a matter of the greatest moment."

Mrs. Dale saw that the woman was tired, distraught, and ill, and as a Christian lady she could not turn her away. "Come into the parlor and I'll let Mr. Caine know you are here." She led Daisy to the room, ushered her into a chair and said, "Would you care for coffee and perhaps a slice of seed cake?"

"Just coffee," Daisy said. "The blacker, the better."

"Are you not feeling yourself today, my dear?" Mrs. Dale said.

"No. No, I'm not."

"Then I'll bring the coffee and get Mr. Caine." Mrs. Dale smiled. "Normally, I don't let young ladies cross the threshold, but I'll make an exception in your case."

"I'm neither young nor a lady," Daisy said. "So you won't be breaking any rules."

"Just so," Gertrude Dale said. "I'll bring the coffee."

A couple of minutes later, she brought coffee and a wedge of cake. "I know you said you didn't want any, but everyone enjoys seed cake."

The woman swept out of the parlor and Daisy was drinking coffee and eating cake when Dan Caine and Crow stepped into the room. Both were dressed and their cartridge belts and holstered Colts hung over their shoulders.

"You look a lot better than the last time I saw you," Daisy said.

"I guess that's not too difficult, Dan said. Then, "What brings you here?"

"Bad news."

"Tell it."

"Mary Jane Hillman is dead."

Dan's face hardened. "How?"

"The Clays."

"What happened?"

"They wanted to know where you were."

"But Mary Jane didn't tell them."

"No. She didn't."

"Then what?"

"Then what? They beat her, raped her, and then hung her. After all, she was only a whore."

Dan looked like he'd been punched in the gut and Crow's sudden, sharp intake of breath revealed his disquiet. He and Mary Jane had grown to like each other.

"When did this happen?" Dan said.

"Early this morning. Mary Jane was still wearing her nightgown when they rode in."

"Did she . . . I mean . . ."

"You're about to ask a stupid question, aren't you, Texas lawman? The answer is she suffered a lot, more than you'll ever know."

"She should've told them."

"She loved you. In Mary Jane's world, love is as rare as a tear at a Boot Hill burying. Once you find it you don't betray it. She found love all right, and she sacrificed her life for it." Dan looked stricken, and Daisy said, "She had a premonition that something was about to come down and I think she knew it was going to be bad. She asked me to come here and let you know when it happened, and I have."

"Where was Wheeler?" Dan said.

"He was around. What could he do to stop the Clays? Besides, Luther has a paper back. He isn't the kind to grab a scattergun and face down men like the Clays."

Daisy Tweed rose from her chair. She wore a tan traveling dress, much frayed around the hem and a straw boater perched on top of piled-up and pinned hair that showed a few strands of gray. A threadbare carpetbag lay at her feet. "Well, I've kept my promise to Mary Jane and now I'm outta here," she said.

"Are you heading back to Wheeler's Crossing?" Dan said.

The woman shook her head. "No. I'm headed for the station to catch a train."

"To where?"

"Anywhere. The West is big and I can choose a place to die. Mary Jane Hillman didn't have that option."

Crow said, "No, lady, you must choose a place to live, not die."

Daisy smiled and nodded. "I'm sure to remember your advice. Now I have to go. I have a Wheeler horse and saddle to sell."

"You're quiet tonight," Crow said. He sat with Dan Caine in the rockers on Mrs. Dale's whittlin' porch under a star-frosted sky. The north wind nipped, reminding everyone that fall was just around the corner. "Mary Jane on your mind? I know she's on mine."

It took Dan some time to answer and when he did, he said, "I wasn't thinking about her just then. No, I was thinking about all the bad things I'm going to do to the Clays."

"My soul is black, just like yours," Crow said. "In my life, I've seldom been in fights, but when I was, I fought to the death. Now I will fight the Clays to the death. There are some people who don't deserve to die, and Mary Jane was one of them. She was a warrior, and for that I gave her my respect."

"She had a revolver," Dan said. "She might have put up a fight."

"The woman who came here didn't mention a fight. I think that after she left her room, Mary Jane didn't know she was walking to her death. She trusted men like Barton Clay to do the right thing."

Dan's face flickered red and black as he lit a cigarette, then he said, "Crow, we're two men, good men, who have no idea how we're going to destroy the Clays and all they stand for. But we will. I swear to God, we will."

"I think we should talk to Luther Wheeler tomorrow," Crow said.

"Maybe I'll shoot him," Dan said.

Crow smiled. "No, don't shoot him, at least not yet. I want to know what happened and who was involved beside the Clays. I reckon there were some mighty low-down punchers in that crowd."

"That makes sense. And here's more sense. From now until this is over, I want to ride with Crow the Apache, not Crow the bagpipe-playing Scotsman."

"My father never played bagpipes, as far as I know."

"As far as you're aware. Listen, all Scotsmen play bagpipes, like the Irish play harps and Germans eat sausage. These are things every educated white man knows."

"I don't."

"That's because you led a sheltered life of ignorance among the savages."

"Did you know that the Mescalero have no word for warrior?" Crow said. "It's because everyone is expected to fight—men, women, and children."

Dan nodded, stone-faced in the gloom. "I know and I'm teasing you, Crow, and I'm sorry. Just . . . be an Apache."

"Dan, to avenge Mary Jane and the great wrong done you, I'll be anything you want."

"A half-Apache, half-Scotsman is good enough for me," Dan said.

"Damn right it is," Crow said.

CHAPTER THIRTY-EIGHT

Two oil lamps cast a warm glow but deepened the shadows in Barton Clay's parlor, and outside under a starry sky nothing moved but the wind. He and his most trusted associates, his two sons and Ruben Webb, sat around the fireplace and stared at the burning logs that scented the room with their piney fragrance. Barton and his sons had been drinking heavily since nightfall, but Webb had nursed a bourbon for hours.

Finally Barton broke the silence.

"All right, where the hell is he?"

Silence was the ear-splitting reply.

The grandfather clock in the hallway tick-tocked away a couple of slow minutes, then Webb, the only one sober said, "They've got to be in Tucson. We've got drovers herding cattle for the fall roundup north, east, south, and west and they've seen no sign of Caine and the breed. After we burned the ghost town, they had nowhere else to go but Tucson."

Decker, drunk, said, grinning, "And with the whore gone, there's no one else to feed them."

"I'd burn down Tucson if I thought it would scorch Caine's tail feathers," Barton said.

Webb said, "Perhaps burning down the pride of the Arizona Territory would be an unwise move for our future governor."

Barton nodded. "Yeah, you're right. But we can get that useless fat slug Bill Roche to hire some people and institute a search. Go house to house if he has to."

"Good idea, Pa," Decker said.

"Of course, it's a good idea," Barton said. "If I thought otherwise, I wouldn't have said it. You're drunk, boy. Go to bed."

"But Pa . . ."

"Go to bed. I won't tell you again."

After Decker left the room cursing under his breath, Barton said, "I worry about that boy."

"He had too much excitement this morning with the woman," Pete said. "He'll be all right."

"If he wants to build himself a rep, he'd better lay off the whiskey," Webb said. "Drinking too much and shooting is a bad mix."

"I know it is, but Pete's right," Barton said. "All that fun with the whore scrambled Decker's brains a little. He'll be just fine after a good night's sleep and one of Quan Wen's big breakfasts."

"Boss, tomorrow do you want me to talk to Roche, put some pressure on him to find Caine?" Webb said.

"Yes, but go easy on him," Barton said. He got out of his armchair, stood with his back to the fire and rubbed his left arm. "Let Bill know what a good job he's doing and how well he looks. Then drop him a couple of tens and tell him what I want him to do. Be nice, Ruben, polite, I'll need scoundrels like Bill Roche when I'm governor, so give him a hint or two that I might find a place for him in my administration."

"I understand, boss," Webb said. "I'll charm the tar out of him."

Barton nodded. "Good. Excellent. Now I must go to my bed. We had a busy day today." He smiled. "It was interesting but tiring."

"Pa, are you feeling all right? You look pale," Pete said.

"I'm fine, son. Just a little tired is all."

"Pa, don't worry about things so much. We'll find Dan Caine for you."

"I'm not worried because I know you will."

"And Roche will help," Webb said. "You have my assurance on that."

"Well said, Ruben. We won't burn Tucson, but we can take it apart, adobe brick by adobe brick and timber by timber," Pete said.

Ruben Webb stood outside the ranch house, smoking a cigar and watching the spectacular sky. He heard an irritated horse kick at a rat in the barn, and then the night fell silent again.

He was busy with his thoughts.

The man who brought in the head of Dan Caine would be rewarded richly, Barton Clay would see to that. Now all he had to do was find the man, perhaps with the help of the idiot Roche. Webb nodded to himself. Caine was a man with nine lives, but he would kill the rube, no one else.

That thought pleased him. He smoked the rest of his cigar and stepped back into the house. The boss was right. It had been an eventful day, and he was ready for bed.5

CHAPTER THIRTY-NINE

After an early breakfast of eggs, salt pork, and soda biscuits, served with some meaningful looks from Mrs. Dale and the other guests, Dan Caine and Crow left for the livery stable, saddled up, and headed east. The morning seemed stillborn, and shadows still clung like gigantic black cobwebs to every nook and cranny of the buildings they passed on their way out of Tucson. And it was unseasonably cool, another harbinger of the coming fall.

The sun was higher in the sky, the morning brighter and warmer, when Dan and Crow reached Wheeler's Crossing. They swung out of the saddle at the mercantile hitching rail and it was Crow, with his sharp eyes, who saw a sight that would haunt him for the rest of his life.

"Dan," he said, his voice quiet and strangely flat, "look."

Dan looked, stared, and whispered, "Oh, my God."

"They stripped her naked but look, they didn't touch her beautiful hair," Crow said. "That's good, isn't it? Say it's good that they didn't touch her hair."

Dan made no answer. "Cut her down, Crow. For pity's sake cut her down." He pulled his Colt and yelled, "Wheeler!" Then, "Damn your eyes, Wheeler, come out here!"

No answer. The mercantile was as silent as a shadow.

The door was open and Dan barged through it, gun in hand. He looked around and saw that the place was deserted.

CLANG! CLATTER! CLASH!

His revolver's hammer back, Dan swung toward the calamitous racket. He fired instinctively, shooting into sound.

"Stop that, you damned ruffian!" A woman's voice from behind a hardware display. And then, "Are you trying to kill me?"

"Come out with your hands where I can see them," Dan said. He was aware of Crow, rifle in hand, beside him.

"You damned scoundrel, you tried to kill me."

"Show yourself."

"Wait just a second, I dropped my buckct."

The woman did not appear and Dan walked to the display of galvanized buckets and milk cans. A small, dark-haired girl was on her hands and knees, dropping coins and banknotes back into the bucket. Dan noticed cheap jewelry and other trinkets in there along with a nicely kept Sharps and Hankins single shot derringer with a box of .32 rimfire cartridges.

"Where is Wheeler?" Dan said.

"Hell, probably," the girl said.

"A straight answer, lady."

"The straight answer is he's dead. He blew his brains out after what happened to Mary Jane." The girl lifted her huge brown eyes to Dan's face. "Luther never cared too much about his whores my ownself included, but something in him changed when he saw Mary Jane's naked body hanging from the cottonwood tree by the stream."

"Where is Wheeler's body?" Dan said.

"In his room, I guess. I heard the shot, but I didn't look." The girl stood, the bucket in her hands. "My name is Rose Richards and I whored for Luther for the best part of two years. Mister, he wasn't much of a man, paper backed, he was. But somehow, after he didn't try to save Mary Jane, he found the balls to kill himself. Don't ask me why because I don't understand it. Maybe God or the devil spoke to him, I don't know." She held up the bucket. "There's more than five hundred dollars in there and I figure I earned it. I'm taking Luther's remaining nag and getting out of here. I'm twenty-three, and I've already got gray hairs, so no more whoring for me. I'm gonna find me a man to marry and settle down and maybe own a small ranch one day." She stepped toward Dan. "Now my speechifying is done and will you give me the road?"

"Take anything else you want," Dan said. "I'm going to burn this place down with Wheeler in it."

"I've got what I need," Rose said. "So long, lawman." She saw the question on Dan's face and said, "Mary Jane told me about you. She had your brand on her heart, poor woman." She shook her head. "Poor whore."

Crow stomped into the mercantile, ignored Dan and the girl, and pulled a blanket off a shelf. He left without a word.

"Good luck with the husband and the ranch," Dan said.

"Thank you and to you, good luck," Rose said.

She left the mercantile, and Dan Caine never saw her again.

Crow stepped back inside, grabbed a couple of shovels and offered one to Dan. "We got a burying to do."

Dan nodded, took the shovel, and he and Crow walked outside.

"Wrapped in the blanket she looks so small," Crow said. "I can't remember her being so tiny."

"She wasn't a large woman," Dan said. He looked at Crow. "How did she look? What did they do to her?"

"I know. Best you don't. Best you never know."

Dan nodded. "Have you seen a good spot for the burying?"

"Yeah. Over there." He pointed. "See the boulder on the rise to the left of the wagon road? It's as tall as a man and standing by itself in the middle of nowhere."

"I see it."

"That's where we'll bury Mary Jane."

Dan looked around him, at the small graveyard behind the mercantile, marked by a few wooden crosses, none of them standing straight.

"Why there?" he said.

"Because I may come this way again and I'll want to visit Mary Jane's grave. The big rock will mark the spot."

"Then let's get it done," Dan said.

CHAPTER FORTY

Mary Jane Hillman was laid to rest in the shadow of the rock. Dan said the Lord's Prayer, the only one he knew, and Crow chanted, mourning the dead in his own way, little of which Dan understood, but he didn't doubt its sincerity.

After a while, Dan said, his head bowed, "Vowing to avenge you over your grave isn't decent, Mary Jane, but I promise that justice will be done."

"I reckon she already knows that," Crow said.

"I'm sure she does," Dan said.

They walked back toward the mercantile, shovels in their left hands, Winchesters in the right. They were on the edge of enemy territory and Dan was taking no chances.

"I haven't seen Wheeler," Crow said.

"Wheeler is dead," Dan said.

"How did it happen? The Clays?"

"No, he blew his own brains out."

Crow looked puzzled, and Dan said, "He didn't try to help Mary Jane and it preyed on him. That's what Rose Richards said."

"The little gal you took a shot at?"

"You heard the bang, huh?"

"Yeah. And I reckoned it had to be you. She made a small target and that's why you missed."

"I didn't see her at first. She dropped a bucket on the floor and that's why I fired."

"You shot at the bucket, not the girl."

"Now you have the right of it."

"Did you hit the bucket?"

"No."

"Good shooting."

"Damn," Dan said. "Crow, you can be an aggravating man. Why did I ever make you my deputy?"

"Because no one else wanted the job?"

"Maybe that was it. I can't remember. Ah well, now we've got some arson to take care of."

"The mercantile?"

"Yeah. We'll make sure the Clays will never use the place again."

"Where's Wheeler?"

"In his bedroom."

"So you'll burn him along with his mercantile?"

"Yeah, burn them both to ashes."

Crow nodded but said nothing.

Dan and Crow took what they needed, boxes of .45 and .44-40 ammunition, tobacco and papers, beef jerky and a fine Winchester sporting rifle in .45-90 caliber that he could not bring himself to consign to the flames. But the greatest find of all were the sticks of dynamite, blasting caps, and fuses he found stored in a small closet under the staircase that led to the upper rooms. Dan Caine was in a fight to the death and the explosives were a powerful weapon.

When he and Crow's burlap sacks were bulging, they

made their way to the saloon to have a drink in Mary Jane's memory, but a large area of the floor was still spattered with her blood. Dan grabbed a bottle and two glasses from a shelf behind the bar and they quickly retreated back into the mercantile.

It proved to be a somber toast to the dead woman's memory that did nothing to ease either man's hurt. Afterward Dan hurled the bottle against a wall where it smashed into shattered glass shards and a shower of amber whiskey.

"Crow, use all the coal oil and kerosene we can find," Dan said. "I want this whole building to burn like the Clays burned Ellie Reynolds' place."

"To the ground, you mean."

"Yeah. To the ground I mean."

One thing Luther Wheeler stocked in plenty was coal oil, and Dan and Crow splashed a dozen cans of the stuff around the mercantile and the adjoining saloon. Dan broke a window, lit an oil-soaked rag and tossed it into the building, starting a blaze that would last until sundown. The timber structure, tinder dry, burned readily and spawned a massive pillar of smoke that spilled like soot across the blue face of the sky. Black powder, confined in barrels, erupted into massive explosions that sent flaming debris in every direction and fed flames that flapped and fluttered frantically like massive yellow and scarlet birds caught in bear traps. The fire raged and roared and crackled like a burning medieval witch, a primitive, elemental force that had a life of its own, and Dan and Crow could only stand at a safe distance and wonder at the destruction they had wrought.

His face made ruddy by firelight, Dan took Crow by the arm and pulled him away from the hypnotic allure of the blaze. "Now we've got more war to wage," he said.

Crow blinked a few times and then said, "Where?"

"We're taking the war right to Barton Clay's doorstep," Dan said.

"You mean, attack the ranch?"

"I mean part of it."

Crow was suspicious. "What part?"

"You'll find out when we get there."

"I hate conundrums."

"Don't worry, you'll have the answer soon."

"The Clay ranch is due east of where we are, isn't it?"

"Yeah, it is and the thirsty and horny Clay boys and their hands made a clear trail from here to there. Civil of them, don't you think?"

"We'll run out of daylight before we get to the ranch."

"I know," Dan said. "In fact, I'm counting on it."

CHAPTER FORTY-ONE

Barton Clay thought he smelled woodsmoke in the wind, but he dismissed it as a campfire made by deer hunters up from Tucson. His attention was on the approaching surrey, City Marshal Bill Roche at the reins, beside him a smallish man wearing a bowler hat, gray ditto suit, and a round-collared shirt with a red bow tie. The little man frowned like a stern schoolmaster, as though he hated everything about this trip.

Roche drew rein and after he and the stranger stepped out, the beaming marshal said with considerable bonhomie, "I think introductions are in order. Mr. Barton Clay, may I present the Honorable Horace Dinwiddie, President Harrison's Under Secretary of Domestic Affairs. He is here on a matter of the greatest moment, concerning the impending move of the territorial capital to Phoenix."

Dinwiddie's hand was lost in Barton's massive paw and he quickly withdrew the appendage, perhaps fearing that it might be crushed.

"Please come inside, Mr. Dinwiddie," Barton said.

"You've had a long journey from Tucson and a drink is in order."

The little man's smile was as fleeting as a wood spark and as he entered the house he said, "I don't imbibe alcohol, and I'm told the territory's water is undrinkable, but a glass of milk or a soda pop would be acceptable."

"Quan Wen, my cook, keeps a quantity of root beer on hand," Barton said.

"That will be quite acceptable," Dinwiddie said as he was ushered into a chair.

A few minutes later, a glass of root beer in hand, the little man said, "I'll come straight to the point. As City Marshal Roche said, I'm here on a matter of the greatest moment. Do you understand?"

"I understand," Barton said. So far, he'd heard nothing that needed understanding.

"Good, then to the business on hand. The territory's capital, just a few weeks ago, has been moved from Prescott to Phoenix. Now for the crux of the matter. There was a governor's mansion, such as it was, in Prescott, but there's none in Phoenix. Do you understand?"

"Yes," Barton said.

"Since Governor Wolfley has just handed in his resignation, you are now the de facto governor of the Arizona Territory."

"Congratulations, Governor Clay!" Roche said.

"Hold hard there, Marshal, I'm still speaking," Dinwiddie said. "And Mr. Clay is not governor quite yet. Mr. Wolfley's resignation does not take effect for a few days yet."

Elation spiking at him, Barton said, "Where should I build my governor's residence?"

"A good question, an excellent question if I may say so," Dinwiddie said. "And the answer is, if you don't care to purchase a property in Phoenix, you can build anywhere you please. Excellent root beer, by the way. Not too sweet."

"Thank you," Barton said. "I can rule the territory from right here."

"Ah . . . you govern the territory, not rule it, Mr. Clay. We live in a republic after all. And yes, if it pleases you, by all means work from here, but may I suggest a dwelling in Tucson might better fit the bill. Do you have someone to run the ranch while you're gone on official duties?"

"Yes, I have two sons."

"Excellent!"

Barton smiled. He looked both handsome and charming and had a bridge to mend. "That rule thing, Mr. Dinwiddie, was just a slip of the tongue."

"My dear fellow, of course it was. We're all guilty of those." He flashed his own here-and-gone smile. "Can I tell the president that you're eager to take on the great responsibility of governorship? Champing at the bit to get started, as it were?"

"Yes, yes indeed," Barton said. "And tell him I'm honored. I'm only a simple rancher and it comes as a great surprise that he's chosen me."

"I'll gladly pass those sentiments on to the president." Dinwiddie finished his root beer and consulted the gold watch he took from his vest pocket. "Now we must go, City Marshal Roche. I have a train to catch." He smiled. "Several trains in fact."

Barton herded Dinwiddie outside to the waiting surrey and when the little man was seated, he said, "I won't let the president down."

"Of course, you won't," Dinwiddie said.

And City Marshal Roche, grinning, said, "Governor Clay . . . Governor Clay . . . Governor Clay . . . I need to get used to saying that."

"Yes, you do," Barton Clay said. He bared his teeth in a smile. "Pronto."

CHAPTER FORTY-TWO

Dan Caine had the tobacco hunger but dare not scratch a match for fear of being seen. In the middling distance, lamps were lit in the Clay ranch house, and the bunkhouse showed as four rectangles of light.

The initial horror of Mary Jane Hillman's terrible death had passed, replaced by a seething anger, so scalding that Dan tasted green bile in his throat and felt physically sick.

Just a few hundred yards away, under a roof of stars, Barton Clay sat cozy in his parlor, content in the knowledge that he'd gotten away with yet another murder. After all, who cared about the life of a two-dollar-a-screw whore? In the scheme of things, she was nothing, a nobody, especially when stacked up against Barton's soaring ambitions. Besides, the boys worked hard and needed a little fun now and again. Who could hold it against them?

Dan's bloodless lips tightened. Sure, Barton was in his parlor, thinking big, thinking himself safe, but Dan intended to blow him the hell out of there, a little reminder that now the war had started he wasn't safe anywhere.

"Squeeze that tree limb any harder and you'll bring

down the whole damn oak about our ears," Crow said, the quietness of the night making him whisper.

Dan realized how tightly he'd been clutching the branch and smiled. "I need a smoke."

"Make a cigarette and chew it."

"It's not the same, is it? Is the dynamite ready?"

"Yes. I shortened the fuses like you said. You're not going to have much time."

"I won't need much time. Just cover me with your rifle."

"Depend on it, Sheriff Caine."

Dan's teeth gleamed in the gloom. "You can keep that title on ice until we're home in Broken Back."

Crow nodded. "Sure thing." Then, "The moon is bright, a good sign. If we die, our souls won't wander forever in darkness."

"A comforting thought."

"I reckoned it might please you."

"Mount up. Let's get it done and wake up Barton Clay."

The dark of night was Dan Caine's friend. He and Crow rode unseen to within thirty yards of the ranch house before he lit the dynamite fuse. The fuse sizzled into sparkling life and Dan kicked his horse into motion. He was at full gallop when he tossed the dynamite in the direction of the door and it cartwheeled through the darkness like a Catherine wheel. Then he was beyond the house, Crow close behind.

BOOM!

The vagaries of a dynamite explosion forced the blast upward and inward so that the ranch house's heavy mahogany door with its polished brass fittings was blown twenty feet in the air, taking with it large pieces of the adjoining timber walls and two glass windows, their panes and frames shattered. With catastrophic violence, debris hurtled into the hallway like a Gatling gun volley and immediately caused flames that were quickly fed by a pair of smashed oil lamps, turning the blaze into an inferno. The blast was devastating, beyond anything Dan Caine could've hoped for, and it sent a cursing Barton Clay, his sons and Quan Wen, all in night attire, fleeing, ears ringing, out of the back door into the night.

After the explosion, hands dressed in hats and long johns spilled out of the bunkhouse, but Crow, who'd been waiting for such a reaction, dusted them with his Winchester, scored no hits, but sent them scuttling back inside.

From somewhere in the moon-glossed darkness, Dan yelled, "Crow! Get the hell away from there!"

Crow raised his rifle over his head, let out a loud, "Yip! Yip! Yip!" and then turned his horse around and cantered in Dan's direction.

Then Dan's voice from the gloom, "I heard the dynamite blow but didn't see what happened."

Crow waited until he drew rein beside Dan and said, "I think that Mr. Clay is going to need a new house."

CHAPTER FORTY-THREE

Barton Clay was beyond anger, beyond rage, his uncontrollable wrath pushing him to the boundaries of insanity. His house, the soon-to-be governor's mansion, almost destroyed by a fatherless nonentity, the spawn of a whore, who called himself Dan Caine. Despite the heroic efforts of a cowboy bucket brigade, it would take months and thousands of dollars to restore the dwelling to its former splendor, if that was even possible. The governor of the Arizona Territory without a roof over his head. It was unthinkable.

The ranch house fire was extinguished but the damage was extensive and the mahogany door, brought all the way from Denver, lay twenty yards from its proper place, a scarred, scorched wreck of its former self.

"I want Dan Caine skun," Barton Clay said. "I want his bleeding hide to nail to my barn door. Are you listening? Do you hear what I'm saying?"

The hands and Pete and Decker Clay were assembled near the corral, the scene lit by guttering lanterns that made them look like a coven of warlocks.

"We hear you, Pa," Pete said.

"Remember, a thousand dollars to the man who finds

him," Barton said. Then, after a string of oaths, "I want that man Caine dead, dead, dead."

"Pa, where do you suppose Caine got the dynamite?" Pete said. "Did Luther Wheeler take a hand in this business and sell it to him?"

"I don't know, but get to Wheeler," Barton said. "Put him to the question and if he doesn't answer set his toes to the fire. Burn him alive, if you have to, but make him tell you where Caine is."

Decker said, "I reckon Wheeler could've switched sides after what we done to his whore."

"Yeah, I've always figured Wheeler for a Judas," Barton said. "Decker, take Webb and a couple of hands and ride to Wheeler's Crossing."

"Now, Pa?" Decker said, surprised.

"Yes, now, damn you. Drag Wheeler from his bed, throw the whore with him out the window, and then do what I ordered you to do."

Ruben Webb was already striding toward the barn and Decker called the names of a couple of punchers to get their horses and saddle up. He grinned. "Boys, we got some toes to tickle."

———

After Decker Clay and the others rode out, Barton instructed Quan Wen to go back into the house and salvage whatever undamaged clothes he could find and to bring the petty cash box from the office. The little Chinaman looked at Barton, then at the blackened house and then back to his boss. He shook his head. "Roof fall down, you bet. Bad thing for Quan Wen."

"Get in there or I'll send you back to the stinking Chinatown swamp you came from," Barton yelled. He wanted to vent his simmering rage at someone, anyone, and he'd found a target.

His face far from inscrutable, Quan Wen looked deeply hurt. The man he admired most in the world had just turned on him, speaking to him as he would speak to a cur dog.

Without a word, the Chinaman turned, walked to the house, his nightgown flapping around his ankles, and disappeared inside. Barton watched him go, then, his mouth twisted into a snarling grin he said to the punchers, "Boys, for his sake, I hope the roof holds."

This brought hearty laughter. In a cowboy's world a Chinese ranked about as low as a saloon swamper. "Buff," Barton said to a tall, lanky hand with a huge mustache, "go get the surrey ready. You'll drive me into Tucson." He saw the question on the man's face and said, "The governor of the Arizona Territory doesn't sleep in a barn, or in a bunkhouse either."

Buff Grant smiled and said, "I'll get it done, boss."

The surrey was readied, the draft Morgan in the shafts, about the same time Quan Wen appeared with a bundle of clothing in his arms, a pair of boots and the cash box on top, and Barton's gunbelt over his shoulder. Without a word of thanks, Barton sorted through the pile, selected a hat, underwear, socks and a shirt and pants. The remainder of his duds he tossed into the back of the surrey. He took off his nightgown and stood as naked as a jaybird in the lantern light until he dressed again and buckled on his gun.

"All right, Buff," he said. "Let's go."

"I go, too," Quan Wen said.

"No, you don't," Barton said. "You sleep in the bunkhouse."

"But boss . . . the hands hate me."

"Too bad. And they don't let Chinamen into the Palace Hotel. I told you, sleep in the bunkhouse or the barn."

For a while Quan Wen ran beside the surrey frantically pleading to accompany Barton, then Buff Grant kicked him away and he sprawled in the dirt and watched his boss abandon him.

CHAPTER FORTY-FOUR

"It looks like Dan Caine is gonna blow up the whole damn territory," Decker Clay said.

"If it was him, he made a good job of it," Ruben Webb said. "I can see that even in the dark."

"It was him all right, no one else?"

"Yeah, I've studied on it and my money is on Caine."

"We have to find him," Decker said. "Find him and skin him alive for Pa."

"For your pa? How about for yourself? It looks like your drinking and whoring days are over at Wheeler's Crossing."

"And yours," Decker said. He looked at the ruin of the mercantile and shook his head. "You're right, I'm gonna miss this place."

"Well, it's no matter, you were killing off all the whores anyway," Webb said.

"Is that supposed to be a good joke?"

"No, I'm just stating a fact."

"Then don't state any more facts. I don't like them."

"All right, no more facts," Webb said, his face shadowed by the brim of his hat. "So where do we go from here?"

"Look at this place," Decker said, ignoring the question. The pair of gun punchers with him looked stunned. The mercantile had been the only place for miles around where a man could buy a drink and a woman, and they already felt its loss.

Wheeler's place was flattened, a few charred spars stuck up at crazy angles, and the ruin stank of burned wood and whatever else had been caught by the flames.

"The question is . . . where the hell is Wheeler?" Decker said.

"If I was a betting man, I'd bet the farm that he's in there, his ashes all mixed up with other ashes," Webb said.

"You reckon Caine trapped him in there and burned him alive?" Decker said.

"That would be my guess," Webb said.

"Why? There was no bad blood between Caine and Luther Wheeler."

"Wheeler didn't intervene when you were trying to cripple Caine with the boot, and he said nothing when you and your boys were murdering the whore. All that could prey on a man like Caine's mind and make him hold a grudge."

"You almost sound like you admire him," Decker said. "And I don't like that word murdering."

"So what do you call it?"

"Execution. We executed Mary Jane Hillman and that's why in the end we hung her."

"But that was after you and your boys had raped her and almost beat her to death. It sounds like something that might've happened in the Dark Ages."

"What the hell were those?"

"A time when you wouldn't want to be alive."

Decker stared at Webb in the waning moonlight and

then said, "Sometimes I wonder whose side you are on, Ruben."

"I'm on your father's side. He's the man that pays my wages. But there are some lines I won't cross, and killing a woman is one of them."

"Hell, killing a woman is just like killing a man, no different." Decker turned in the saddle and said to the two punchers behind him, "Would you boys kill a woman?"

"Sure," one of them said, "if you pay me enough, I'll kill a woman. Give me five hundred dollars and I'll also gun her mother and her grandmother and her great-grandmother and all her female children."

"How about you, Luke?" Decker said, smiling.

"Me, I shot a whore in El Paso one time for stealing my wallet. It didn't bother me none." The man called Luke's eyes went to Webb. "Seems like we got a man here who spent too long in the shadow of his mama's apron."

Webb's smile was a warning. "Luke. It's Luke Prentice, isn't it?"

"Yeah, that's what I call myself."

"Well, Luke Prentice, I'm not on the brag, you understand, but in my time, I've killed fifteen men and all of them died facing me with a gun in their hand. I'd like to even that number up. I believe you just insulted me and as a Southern gentleman I safeguard my honor and must now demand satisfaction."

"Luke, tell the gentleman you didn't mean it and say you're sorry," Decker said. "You can't shade Webb, not on your best day."

When he was just out of his teens, Luke Prentice shot and killed a city policeman in Houston and he'd been in several shooting scrapes since then but had scored no more kills. The man had sand, but he wasn't about to brace a shootist of reputation like Ruben Webb.

"I'm sorry," he said. "I didn't mean to insult you, Mr. Webb."

"Apology accepted," Webb said. He reached into the pocket of his shirt and said, "Have a cigar."

Prentice took the cigar with as much grace as he could muster and Decker Clay said, "Boys, that ends it. We don't need to fight among ourselves."

"I agree with that," Webb said. "Now tell us, Decker, where is Dan Caine?"

"I'm drawing a blank. Any ideas?" Decker said. He settled his restive mount and added, "I'm open to anything."

"We burned down the Amitola ghost town," Webb said. "But could Caine still be using it as a hideout?"

"He wouldn't expect us to hunt for him there," Decker said. "The place is only a pile of ashes, but there's a spring nearby and graze for his horses."

Webb said, "The ghost town . . ."

"What's left of it," Decker said.

"Was close enough to both Wheeler's place and the Clay ranch to make Caine figure it was worthwhile roughing it until his war was over."

Decker considered this and then said to Prentice and the other gun hand, a small, hatchet-faced man named Stan Mathers, "What do you boys think?"

"Makes sense," Mathers said. He spoke in a forced whisper, the result of a cutting, a wound to the throat he'd gotten in a Dodge City saloon.

To this day, some antiquarians claim the knife man was Doc Holliday, who was in Dodge in 1879 and in June of that year was a dealer in the Long Branch saloon. On June 16, the *Ford County Globe* reported, "The boys and girls across the deadline had a high old time last Friday. They sang and danced and fought and bit, and cut, and had a good time generally, making music for the entire settlement. Our reporter summed up five knockdowns, three broken heads, two cuttings and several incidental bruises. Unfortunately, none of the injuries will prove fatal." It's possible that both cuttings can be attributed to Doc, with Mathers on the receiving end of one of them.

"Luke, how about you?" Decker said.

"I'm with Whispering Stan," Prentice said. "I helped burn down the ghost town and I reckon it's worth paying it a visit."

"All right, it's due north of us," Decker said. "Should we wait for sunup?"

"I wouldn't," Webb said. "If Caine and his breed are there, we can catch him in his blankets."

Decker nodded. "Then let's ride."

The moment Decker Clay and his gunmen rode north, it set the scene for the collision of two fates . . . one Decker's . . . the other a rabid wolf in the guise of a man, a monster called Asher Starbuck who gave lawmen across the length and breadth of the West screaming nightmares.

CHAPTER FORTY-FIVE

With hearing sharper than that of a lobo wolf, Asher Starbuck heard the distant sound of approaching riders, rose from his blankets and tilted his nose to the south wind. Yes, at least four men and horses and that could only mean a posse. Starbuck growled deep in his throat. He'd make them pay for disturbing his slumber. He buckled crossed gunbelts around his slim hips, each scabbard holding a Smith & Wesson Model 3 revolver in .44 caliber. He kicked dirt on the small fire at his feet and stepped back, fading into the night. His mount, a big American stud, grazed on a patch of grass. The horse was black and almost invisible in the darkness, and Starbuck let it be. When the guns started firing it would stand.

Asher Starbuck was four inches over six lanky feet that summer and was possessed of great strength and lightning reflexes and when cornered, he would fight like a cougar. His complexion was dark, his eyes black and the hair that fell straight over his shoulders under a flat-brimmed hat was the color of a raven's wing. Some said he was a breed, others that he was Mexican, but most pegged him as a son of the devil. He was thirty-four years old and was in fact the son of a Texas farm couple. His mother he never knew because she died young. She'd had the reputation as a witch who practiced black magic and she burned to death in a fire that may have been lit on purpose. His father, a profane, drunken lout, beat young Asher every day of his life until the boy turned twelve and bashed his sleeping papa's head in with a rock. Young Asher killed his second man when he was fourteen, taking his horse and guns. About that same time, he raped and then murdered a married woman in an isolated farmhouse and enjoyed it so much he raped and strangled a second a month later.

Asher then fled Texas with a hemp posse on his heels. He landed in the Oklahoma Indian Territory where he made a good living waylaying and robbing travelers and peddlers. None survived these encounters and his kill count rose to eighteen men and women of all races. Then in 1878, he kidnapped, raped, tortured, and murdered a thirteen-year-old Choctaw girl and again had to make a run for it. His animal instincts and skill with a rifle kept his angry pursuers at bay and Asher escaped into Texas. For the next five years he conducted one-man raids in central and west Texas and became the Rangers' most wanted outlaw. During that time, he killed another eight men and three women and, his violent and unhinged personality forged by a childhood of deprivation and beatings, he developed a taste for torture. It took his prisoners, both male and female, a long time to die.

In 1883, ten miles south of El Paso, he shot and killed a circuit judge for his watch and wallet and the Rangers said enough is enough. They chased him into the New Mexico Territory where they lost him. After several more killings, all of them saloon brawls, Asher rode into the neighboring Arizona Territory where his reign of terror along the

Mogollon Rim became legendary. And here it gets murky. The most current research suggests that when Asher came down off the Rim and headed south, he planned to go all the way to Sonora, Mexico. By 1889, the law was closing in on him, and he no doubt figured it was time to get out of the United States for a spell. That assumption is probably correct, as is the belief that when Asher encountered the Clays in the old Amitola ghost town he had killed at least a hundred and twenty-five people, making him the most murderous gunman in Frontier history. To sum it up, Asher Starbuck was a dangerous psychopath, in all likelihood deranged, and his brush with the Clays was a wild card twist of fate.

"I can't see a thing out here," Decker Clay said.

"Me neither," Ruben Webb said. "But since we've come this far, I guess we should fan out and take a look." He swung out of the saddle and looked around, the shadows deep, dark, and mysterious in the waning moonlight. "Decker, the place is just as we left it."

Decker stepped beside Webb and yelled, "Hey, Caine, don't cower in the woods. Show yourself."

No answer.

Unseen in the gloom, Asher Starbuck smiled and his eyes glittered.

"He ain't here, boss," Luke Prentice said.

"Seems like it," Decker said. He thought about it for a while and said, "Luke, you and Mathers stroll down the street to the spring, see if you spot anything. Me and Webb will comb through the ruins. If Caine is hiding out here, we'll find him."

Still smarting from his run-in with Webb, Prentice was

sulky. "Hell, boss, it's a waste of time," he said. "Caine ain't here."

"We won't know that until we look, will we?" Decker said. "Now do as I told you."

With ill grace, Prentice followed Mathers down the road and soon lost sight of him in the darkness. He walked at a snail's pace, content to let Mathers, an idiot, check out the stream. Then a few more yards he stopped. What was that smell? Woodsmoke . . . made by recently burned wood. It seemed to be coming from a dark space between the blackened ruins of a couple of structures, stores probably. Barton Clay said a thousand dollars to the man who kills Dan Caine and if it was Caine, Prentice wasn't about to share the reward with Mathers. He pulled his Colt and peered into the darkness. It was like looking at a black-painted wall. There was no sound and nothing moved. Prentice took a couple of wary steps, his alert, restless eyes searching the murk of the night. Then, his gun up and ready, he stood and whispered, "Caine? Are you in there?"

The silence mocked him.

But then he felt warmth seep through the thin sole of his left boot. He kneeled and searched around with his hand and discovered the remains of a small campfire. Caine had thrown dirt on the flames, but some heat remained, not much, but enough to tell Prentice that fire had only recently been snuffed out.

Damn it, Caine was here, and he was close, and damn this infernal darkness.

Prentice got to his feet again and again whispered, "Come out, Caine. We got you surrounded." He heard the steady thump of his heart in his ears, and his breaths came in a series of quick, short gasps. The Peacemaker's muzzle was still up and ready, and he swallowed hard and said, "Caine, I'm coming after you, so before you piss yourself, come on out with your hands where I can see them."

Then a rustle in the grass. Caine was trying to hightail it.

Scenting blood, Luke Prentice took a quick step forward . . . into a bowie knife blade that buried itself to the hilt in his chest. A split second later a huge man emerged from the gloom. He put his right hand over Prentice's mouth to stifle any screams and at the same moment his left twisted the gun from the dying man's hand. Asher Starbuck slowly lowered Prentice to the ground and then tugged his knife from the man's chest. It looked like he was still alive and Asher slashed his throat swiftly and efficiently, killing him twice over. As he wiped the bloody blade clean on the dead man's shirt, Asher did a count in his head. Four lawmen, one dead, three to go. He had to improve those odds.

His chance came a couple of minutes later as Stan Mathers returned from his fruitless stroll to the stream and back. That Prentice was nowhere in sight didn't enter his thinking as strange.

A creature of darkness and soundless as a ghost on his feet, unseen, Asher got behind Mathers and shattered his spine with a shot in the back. The man dropped fast and hard and chewed on gravel before he died.

Asher Starbuck figured it out. Four lawmen, two dead, two alive and that number he could handle.

He adjusted the lie of his gunbelts and then set out on a gunman's walk toward the two men he could now see in the graying gloom.

CHAPTER FORTY-SIX

"What the hell?" Decker Clay said. "Who is he?"

"It ain't Caine. I can tell you that," Ruben Webb said.

"Then who is it?"

"Ask him."

"Hey, who are you?" Decker yelled.

Four horses and saddles, guns and whatever they had in their pockets, Asher Starbuck knew he could realize a tidy profit from this night's work. He smiled to himself. This day's work. The night was fading fast.

"You know who I am, lawman. Now don't talk to me," Asher said. "I'm not here to talk, so don't ask me any more questions. Just pull those pistols, open the ball and get to your work."

Asher drew his own guns and continued his walk toward Decker and Webb. The range was now twenty-five yards . . . and he was almost ready to fire.

It's highly doubtful, but possible, that Asher Starbuck, a common murderer, had never pulled a gun on a named shootist, a cool-headed man of skill and reputation. What's more to the point is that he'd probably never before encountered the new breed of Texas drawfighters exemplified by men like Wes Hardin and Ruben Webb.

He encountered one of them now.

Barely believing what was happening, Webb stood his ground as one of Asher's bullets *zinged!* past his ear and another kicked up a startled V of dirt between his feet. Webb drew, a practiced movement, very smooth and fast, and thumbed off two shots that thudded into Asher's belly. Beside Webb, young Decker Clay fanned his Colt, a marquee play that missed Asher with three shots. No matter. A pair of .45 bullets to the belly are killing hits that can pull a man up by the roots. Screaming his rage and disbelief, Asher dropped to his knees and then, by superhuman effort, managed to trigger both his Smith & Wessons. One .44 bullet went nowhere, but the other hit Decker Clay, a through-and-through shot that entered the left side of the young man's waist and exited his lower back. He yelled, "I'm hit!" and staggered back. Webb fired at Asher, another hit, but it was unnecessary, the man was already dead. He fell forward on his face and lay still.

Ruben Webb had rid the West of a great evil, but the way the cards were later to fall, he never knew it.

He kneeled beside Decker and said, "Lie still. You're badly wounded."

"Am I going to die?" Decker said.

Webb managed a smile. "I've seen men survive worse."

"Where are Prentice and Mathers?"

"Mathers was shot in the back and is dead, and I suspect Prentice is too."

"Who the hell was he?"

"I've no idea." He shook his head. "He was game or crazy, I don't know which."

"He thought we were lawmen."

"I know, so I peg him as an outlaw of some kind."

"I need a doctor, Ruben."

Webb's eyes went away from Decker's. "That means Tucson. It's a hell of a ride for a wounded man."

"I don't want to stay here by myself."

"With three dead men."

"Ruben, you've got to get me to Tucson."

"Don't worry, I'll get you there."

"You could make a travois."

Webb shook his head. "Too much rough country between here and Tucson for a travois. I'd never get you there."

"My pa is in Tucson by now."

"Good. You'll meet him there."

"I'm in pain, Ruben."

"Hold on. When we reach Tucson, the doctor will give you something to ease it."

"Damn, we're in the middle of nowhere," Decker said.

"That's the way of the West. Most times when a man stops for a moment and looks around, he realizes the only thing he can see for miles in all directions is the back of beyond." Webb laid his hand on Decker's chest. "I'll bring your horse."

"Suppose we run into Dan Caine?"

"Don't build houses on a bridge we ain't crossed yet. If we meet up, I'll take care of him."

CHAPTER FORTY-SEVEN

"I heard you come in, Mr. Caine," Mrs. Gertrude Dale said. "You were very late. And who sounded the dinner gong?"

"That was me, Mrs. Dale," Crow said. "I hit it with my knee in the dark."

"You scared poor Mr. Mulholland half out of his wits."

"Indeed, you did," Mr. Mulholland said, a forkful of scrambled eggs poised at his mouth. He was small, slight, bald, and inoffensive, a ladies corsets drummer by trade. "I thought the gong had sounded for Judgment Day." He shoved the eggs into his mouth and said, chewing, "You must understand that I'm under a doctor's care for nervousness. Nervous by name and nervous by nature, that's me, my wife always says."

"Poor Mr. Mulholland," Mrs. Dale said. "Perhaps a brandy?"

Mulholland shook his head. "No thank you, dear lady. Long ago I promised my dearest wife back in Austin that ne'er would I let demon drink touch my lips. Like me, Mrs. Mulholland is of a nervous disposition and she's taken a set against John Barleycorn. Alas, she's very much prone to fainting, poor little thing, and since she weighs three-hundred pounds, getting her on her feet again can be quite a chore." The little man stared at the ceiling for a moment, his mind working. Then he nodded to himself, returned to his plate, and said, "My word, yes, quite a chore."

Four other guests, including Dan and Crow, maintained a sympathetic silence, but a young warehouse clerk with bad acne named Marvin, nobody ever cared to ask for his last name, grinned and said, "Get yourself a skinnier wife, Mr. Mulholland. She'd be easier to pick up off the floor."

"Oh, dear me, no, never," Mr. Mulholland said. "I will never desert Mrs. Mulholland. 'Leave her,' people say or 'She's too fat, get rid of her.' But I will never discard Mrs. Mulholland, no matter what well-meaning people urge me to do." He thought about that and added, "No, I will never desert Mrs. Mulholland."

"Well, good luck, Mr. Mulholland," Dan said. He rose to his feet and said, "Crow, we have business to discuss."

"Can I plan dinner this evening for you two gentlemen?" Mrs. Dale said, frowning slightly.

Dan and Crow exchanged glances. "Yes," Dan said. "You can depend on it."

"What's for dinner, Mrs. Dale?" Crow said.

"Pigs feet in a batter, Mr. Crow, and buckwheat cakes and honey for dessert."

"My favorites, ma'am," Crow said.

"Anything that's edible is your favorite," Dan said.

He and Crow walked out into the gray, overcast morning, the clouds curling across the sky like sheets of lead. Thunder grumbled in the distance and the rising wind banged Mrs. Dale's screen door at the back of the house open and shut. She insisted on keeping the door closed to provide relief from the indoor heat and to keep out bugs, but her guests, on their way back from the outhouse, invariably left it ajar.

Dan built and lit a cigarette before he spoke. "Well, Crow, any ideas?" he said.

"No, I'm all out of ideas."

"Try harder."

"Dan, you killed Ben Clay, dynamited his pa's house, and burned down the mercantile. Maybe enough is enough."

"And maybe it isn't," Dan said. "We also buried Mary Jane, remember?"

"I remember, but where do we end it?"

Dan smiled. "My vigilante vendetta?"

"Yeah . . . whatever the hell that means."

"It means that the reckoning is still to come."

"The reckoning. I think that those words are carved on your heart."

"After what the Clays did to me, and what they did to Mary Jane Hillman, it may never end. Destroying the Clays and all they stand for could be my life's work, like one of those authors who spend an entire lifetime working on a single book." He stared at Crow. "Are you catching my drift?"

"No. I don't know anything about authors. It's you I'm talking about."

"Decker and Pete Clay tried their best to kill me and they murdered Mary Jane. They're still above ground, and I can't live with that."

"Those boys are right fond of whiskey and whores,"

Crow said. "Now the mercantile is gone they'll come to Tucson."

"And I'll be waiting for them," Dan said. "How many saloons do you reckon are in this town?"

"I don't know."

"Maybe a dozen. I'll patrol all of them, then one day they'll be standing at the bar and I'll call them out."

"How many days or weeks will that take?"

"It depends on the Clays. How long can they go without a woman? I don't rightly know."

"Our money will soon run out. Mrs. Dale isn't going to let us live there gratis."

"Any ideas?"

"Rob a bank? I don't know."

"It won't take too long," Dan said, more in hope than certainty.

"Call them out," Crow said.

"Huh?"

"That's what you said. You said that you'd find the Clays in a saloon and call them out."

Dan nodded. "Yup, that's what I said."

"They travel in a pack. It won't be just the Clay brothers. They'll have hard cases with them."

"Too bad for them," Dan Caine said.

CHAPTER FORTY-EIGHT

Thunder rumbled and lightning shimmered. Driven by a gusting wind, gravel rattled on the boardinghouse windows and ozone stung the air. The morning had grown darker as though a curtain had been rudely drawn across the face of the rising sun. Rain ticked on the leaves of the surrounding hardwoods as Mrs. Dale opened the front door, stuck her head out the better to see and tut-tutted at the rambunctious day before going back inside.

Crow said, "Somebody coming."

A man wearing a bloodstained white apron over a shabby black coat and pants, the top hat on his huge head worn at a jaunty angle, stepped up to the porch and said, "'Mornin', gents. Is the widow Dale to home?"

"She's inside," Dan said. "Looks like it's fixing to storm."

"That's Arizona Territory weather for you, sun one minute, rain the next." The man showed the paper-wrapped contents of the wicker basket he carried over his arm. "Pork sausages and some pigs' feet." An affable gent, he smiled and said, "Tonight's dinner I'll be bound, or me name's not Bill the butcher."

"Mrs. Dale is cooking them in a batter," Crow said. "Or so she says."

"Well, that's one way," Bill said. "But meself, I prefer them soused."

The man walked up to the door, knocked sharply and when it opened, he and Mrs. Dale spoke briefly about the unusual weather, the fragrant freshness of the pigs' feet and the plumpness of the sausages, and then coins chinked into the butcher's palm and the door closed again.

The man lifted the basket over his head so that it hung over his back and the handle crossed his chest. A talking man, he said to Dan, "A hell of an excitement downtown, did you hear?"

"Hear what?" Dan said.

Bill sounded pompous. "Why, only that the future governor of the Arizona Territory has just taken rooms in the Palace Hotel. He's a wealthy rancher by the name of Barton Clay and he's a Democrat by God. They say he's now just a hair's breadth from the presidency itself."

Dan pretended ignorance. "Why is he here in Tucson?"

"It seems that his ranch house was damaged by a fire and he's here until the repairs are completed, probably in a couple of weeks. City Marshal Bill Roche had just called on his excellency when I left with the sausages and pigs' feet."

"And Clay's sons?" Dan said. He had a handsome, pleasant face, but his stony features were anything but pleasing that morning.

"I heard he has sons but I don't know anything about them," Bill said. "I guess they'll join their father at the Palace."

"You mean the Palace Hotel," Dan said.

The butcher looked puzzled. "Yeah, the hotel." He

glanced at the sky. "I got to be going before the storm kicks up in earnest." He waved a hand. "Enjoy your pigs' feet, gentlemen."

Lightning flashed, thunder banged, and the slanting rain rattled through the tree canopies. The door opened and Mrs. Dale, a feather duster in her hand, stood in the shelter of the porch roof and said, "Mr. Caine, Mr. Crow, you'd better come inside. This is shaping up to be a bad storm."

"We'll be right in, Mrs. Dale," Dan said.

"I'll put more coffee on," the woman said. "It looks like you won't be going anywhere for a spell."

The door closed behind her and then Crow said, "So . . . do we blow up the Palace Hotel?"

"I'd like to, but a lot of innocent folks might die," Dan said. "I only want Barton Clay and his sons."

"Gunning the newly appointed governor of the Arizona Territory might be less than wise," Crow said. "It could be like what happened after Lincoln was shot, only this time the hue and cry could go all the way to Broken Back."

"You think he's that popular?"

"Yeah, I do. He's the new governor. The last feller didn't really want the job, but Barton Clay does. He's a Democrat and folks think he'll do great things for the territory."

Dan waited until a roll of thunder passed, smiled and said, "How do you know these things, Crow?"

"You heard the butcher call Barton his excellency. Seems to me that Mr. Clay is mighty popular around these parts. They're bound to believe that he'll put Tucson on the map, and Bill the butcher will sell a heap more pigs' feet, him and the other town merchants."

"They all don't sell pigs' feet."

"You know what I mean."

"Would Barton Clay be as popular if the good citizens

of Tucson knew that on his orders, his sons beat, raped, and then lynched Mary Jane Hillman."

"No, he wouldn't be as popular, but it's a serious charge that a couple of nobodies like us can never prove," Crow said.

"A hick lawman and an Apache breed, you mean."

Crow smiled, "That's what I mean. Can you imagine us in the witness box facing a battery of Clay's lawyers? Our testimony would be shot to pieces, and us with it."

The wind grew stronger, carrying with it torrential rain, and the heavens were being torn apart by thunder and lightning. A gray fox galloped around the front of the porch and came to a startled halt when it saw two humans. For a moment, ears pricked, the fox studied Dan and Crow and then it dashed under the house. The Apaches considered the gray fox to be the herald of impending death and he was visibly upset by it.

"Did you see it?" Crow said.

"Yeah, it was a fox or maybe a small coyote."

"It was a gray fox and it warned us that death is just over the horizon."

"It was here because it was looking for shelter from the rain," Dan said.

"I had a vision," Crow said.

"It must have been quick."

"It was, like a flash of lightning."

"What did you see?"

"I saw Barton Clay astride the world and then he broke up into pieces and fell to earth like a broken earthenware pot."

"It doesn't sound good for Barton, does it?" Dan said.

"Maybe, but I don't know what it means."

"It means he'll ride high for a spell and then collapse," Dan said.

Crow shook his head. "Visions can have many possible interpretations. Geronimo would've told me what it means."

"And he's not here."

"No, he's not, so your meaning may be the right one."

"Let's hope so," Dan said.

The door opened and let the relentless thunder come inside. "Coffee is ready, mostly warmed up from this morning's breakfast, but I have bear sign to go with it."

Dan Caine rose to his feet and said, "Mrs. Dale, you're so good to us."

"A heart of gold," the woman said. "That's always been my problem."

CHAPTER FORTY-NINE

Riding through the wild tunnel of a thunderstorm, Ruben Webb brought Decker Clay into Tucson draped across his saddle, leading the young man's horse. His face a study in stunned surprise, a passerby stopped and looked at Webb, then at Decker and back to Webb again.

"Doctor?" Webb said, drawing rein.

The man he addressed, young, skinny and insignificant, said, "Next block, Dr. Simpson. Three doors down."

"Obliged," Webb said, touching his hat brim.

The youth called after him, "He was with General Grant at Chattanooga, so he knows all about taking bullets out of folks."

Without looking back, Webb raised a hand.

Dr. Henry Simpson was a middle-aged man with the face of a poet and a picture of Grant on his waiting room wall, a brave or extremely foolhardy thing to do in Tucson.

"Nurse Hartmann, help me get this man onto the examination table," Simpson said. And to Webb, "Stand aside."

Nurse Hartmann was a tall, wide-shouldered Teuton with black hair scraped back in a bun and startling sky-blue eyes. Her habitually disdainful scowl seemed to be engraved onto her face. Webb relieved Decker of his gunbelt and holstered gun, and the nurse and the doctor got Decker onto the table

After a cursory examination, the physician said, "He's lost a lot of blood. What happened?"

"He got shot," Ruben said.

"I can see that," Dr. Simpson said. "Who shot him? City Marshal Roche insists that he gets a report on all shootings and cuttings in Tucson. I don't know why, he never does anything about them."

"It was road agents," Webb said. "They killed two Clay ranch riders and our return fire killed one of the outlaws."

The doctor was surprised. He looked down at Decker. "Is he one of the ranch hands?"

"No, his name is Decker and he's one of Barton Clay's sons."

"Soon to be Governor Clay, I'm told."

"Yes, he is."

"Interesting. Now please leave while I try to save this young man's life."

Ruben Webb was stunned. "Save his life? It's as serious as that? The bullet hit the left side of his waist."

"Where there are parts of the liver, the pancreas, kidney and the colon just to name a few. If the bullet passed through a vital organ, it's very serious indeed. Does the governor know?"

Webb shook his head. "He doesn't. Not yet."

"Then I suggest you go tell him. He'll want to be here."

"I'll see you out," Nurse Hartmann said.

"Can you save him, Doc?" Webb said as he made for

the door. The woman walked close beside him like a prison warden.

"I don't know," Dr. Simpson said. "Sometimes patients don't need a doctor, they need a miracle."

"And Decker?"

"Decker needs a miracle," the doctor said.

Ruben Webb stopped at the door and said to Nurse Hartmann, "What's the best hotel in town?"

"The newest is the Grange, but the most expensive is the Palace."

Webb touched his hat. "Obliged."

Governor Barton Clay would be at the Palace.

"How did it happen?" Barton Clay said. He had dressed in haste, talking to no one. But now as he waited outside the hotel door for his surrey, he said, "Tell me again that it wasn't Caine?"

"No, boss it . . ."

"Call me governor."

"No, Governor, it wasn't Dan Caine."

"Then who?"

"I don't know his name. He was a man who seemed to have camped overnight in the ruins of Amitola."

"This man shot my son and killed Luke Prentice and Stan Mathers."

"He did. But Decker got his work in and we killed the man."

"You, Prentice, and Mathers couldn't stop him, all three

of you gun hands couldn't stop one man and left my son twisting in the wind."

"Boss . . . Governor . . . he was no ordinary man. He just took us by surprise, a gun in both hands."

Barton's huge physical presence dwarfed Webb, and now he took a step back as though to bring the little gunmen's entire body into focus. "I hired you because I thought you were no ordinary man," he said. "It seems I was wrong."

"I did kill him," Webb said. "He was good with his pistols and I killed him."

"Why could you not save my son? You're the paid draw-fighter and it's your job to engage two-gun men. Decker shouldn't have been involved."

Webb's anger flared. "Decker has killed his man three times over and he wanted to be in on the fight. I couldn't stop him. Hell, it all happened so fast I didn't have time to stop him."

Barton Clay stared at Webb for a long time, his thoughts concealed. Finally he said, "Ruben, you can leave my employ anytime you feel like it."

"Not until I've done for Dan Caine."

"When I'm governor, if I decide to keep you around, you'll wear a dark suit and a celluloid collar and tie. Can you live with that?"

"Sure, I can. I look forward to it."

"We'll see," Barton Clay said. "Ah, here's Buff Grant with the surrey. Lead us to the doctor's office, Ruben."

"I'm sorry, your son had lost a lot of blood, and I couldn't save him," Dr. Henry Simpson said. He shook his head. "I tried my best but he slipped away from me."

"Doctor Simpson worked very hard to save him," Nurse Hartmann said.

"I'm not blaming the doctor," Barton Clay said. "He looked at Webb who'd joined them in the surgery and said, "First Ben, now Decker, dear God, is there a curse on my house?"

"There's Dan Caine and his black magic," Webb said. "A hundred years ago they'd have burned him at the stake."

Dr. Simpson said, "It was a bullet that killed your son, Mr. Clay, not magic."

Barton shook his head. "No, no, don't tell me that. I must consult with Paola Gaudet. She knows how to lift the curse."

"Mr. Clay, I know you're grieving and not thinking straight," the physician said. "Perhaps you should speak to a clergyman."

"No clergymen," Barton said. "They're a useless bunch. I'll bury my son and then visit someone who can really help me."

"I've had trouble with Paola Gaudet in the past," Dr. Simpson said. "She's a charlatan and she's caused the deaths of people who thought she'd cured them, people who should've had surgery."

"You couldn't save my son," Barton said.

"He was too far gone."

"Paola Gaudet could've saved him. Ruben Webb, you should've brought Decker to her."

Webb and the doctor exchanged glances, and then the little gunman said, "Maybe I should."

Barton said, "Doctor, I'm sure you can recommend an undertaker."

"Yes. I'll send for one and I can arrange a burial plot in the Court Street cemetery.

"How much do I owe you?"

"Nothing. I don't want your money, Mr. Clay."

"That should be Governor Clay."

"You're not quite governor yet, but as you wish."

"I'm at the Palace Hotel, and I want to be told when the arrangements are made."

"Because of the city ordinance concerning deaths, the funeral will be tomorrow. If you send someone, I can tell him the time."

There was a look in the doctor's eyes that Barton could not ignore and he said, "We all grieve in our own way. When someone close to me dies, I want to lash out, seek revenge for his dying."

"You can't lash out at death, Governor Clay," Dr. Simpson said. "Death just is. It's not the opposite of life but a part of it."

"My son is lying cold on your table, and I won't bandy words with you. I'll send a rider for the funeral details." Barton Clay leaned over and kissed the dead man's forehead, "Decker . . ." he said.

There was a world of emotion, of grief and loss and anger, in that single word.

CHAPTER FIFTY

Bill the butcher was a mine of information. He made a regular visit to Mrs. Dale's boardinghouse but recently, since she had a full complement of boarders, he came around daily.

"How were the pigs' feet and the pork sausages?" he asked Dan and Crow as they drank coffee on the porch.

"Just fine," Dan said. "Mrs. Dale is a good cook."

"I know. That's why I've asked her to marry me three hundred and forty-seven times. Today will make three hundred and forty-eight."

"And she's always said no?" Crow asked.

"Well, the first three hundred and forty times she said no, but recently she's said maybe."

"That's a lot better than a no," Dan said.

"You're right, it is. But a yes would be better still. Ah well, I'll ask her again this morning." He lifted a corner of the checkered blue napkin that covered his basket. "Two plump hens for tonight's chicken and dumplings and a couple of pounds of calf liver. Do you like liver and onions?"

"No," Dan said.

"That goes for me too," Crow said.

"Well, that's a pity, but eat it anyway." Bill put a foot on the porch step, stopped and said, "Say, have you heard what happened?"

"No, what?" Dan said. His cartridge belt and holstered Colt hung over the back of his rocker where it would be handy in an emergency.

"Governor Clay's youngest son was killed by outlaws."

Thunderstruck, Dan leaned forward in his chair. "Decker?"

"Is that his name?"

"Yes, he's Barton Clay's youngest."

"Well, he died on Dr. Henry's examination table. From what I hear, he was shot through and through. The funeral is tomorrow, and the governor is in deepest mourning."

"How did it happen?" Dan said.

"I already told you, he died on Dr. Simpson's . . ."

"I mean, who pulled the trigger?"

"I don't know. It happened east of here when young Decker and another man were beset by road agents. The other man fled, but the governor's son bravely stood his ground and killed all five of the scoundrels before he succumbed to his wounds. Mr. Clay is devastated and there's talk that in a few days when he officially becomes governor, he'll put the whole territory in a state of mourning for a month." Bill shook his head. "I still can't believe it, an innocent young man gunned down by outlaws. We live in terrible times, but Governor Clay, an honorable man, will set everything to rights."

Bill stepped to the door to give the desirable Mrs. Dale her chickens and once again pop the question.

* * *

"Another one down, two to go," Dan said.

"Barton Clay wasn't with the brothers when they tried to kick you to death," Crow said.

"No, but it was him gave the order. Barton Clay, that piece of dirt, the governor of the Arizona Territory, the very thought of it makes my blood boil."

"What's our plan, Dan?"

"I don't have one."

"We can't sit on Mrs. Dale's porch much longer and eat pigs' feet."

"I agree with you, Crow, we can't. We've got to bring this thing to a head."

"And that will be?"

"When Pete Clay and his pa's shadows no longer pollute the ground they walk on."

"Can y'all tell me how we manage that?"

"I don't know. But I'll find a way."

"You just gonna gun them, first chance you get?"

"Something like that."

"There ain't something that's like gunning a man. It doesn't exist."

Dan glanced at the blue sky, smooth as silk, washed clean by yesterday's rain.

"By usual habit, Pete Clay's not a barfly," he said.

"Just as well," Crow said. "A saloon gunfight is always chancy. Guns start firing and put out all the oil lamps and you end up trying to dodge bullets in the dark."

"You know that, do you?"

"Happened to me only once, and that was a long time ago when I was bounty hunting. I was after a ranny by the name of Lucas Akers. He was wanted for murder and arson and there was a reward of five hundred dollars on his head. He saw me in the street, this was in Abilene, and ran into Jack Ryan's Saloon. I followed him and he stood by the bar and started shooting. It was ten at night and when I shot back, everybody was hugging the floor by that time, the lamps went out and me and Akers shot at each other in the dark."

"And what happened?"

"He ran out the back delivery door of the place, and I never saw him again. Paddy Ryan said that between us, me and Akers fired fifteen times and scored no hits, except for a parson who got an earlobe shot off."

"What was a parson doing in a saloon?"

"He was fond of whiskey and he liked the ladies."

"And the moral of this story is . . ."

"Don't gunfight Pete Clay in a saloon, especially after sundown."

Dan nodded. "I'll heed your advice, Crow, and shoot him in the daylight."

"Dan, wiser words were never spoke."

"And those words also go for Barton."

"You know if you gun Barton Clay, the respected, and let me say beloved, de facto governor of the Arizona Territory, you're going to face a noose."

"Crow, where the hell do you get a ten-dollar word like de facto? I don't even know what you're talking about."

"When I was a young man, a United States Army colonel told the people of our rancheria that Geronimo considered himself the de facto chief of the Chiricahua and Mescalero and that we must undertake to banish him from our lands and our lives. I didn't know what de facto meant, and I asked an old and wise elder what was its meaning and he told me it was the white man's way of describing something that had happened but wasn't yet official. So Barton Clay is the de facto governor of the

Arizona Territory until he's sworn in or whatever it is that governors do."

"Well, don't use those words again," Dan said, irritated. "It doesn't become an Apache, even half an Apache, to mouth jawbreakers like that."

"All right, I won't, ever again, even though your education is sadly lacking. Now tell me how you're going to avoid the death penalty after you gun the de facto governor."

"I'm ignoring that, because I didn't hear it," Dan said. "After I talk long and sincere to the jury those chosen men will realize what kind of monster Barton Clay really was."

"That, or they'll think you're a damned liar, and then you'll get sentenced to the big drop."

Sunlight flashed behind a solitary white cloud, and for a moment Crow thought he was having a vision. But the cloud moved on, and he realized he wasn't.

"I'll back you every step of the way, Dan. But I just don't see a happy ending to this story. I mean, for me and you."

Dan nodded. "One way or another it will be over soon. It's just about time to open the ball."

The door of the house opened and Bill the butcher stepped onto the porch and slung his basket on his back.

"Well?" Crow said.

"Well what?"

"Did she say yes?"

"No, she didn't," Bill said. For a moment he was crestfallen, but then he brightened and said, "But she's thinking it over."

"Thinking it over is better than an outright no," Dan said. "And when a woman says she's thinking a thing over, it's always a good sign. Women do a lot of thinking, and they're very good at it."

The butcher smiled. "Well, you boys have been very encouraging and you've shown me that there's light at the end of the tunnel of love." He stuck out his hand to Dan and said, "Bill Souter. Put it there."

"Dan Caine and the yellow-haired giant over there is called Crow."

Bill shook hands with Crow and said, "It's a pleasure to meet you."

"Likewise," Crow said.

Friendly, innocent handshakes all round . . . that very soon would hurl Dan Caine and Crow into the gaping jaws of disaster.

CHAPTER FIFTY-ONE

The funeral for Decker Clay took place very early in the morning while the sky was still ribboned with red. Barton wanted it that way. A dead son above ground preyed on his mind and made him uncomfortable. The quicker Decker was laid to rest, the better.

An atheist, Barton at first refused having a clergyman graveside, but at the urging of Pete an elderly Catholic priest with tired eyes named Father John O'Rourke agreed to do the burial service. A chaplain attached to the Union's Irish brigade during the War Between the States, he'd seen much of death.

The service was brief, marred by a loose horse in a lot adjoining the cemetery that galloped in circles and neighed loudly and constantly, putting everyone on edge, especially the six Clay cowboys in attendance, a superstitious breed who exchanged worried looks and wished the damned horse would settle. It never did.

After the service, when everyone present had thrown a handful of dirt onto Decker's coffin before leaving, Barton told Pete to take Ruben Webb and the rest of the hands to a saloon and to buy rum punches all round to offset the unseasonably cool weather.

"Are you going back to the hotel, Pa?" Pete asked.

"Not yet," Barton said. He seemed distracted, distant and strange, for such a large, muscular man, strangely pale and fragile. "Tell Buff Grant to come here."

"Is there anything I can do, Pa?" Pete said.

"Nothing, unless you can lift the curse from us," Barton said.

"Pa, there is no curse," Pete said. "Some bad luck, that's all."

"Ben's death was bad luck? Then Decker's? Luke Prentice and Stan Mathers both dead. Jess Gentry too. It's more than bad luck. There's a curse on my house and Princess Paola Gaudet will lift it."

"Pa, don't . . ."

"Pa, nothing. You're now my heir, my hope for grandchildren and the continuance of the Clay bloodline. Damn it, boy, I want to found a dynasty and it begins right here today with Paola Gaudet." He looked over Pete's shoulder and yelled, "Buff, I'm ready to go." Barton again focused on his son. "Pete, I've decided to send you East, to one of the big cities. The idea came to me at Decker's grave."

"But the ranch . . ."

"It won't be for long, just long enough to find a bride, an innocent, healthy girl who can birth lots of children."

"Pa, there are lots of those in the Territory."

Now Buff Grant stood between the two men, an interested onlooker.

"Whores! Grubby women like the one we hanged. You'll go to Richmond or some other city of the old Confederacy and find a pretty Southern belle we can both be proud of."

"When?" Pete said.

"Soon. I'll let you know, but I have to dispose of Dan Caine first." Barton looked at Grant. "Buff, let's go. You know the place."

"I sure do, Governor," Grant said.

Barton Clay lay on Paola Gaudet's silken bed, his head on her lap as she stroked his hair. Her boudoir smelled of incense and exotic spices and other fragrances Barton could not identify. He was fully clothed but for his spurred boots that stood together neatly on the floor like a pair of bookends. There was a calavera in the shape of a human skull on the bedside table, painted in the old Day of the Dead Mexican style. Beside it lay a curved, sacrificial knife in a jeweled sheath and a bottle of Old Crow bourbon. A portrait of a turbaned Marie Laveau, the most powerful voodoo queen of them all, hung on the wall.

"You have the potential to be a great man, Barton Clay, but the curse is real, and it slows your progress. A warning . . . in the crystal ball I saw a white man and with him an Indian and they wish you harm."

"His name is Dan Caine and the Indian is an Apache breed who calls himself Crow. Is Caine the one who put a curse on my house?"

Paola Gaudet nodded. "Perhaps. Two dead sons, both fine young men, indeed the curse is a powerful one."

"Is it too powerful for you?"

"No. It's not."

"Can you lift it?"

"Perhaps. But there is a shadow in the crystal, a twilight that troubles me. It warns of a dark deed recently committed that may have been carried out by you or someone close to you. Do you know about this? If I am to banish the curse I need honesty, Barton Clay. In voodoo, there can be no lies, no deceptions, no half-truths. The reason for voodoo's existence is *sevi iwa* and that means to serve the spirits, and I hear a voice crying out for justice."

"What kind of voice? Does it belong to a man or a woman?"

"It is neither male nor female . . . it is the sound of a tormented soul that speaks to me."

Barton sat up on the bed, then got to his feet and poured himself a bourbon. He downed a shot and then poured another.

"Lift the curse, Paola. I'll pay you anything you want."

"I think she was a woman."

"Enough of that bilge," Barton said, angry. "Lift the curse."

"The curse of a dying woman is a formidable one. How many times in the Dark Ages did a witch curse those who burned her? Many times the men who carried out the deed died terrible deaths themselves, and most of them clergy that an angry God no longer protected."

"All that matters little," Barton said. "Some lives are worthless."

"All lives are precious in the eyes of the Deity."

"Damn you, woman, lift the curse on me and my house. I'll pay you five thousand dollars to free me from this scourge." Barton poured another drink and rubbed his left arm. "And give me something for this damned pain."

"Who was she?" Paola Gaudet said.

"What do you mean?"

"The dying woman who cursed you and yours, who was she?"

"I don't know what you're talking about."

"Then I can't help you any longer. I won't become party to your misdeeds, Barton."

"All right, she was a cheap whore. Pay her two dollars and a man could have her all night."

Then, after a long pause, Paola Gaudet's unblinking eyes on him, "What did you do to her?"

"I hanged her, me and my sons."

"You hanged her from a tree?"

"Yes, I did."

"Why?"

"Because she was a stubborn slut who refused to tell me where Dan Caine was hiding out." Barton Clay's eyes were wild. "Oh, she knew all right, she knew damn well, and I needed to get it out of her. I thought the threat of the noose would be enough to loosen her tongue, but it wasn't. Well, she paid the penalty for her bullheadedness, the tramp."

"You murdered her, Barton."

"If you want to call it that. I say I executed her."

"You must go to City Marshal Roche and confess to what you have done. Only then can the curse be lifted."

"I did nothing. What happened is just between you and me. No one cares about a dead whore. She's already buried and forgotten."

"Go to City Marshal Roche, Barton. That's the only way the curse can be lifted."

Barton Clay slid the knife from its sheath, the blade curved and razor sharp. He studied the gleaming steel closely and said, "In a couple of days I'll be the governor of this territory. I can't afford to get involved with Roche and a noisy and ultimately useless investigation into the death of a whore. Paola, let sleeping dogs lie. Find some other way to end the curse. And answer me this, who deserves more to live? Me, a rich and respected rancher, a governor who's charted a course for the presidency, or Mary Jane Hillman, flat backer."

"You remember the prostitute's name. I would've thought you'd forgotten it by now."

"What does it matter? I remember lots of names."

"Barton, I'm a voodoo princess, I talk to the living and the dead, but I'm also a citizen of these United States and the murdered woman's voice clamors in my head, asking me to do the right thing."

"And what's the right thing, Paola?" Barton said, his voice rising with every word of his question.

"The right thing is to ask the authorities to investigate the murder of Mary Jane Hillman."

"I'll give you money, set you up in Washington one day and all you have to do is keep your mouth shut." Barton smiled without warmth. "You're an attractive woman, Paola, and I'm willing to make you my mistress. You'll never lack money again in your life."

"I have money, Barton, and I'll be no man's mistress."

"I'm sorry to hear that."

"And now I'm asking you to leave."

"What about the pain in my left arm and leg?"

"Use the magic and medications I've already given you."

"You won't really talk to Bill Roche, will you?"

"I believe I will. The voice of Mary Jane Hillman will give me no rest."

"Then I'll still that voice in your head forever."

For such a big man Barton Clay moved as fast as a lightning bolt, the backward slash of the knife in his left hand flashing across Paola Gaudet's throat, immediately opening up a ribbon of scarlet on the woman's slender neck. Paola staggered back, her black eyes registering surprise and fear, and Barton, enraged at her treachery, struck again, the blade thrusting between her breasts. The woman fell on her back, knocking over a bedside table and lay there in a heap, her yellow robe stained with her blood. Her silent lips moved and then stilled and dead eyes stared at Barton as he looked in horror at what he'd done. The knife in his hand was bloody, and he threw it away from him in disgust. He pulled on his boots, a plan coming to him piece by piece as he ransacked the house. He found what he was looking for in what seemed to be Paola's parlor, a metal money box, inside it eighty dollars and some change. Barton pocketed the cash and threw the box in the middle of the floor.

He smiled to himself. By all that's holy, someone would pay for Paola Gaudet's atrocious murder . . . but it wouldn't be Barton Clay.

CHAPTER FIFTY-TWO

The morning after Paola Gaudet's murder, a cleaning lady, a widow by the name of Sarah Willis, discovered the blood-splashed body of Paola Gaudet and raised the hue and cry. Church Street was a business area, and hearing Mrs. Willis's cries of "Murder! Murder!" she was soon surrounded by concerned warehouse workers and office clerks.

"In there!" Mrs. Willis pointed to the door of the Gaudet house and promptly fainted.

This dreadful, but exciting news, was delivered to Mrs. Gertrude Dale and her assembled guests by Bill Souter on his daily morning visit with fresh meat supplies. Like the others, Dan Caine and Crow were just finishing breakfast when the appalling news broke like a tidal wave over the stunned boarders.

Mrs. Dale was the first to recover her composure. "This doesn't surprise me in the least," she sniffed. "The Gaudet woman dabbled in the dark arts and sooner or later something terrible was bound to happen. Mark my words, this was the work of the devil."

"It seems that robbery was the motive," Souter said.

"Her empty money box was found on her parlor floor. Nothing else was taken."

"What does Marshal Roche think?" Dan said.

"I don't know, but he was consulting with Governor Clay when I left. By the way, Mrs. Dale, those are excellent steak-and-kidney pies today. I made them myself."

"Thank you, Mr. Souter," the woman said. "I know they will be excellent." She waved a hand. "And so do my guests."

"Of course, we will," one melancholy-looking man said. "As long as the beef isn't full of gristle and the kidneys are fresh."

"Fresh as the day is long," Souter said. He was anxious to return to the subject of Paola Gaudet's murder. "I did hear City Marshal Roche say that the murderer was not a stranger, but someone who lives in Tucson. A man who knew Miss Gaudet lived alone and kept money in her house."

"Nothing good comes from heathen religions, Mr. Souter," Mrs. Dale said.

"Indeed, dear lady," the butcher said. "Voodoo is the religion in question. Its practitioners believe they can raise the dead and use them as slaves."

Mrs. Dale's hand flew to her throat. "Oh, dear God in heaven, say it isn't so, Mr. Souter. I'm suddenly sore afraid."

"Fear not, widow Dale, Paola Gaudet is dead and the danger is past," Souter said. He made so bold as to reach out and squeeze the woman's hand. She seemed to enjoy it and didn't pull away.

Dan got to his feet and said, "I'll finish my coffee on the porch."

"I'll join you," Crow said.

"And I must be going," Souter said. He smiled at Mrs. Dale. "As always, dear lady, you are a sweet beguilement and I'd love to tarry, but duty calls."

"Until tomorrow then, Mr. Souter," Mrs. Dale said. She smiled. "And I haven't yet made up my mind about the proposal closest to your heart."

"Then I will impatiently wait a little longer," Souter said.

Mrs. Dale lifted the coffeepot and to the men sitting around the table she said, "More coffee?"

"You're not going to get close to Barton Clay or his son," Crow said. "He's the governor now and I reckon he'll never be alone. He probably has a guard on his hotel room door."

"What are you telling me, Crow?"

"That it's time to go home."

"Forget what he and his son did to me and Mary Jane Hillman?"

"Dan, I'm not a quitter, and neither are you, but sometimes the game ain't worth playing anymore. The best revenge you can get on Barton Clay is to go home and live happily with your wife. Maybe have a passel of young'uns to keep you busy."

"I want to kill them both, Barton Clay and his son, and rid the earth of their shadows."

"Dan, you've been a sheriff, and a vigilante, and you've killed men but what you've never been is an assassin."

"An assassin. Maybe that's what it takes to get rid of the Clays."

"And it's something you ain't. You'll go in with guns

blazing and end up dead on the floor and make Helen the prettiest widow in Texas."

"All right, I'll study on it," Dan said. "But I don't want folks to think that Barton Clay put the crawl on me."

"Folks don't give a damn what happens to you, Dan. The person they see in the mirror when they comb their hair in the morning is the only ranny they take an interest in. Believe me, they don't give a tinker's damn about Dan Caine and his problems."

"All right, Crow, I'll study on it some more."

"Just don't take your time about it. We got enough money to spend two more nights in the boardinghouse. After that, we're out on our ear."

Dan's smile was faint. "Do you remember when Mary Jane gave us the money, forty dollars, her life savings?"

"Sure, I remember. It's what we've been living on this past week."

"Now here's an idea, we could get the dynamite from where we stashed it and blow up Barton Clay's place again," Dan said. "It's a thought, ain't it?"

"Blow up what? You already demolished his house, what's next? The bunkhouse? The barn? A corral? An outhouse or two maybe?"

"Enough, Crow, I got your drift. It was a bad idea."

"Then here's a good idea. We wait for two days and if an opportunity doesn't arise to cut the Clays' suspenders we head back to Texas."

"It's a deal," Dan said.

He recalled Mary Jane Hillman, her face, her wonderful smile, how the sunlight tangled in her hair, a woman who loved him and nursed him back to health after the beating he took from the Clays almost killed him. Now Mary Jane lay in a cold grave. He saw in his mind's eye Governor Barton Clay lording it over the Arizona Territory, occupying the White House, his son Pete getting rich at his side. How can a man rid himself of those visions? He can't, not if he lives a hundred years. Dan Caine realized he'd endure crushing guilt for the rest of his life. It was a grim, heartbreaking prospect.

CHAPTER FIFTY-THREE

Barton Clay, red in the face, was furious.

"Find the murderers, Bill, and string them up without benefit of a trial," he said.

"How do you figure there was more than one killer?" City Marshal Roche said.

"A hunch points me in that direction."

"And I believe there was only one."

"One, two, what difference does it make? Your job is to find out who killed Paola Gaudet."

"Did you know her?"

"I met her only briefly. She sold me something to ease my headaches, but it didn't work."

"I think she knew her killer. She wouldn't invite a stranger into her boudoir."

"Unless she was whoring on the side."

"There's always that."

"Raise a posse, Bill. Search this town. I'll help."

"What does a woman killer look like?"

"I don't know."

"And that's why a posse is useless. We don't have any idea what we're searching for. Was he young, old, fat, thin?

Maybe the killer was another woman. There were no witnesses so who knows?"

"Bill, are you taking this investigation seriously? After all it happened on the governor's doorstep."

"Barton . . ."

"Governor."

"Governor, I'm taking it very seriously. I'll find the woman's killer, be assured of that."

Barton almost laughed aloud. Bill couldn't find an egg in a hen house.

"I'm glad to hear that," he said. "For the good of this town the murderer must be brought to justice and quickly."

"Yes, I know," Bill Roche said. "I know that only too well."

City Marshal Bill Roche walked back to the large brick courthouse at the corner of Church and Pennington streets, his mind working. Paola Gaudet and he were not lovers in the romantic sense, but they occasionally slept together, satisfying a need they both felt. Her murder had shaken him to the core. It was such a savage, mindless killing, and money wasn't the motive. Paola Gaudet was free with money, and she gave a handout to every down-and-out bum who knocked on her door. Roche had chided her several times for her generosity. If a man had entered Paola's house to rob her, she would've laughed and given him her money box and maybe a voodoo blessing along with it. There would be no reason to kill her. And the clue he found on the plush Persian rug in her bedroom disturbed him. It was hard to see, but it was there all right, the print of a round-toed, high-heeled riding boot that cattlemen wore. Paola's murderer wasn't a townsman. He was no warehouse or counting-house clerk, tradesman or merchant, but a puncher . . . or a rancher. Roche was determined to solve the riddle, knowing full well he was treading on dangerous ground, and suddenly he needed a backbone and the sand to go with it. He doubted that he had either and that troubled him.

Barton Clay sat in his two-room hotel suite with Ruben Webb, a bottle of whiskey on a table between them. Webb wasn't much of a drinker, but he was a good listener.

"So, when she said she was going to the law, you killed her," Webb said.

"Of course, I killed her," Barton said. "What else could I do?"

"You done right, Governor," Webb said. "She gave you little choice."

"I wasn't thinking straight, right after burying Decker, and I guess she scared me."

"Then the fault was hers, scaring folks like that."

"I hated to do it, Ruben, because I needed her magic."

"There are plenty of them witchy women. We'll get you another."

"Yeah, once I'm officially governor . . ."

"In a couple of days."

"I'll take a trip to New Orleans and find me another voodoo queen. Once my house is rebuilt, damn Dan Caine, I'll install her at the ranch permanently."

"How is City Marshal Roche taking all this?"

"Bill Roche is an idiot, about half as smart as a wooden Indian, but he's sniffing around asking questions and I guess he could make trouble."

"Just give me the word and I'll gun him," Webb said.

"Clumsy, a shade ham-handed, but it may come to that," Barton said, his eyes hard.

He stood, stepped to the window and watched intently as a brewer's dray trundle passed, the barrels chained together like so many rotund convicts.

"Damn it all, I have an idea," he said. He turned and looked at Webb. "I know how to get Roche out of the way."

"I'm listening, Governor."

"We find a nonentity to blame for the murder. We'll have another nobody as an eyewitness who'll swear he saw the nonentity leave Paola Gaudet's house in the early hours of yesterday morning." Barton smiled. "And there was blood on his hands."

Webb smiled. "It could work . . . if we can find the right nonentity and nobody."

"The nonentity should be any stranger in town we can kill right here at the hotel. And the nobody . . . well, any drunken good-for-nothing will fit the bill so long as he can identify a corpse as the man he saw leave Paola Gaudet's house."

"Governor, why do we have to kill the stranger, whoever he is?"

"To shut his mouth. It's best we don't give him a chance to protest his innocence to Roche. The setup is simple. A lunatic tries to assassinate me and is shot by one of my associates. The drunk then identifies him, in Roche's presence, as Paola Gaudet's killer. Case closed."

"All right, I'll ask around town, see what I can do," Webb said.

"Be quick about it, Ruben. We don't have much time to set this plan in motion," Barton Clay said. "You must bring the stranger here. Tell him the governor wants to talk with him on an important matter and he'll come running."

"And the drunk?"

"Tell him what we need him to do, and then stash him somewhere until I'm ready for him."

Webb smiled. "Boss . . ."

"Governor . . . please."

"Governor, I must hand it to you, when it comes to plotting a killing, you're a master."

"No, Ruben, when it comes to my survival, I'm a master. In my time I've shot, hanged, and burned alive at least two score men, and if the truth be known, a few women as well, and that, my friend, is why I'm still here. The suffering of other people makes Barton Clay thrive. That's the way of it."

Ruben Webb wanted to say, "You're thriving, Barton, but you've buried two sons."

He did not, however, think it was wise.

CHAPTER FIFTY-FOUR

I'm on a wild-goose chase, Ruben Webb thought to himself. The governor needs to find another way. Think about it. How easy would it be to lure a perfect stranger to the Palace Hotel, gun him and then bring City Marshal Bill Roche running to the scene? Tell Roche the dead man tried to assassinate the governor, and by the way that's not all, Marshal, this drunk here recognizes him as the man he saw leaving Paolo Gaudet's house after she was murdered, and he had blood on his hands.

Even Roche, whom Webb suspected wasn't nearly as stupid as the governor thought, wouldn't swallow that story hook, line, and sinker. In fact, he probably might not believe a word of it.

The noon sun was high and hot as Ruben Webb stepped out of the hotel and almost bumped into Bill Souter who carried a basket loaded with paper-wrapped packages, some stained with blood.

"Sorry," Souter said. "I didn't see you there."

"No harm done," Webb said. "What do you have in the basket."

"Meat from my butcher shop for the hotel restaurant,"

Souter said. "The chefs are mighty picky and require a fresh supply every day."

"Do you only deliver here?" Webb said, an idea forming in his mind.

"No, sir, I deliver all over town. Tucson is growing and I'm getting so busy I plan to buy a wagon and a horse to pull it."

"I don't want to detain you, but may I ask you a question?" Webb said.

"Ask away. I've got a few minutes."

"I have a friend arriving in Tucson, but the trouble is, I don't know when."

"That's a problem."

"Yes, it is. Have you by any chance met any strangers who recently arrived in town?"

Souter shook his head. "I can't say as I have. Tucson is a big town and people are always coming and going."

Webb nodded. "Well, if you think of anything, I'm staying here at the hotel."

"The governor is here, you know."

"Yes, I know. I'm on his staff."

Souter looked Webb over, a smallish man, mild-looking, dressed in black like a parson. No gun or knife showing.

"Well, congratulation. You must be very proud. I'm told the governor is a fine man and a Democrat. Do you live at his ranch?"

"Some of the time. I go where the governor goes."

"Wherever his duties take him."

"Yes, but he isn't officially the governor yet."

"No, it's a couple of more days before he's sworn in."

"At the moment he keeps busy with his charitable work, helping the poor and sick, you know."

Souter smiled. "A wonderful man. I hope the murder of that strange Gaudet women hasn't upset him too much."

"He was naturally distressed by the murder, but he took refuge in prayer."

Souter shook his head. "Is there a more honorable man in the territory? I don't think so." He smiled. "Now I must make my way to the kitchen. It's been a pleasure talking with you . . . mister . . . ah . . ."

Webb was a named man and decided to play it safe. "Brown, Tom Brown."

"And I'm Bill Souter. Please give my regards to the governor-elect."

"I certainly will."

The butcher walked away a few steps and then stopped. "Wait," he said to Webb's retreating back. When the little gunman retraced his steps, Souter said, "You told me you're expecting the visit of a friend, but I just remembered that two strangers recently rode into town. They're both nice fellers and they're boarding at Mrs. Dale's boarding-house on Cemetery Street. She only takes in good Christian white gentlemen, but she made an exception for one of the fellers who's half Apache but doesn't look too much like a savage."

Suspicion burst like a bubble in Webb's head. "My friend's name is Dan Caine," he said. "Does that perhaps ring a bell with you?"

"Why yes, yes, of course. That is one of the men's names, the smaller one, it's strange to call a man small who's stands at least six feet, but compared to his friend Crow, he is."

"Yes, that's him, good old Dan," Webb said. "Like Crow, he preaches the gospel to the savages."

"Odd that men who took up that calling both wear guns," Souter said.

"I know, but they're only for protection against snakes and, God forbid, rogue Apaches and road agents. Dan and Crow are men of peace, and holy scripture guides their every action. When are they available so that I can visit my old comrades in Christ?"

"Mrs. Dale serves supper at seven. Gertrude, that's Mrs. Dale, says that Mr. Caine is a picky eater, but Crow devours everything in sight, so suppertime is your best bet."

"One more question, if I may," Webb said.

"I am in a hurry," Souter said.

"Then I'll get right to the point," Webb said. "Who is the town drunk?"

Without a moment's hesitation, the butcher said, "I don't know if he's *the* town drunk, but he's one of them. His name is Bobby Dates, and he claims to be the best bottle man in the territory."

"What does a bottle man do?"

"He scrounges bottles all over town. Bates searches the alleys and waste ground and sells the bottles he finds back to the saloons. When you see him, he usually carries a sack over his shoulder that clinks when he walks. Children are scared of the bottle man, but he's harmless."

"Any idea where he is? I'd like to help him."

"Try the saloons. There are five thousand people in Tucson, but sooner or later you'll find the bottle man. Now I must be going. I'm right glad I could help you find your friends."

"And so am I," Webb said. "Believe me, so am I."

CHAPTER FIFTY-FIVE

"They're living in a cheap boardinghouse in the north of town," Ruben Webb said.

"Are you sure it's them?" Barton Clay said.

"It's them all right."

"What about the nonentity?"

"He's a drunk by the name of Bobby Bates, but most folks call him the bottle man.

"What does a bottle man do?"

"He goes around town collecting bottles and sells them back to saloons. I guess he makes enough to keep him in whiskey."

"Where is he?"

"I've got him downstairs in the lobby. I convinced him to leave his bottle sack outside, but the desk clerk and the manager still don't like it."

"Bring him up here," Barton said. "I'll tell him what he has to do. Wait, does he have a brain left?"

"I'm sure he does, when he's sober."

"Good, then we'll bring Dan Caine here and shoot him. The nonentity can witness it."

"I know you're set on that idea, Governor, but it's clumsy."

"I'm not clumsy," Barton said, irritated now. "Nothing I do or have ever done is clumsy."

"I know that. But the plan can be improved with less risk to ourselves. Sure, killing Dan Caine can be written off as an assassination attempt, but since the shooting was in the Palace, touted as the finest hotel in the territory and with a pile of investors' money at stake, it might be investigated by the county sheriff. This may be the Wild West but we don't want to scare away high-rolling customers, do we? The bottle man couldn't stand up to that kind of pressure without breaking."

"Easy enough to kill him after he identifies the assassin Caine as the man who murdered Paola Gaudet."

"Another killing?"

"All right, explain your idea to me."

And Ruben Webb told him.

"Damn it all, I like it," Barton said. "We let the churnhead Bill Roche do the dirty work and we do the hanging. Brilliant! Pete will like this idea. It's perfect."

"It is, if everybody does his part."

"Ruben, I'm not stupid," Barton said. "Of course, everybody will do their part."

"Sorry, Governor, I should've known that."

"Yes, you should've. Now bring the nonentity up here. I want to talk with him."

"He doesn't smell too good."

"Then open a window," Barton said.

* * *

"Your worship, I'm the best damned bottle man in the Arizona Territory, so if it's bottles you're after, I'm the man to ask," Bobby Bates said.

He was a small, bent man with a brown, deeply lined face, a few strands of wispy black hair clinging to his sweaty scalp. He wore somebody's castoff ditto suit and a collarless shirt, the clothing ragged and stained. His footwear consisted of laceless shoes with run-down heels and no socks. But the man's mud-colored eyes held a glint that suggested a certain level of sly intelligence. As one newspaper reporter would later say, "Bobby Bates was probably a tad smarter than a red fox."

Barton Clay held up two double eagles. "Would you like to have these?"

Bates' mouth dried up and he swallowed hard before he said, "I sure would, Governor, your worship."

"I want you to lie for me but pretend it's not a lie. Tell yourself it's the truth. Understand?"

Bates looked blankly at Barton.

"You heard that a woman was murdered, didn't you?"

The little man nodded. "Sure, Miss Paola Gaudet on Church Street. Every Friday evening she'd toss out wine and small medicine bottles. They're all right as bottles go, but the big money is in whiskey and beer."

"A very bad man, no, two bad men murdered Miss Gaudet," Barton said.

Webb looked at him. Barton was adding to the plan. There were now two men instead of one.

Bates had his eyes on the shining coins as Barton added, "But they'll escape just punishment because nobody saw them do it. Understand?"

His mouth open, as though he found it hard to breathe, Bates said, "That's a very bad thing."

"Yes, it is, a very bad thing. Now, all I want you to do is to tell City Marshal Roche that you saw two bad men leave the lady's house and their hands were covered in blood."

"I don't like City Marshal Roche," Bates said. "Every time he sees me, he kicks me in the ass."

"I won't let him do that to you ever again, and all you have to do in return is testify that you saw two bad men leave Paola Gaudet's house with bloody hands. That way they'll get what they deserve. You saw them and heard them, didn't you, Bobby?"

"Huh?"

"You heard them talk to each other and one was named Dan and the other was called Crow. You saw them and heard them talking about killing Paola Gaudet, didn't you, Bobby?"

"I saw them . . . heard . . . what did I hear?"

Bates sounded uncertain.

"Governor, maybe you're giving him too much to remember," Webb said. "He's an idiot."

"Don't listen to him, Bobby. Sure, you did, you saw them. You stood in the shadows and saw Dan Caine and the breed named Crow leave Paola Gaudet's house, and they had blood on their hands."

"That's right, they had blood on their hands."

"Of course, they did," Barton said. "And you saw and heard all that while you were collecting dead men."

Bates smiled, showing few teeth and all of them black. He looked like he was seventy years old. In fact, he was three years shy of forty. "Dead men . . . that's what people call empty bottles."

"Yes, they do. You're smart, Bobby, and you're nobody's fool. I like that. I may have a job for you real soon."

"Picking up bottles, your worship?"

"Yeah, something like that." Barton held up the double eagles, "Now tell me again what you saw and heard the night you were collecting dead men in Church Street."

"I saw . . ."

"Go on," Barton said. "You're doing good, bottle man."

"I saw two men, one was called Dan and the other one was called Crow, after a bird, and they had blood on their hands."

"If it was dark, how did you see the blood?"

"They stopped and lit cigarettes. I saw the blood when they struck a lucifer."

"Very good, Bobby. You're a sight cleverer than you look. I'm going to find a place for you in my administration."

"Your worship, what does that mean?" Bates said.

"It means you're going to help the governor rule the territory," Webb said.

Bates smiled. "That means I can collect bottles everywhere, Phoenix, Mesa . . ."

"Yeah, everywhere and anywhere," Barton Clay said. "You're a sharp one, Bobby, mighty sharp." He handed the gold coins to Bates. "Here's your money." The little man's face lit up and Barton said, "Don't be in a hurry to spend it. You're staying right here until you tell the marshal what you know."

"Tell him what you say I know."

"Step carefully, Bobby. I won't bandy words with you."

"I'm sorry, your worship," Bates said. He rubbed his mouth with the palm of his hand. "I need a drink."

"Ruben, get him a whiskey. There's a bottle and glasses in the other room."

"You want me to play waiter to a bum?" Webb said. "Look at it. It's barely human."

"Please do as I told you, Ruben," Barton Clay said. "A lesson in humility won't do you any harm." He stepped closer to Webb and whispered in his ear, "You can kill him later, if that will help you feel better."

"It will," Webb said.

When Bates had his whiskey, Barton opened the hotel door and called out for Buff Grant. He and Pete Clay and a couple of gunmen shared two rooms farther down the hallway.

"You need the surrey, Governor?" Grant said.

"No, not now. Buff, I want you to go to the courthouse and bring City Marshal Roche here."

"What do I tell him, Governor?"

"Tell him I know who murdered Paola Gaudet and that I want him to act on that knowledge and arrest the men responsible."

Grant smiled. "Sure thing. Is there gonna be another hanging?"

Baron Clay grinned. "You can depend on it," he said.

CHAPTER FIFTY-SIX

"Bill, as governor of this territory I can make or break you," Barton Clay said. "As easy as snapping my fingers."

"I was appointed by the city of Tucson," Bill Roche said. "Not the territorial government."

"You want to stake your career on that?"

"No, I guess not."

"I thought as much. The governor is the real power in the Arizona Territory and if he's not, I'll make it so. The citizens, and the remaining Indian savages, will learn that they have to play on my terms."

"Bob Bates is a hopeless drunk. He sees snakes and lizards crawling all over him when he wakes up in the morning."

"Where does he wake up?" Ruben Webb said.

"I don't know. Anywhere he can flop."

Barton Clay said, "Let's get back to the business at hand. Bill, you heard Bobby Bates testify that on the evening of her death he saw and heard Dan Caine and the breed talking outside Paola Gaudet's door and that their hands were bloody."

Roche said, "He heard the name Dan, or so he says."

"And Crow. He heard that too, the name of the breed."

"Your case is all packaged up neat and tied together with string, isn't it, Barton?"

"Yes, it is, and Governor Clay, please. This is official business."

"The testimony of a known drunk will not stand up in court," Roche said.

"One day, I'll own United States senators, congressmen, and federal judges, the lawmakers who decide who stood up in court and who didn't. In the meantime, I reckon I can convince eight small-town hick jurymen of Dan Caine's guilt."

"You'll act as a prosecuting attorney?"

"No, I won't need to. Money talks, Marshal. Remember that."

"Why do you want Caine dead so badly, Barton?"

The man made no mention of governor, and Clay was aware of the slight, but he let it go and said, "He shot down my son Ben in cold blood, and because of him Decker died."

"Caine killed Ben in a fair fight. I'm convinced of that. And Decker was shot by a road agent, and Webb evened the score."

"Webb didn't even the score. Decker was worth more than a hundred, a thousand, any number you care to choose, road agents," Barton said.

Roche said nothing, his mind working.

Decker was a poisonous little snake who enjoyed beating up whores.

"All right, I'll simplify it for you, Bill," Barton said. "I want Dan Caine dead because I hate his guts. There, does that satisfy you?"

"You make more sense than Bob Bates does," Roche said.

Barton Clay's easily inflamed anger scalded him. "All right, I'll lay it on the line. As governor of this territory, I order you to arrest the murderers Dan Caine and the breed known as Crow. You will take them to the courthouse and lock them up in the holding cells pending trial. Is that clear?"

"Barton, you ain't governor yet," Roche said.

"You're splitting hairs, Bill. I'll be installed as governor of the Arizona Territory in a couple of days. Keep Caine in the cell until then." Barton Clay read the hesitation in Roche's face and said, "I can ruin you, Bill. I can wreck your life so bad you'll be glad to pick up bottles alongside Bobby Bates. Take some well-meant advice, don't test me."

Ruben Webb grinned, and Bill Roche was aware that Pete Clay and a couple of grim-faced men, Barton's hired guns, had crowded into the room. There was not a friendly face to be seen. Even Bates, half-drunk, was scowling.

"Cheer up, Bill. I'm sure I can get you a job as saloon swamper for fifty cents a day. You can eat scraps from the kitchen and sleep on a rope hung across a lice-infested room for five cents a throw." To laughter, Barton added, "Who knows, save your money one penny at a time and you could get rich like me."

Bill Roche knew he had it good in Tucson. He levied his own tax on prostitutes and gamblers, and he leaned on the city's merchants for protection money. But now the writing was on the wall, and the only way to wipe away the words was to agree to Barton Clay's terms and sell his soul to the devil, as he'd been doing for years.

"All right, Barton, I'll do as you say," Roche said, hating

himself for his weakness. "Where is Dan Caine and the breed?"

"Mrs. Dale's house for . . ."

"Christian gentlemen. I know the place."

"Seven o'clock is a good time, when Caine will be sitting down to supper," Barton said.

Roche managed a smile. "I've got one of those newfangled paddy wagons in the barn behind the courthouse. I guess I'll hitch it up for the first time and give her a run."

"I know, I helped pay for it."

"You're a generous man."

"Lock up Caine and the breed as tight as Dick's hatband," Barton said. "We'll put him before a beholden judge tomorrow morning."

Roche nodded and made to leave the room, but Barton stopped him. "One more thing, Bill," he said.

As Roche turned, Barton Clay backhanded him across the face, the sound of the blow loud as a pistol shot. It was a hard hit from a big man, and it staggered the marshal. For a moment Roche was too shocked to be angry, but then he flared, and his fisted hands came up fast.

"I wouldn't." Webb had pulled his gun, the unwavering muzzle pointed right at Roche's belly. He was smiling. "I can drill you from here."

"Lower your mitts, Bill," Barton said. "I was a little riled up, and I had to show you who's the boss in this town, that's all. Why, I'll make the slap up to you once Caine's neck is stretched, and I've paid you a bonus. We'll sit with a bottle of good bourbon, you and me, and talk about this and that and be perfect friends again." Barton looked around the room at the assembled men. "What do you reckon, boys, can I say any fairer than that?"

"You sure can't, Pa," Pete said, answering for the others.

Roche's anger simmered. "I would have killed any other man for that slap."

"Yes, any other man, but not this man," Barton said. "I have your destiny in the palm of my hand, Bill, and if I'm forced to put the squeeze on it . . . well, your future will break into a million pieces and fall into the gutter." Barton Clay smiled. "Do you catch my drift, old buddy, old pal? You're a delight to know, Bill."

Stifled giggles from Pete Clay and the two gunmen raked Roche like talons as the marshal walked out of the room without ever finding a backbone.

CHAPTER FIFTY-SEVEN

"I'm sorry to intrude on your supper hour, ma'am, but I need to talk with one of your boarders."

"And which boarder would that be?" Mrs. Gertrude Dale said. She looked at the city marshal's shield on the lapel of Bill Roche's coat and glanced over his shoulder where the black bulk of the paddy wagon, pulled by a bony gray horse, was parked at the porch. "What is that contraption?" she said.

"It's a wagon for moving prisoners," Roche said. Then with a measure of pride, "It's the first of its kind outside of the big eastern cities."

"Well, there are no prisoners in this house," Mrs. Dale said.

"Not yet perhaps, but I must talk with Dan Caine and the man called Crow who's with him."

"Can't it wait until after supper?"

"I'm afraid not, ma'am. I'm City Marshal Bill Roche, and I must speak to Mr. Caine on a matter of the greatest importance."

Mrs. Dale sighed. "Then you'd better come in. Do you really need that rifle?"

"It's a shotgun, ma'am. And yes, I really need it."

"Then come inside."

Roche followed Mrs. Dale into the dining room where eight men sat around a rectangular table, one of them Dan Caine and another Crow.

Dan put down his fork and said, "We meet again, Marshal Roche." Then, "Why the scattergun?"

"Because I have to take you in, Mr. Caine, you and Crow."

"On what charge?"

"Murder," Roche said.

Mrs. Dale's hand flew to her throat. "Lord a mercy!" she said.

One of the guests choked on a piece of chicken and the man sitting beside him thumped his back. The other guests stared at Roche's shotgun like rabbits mesmerized by a cobra.

"Who are we supposed to have murdered?" Dan said.

"Miss Paola Gaudet."

"Never heard of her," Dan said.

"She is, she was, a voodoo princess out of New Orleans."

"What in hell's blue blazes is a voodoo princess?" Crow said.

"Language, Mr. Crow," Mrs. Dale said. "I know this is a stressful occasion, but we should observe the proprieties."

"Sorry, Mrs. Dale, but the marshal isn't making any sense."

Roche had the shotgun cradled in his left arm and he turned until it was pointing at Crow. "A witness has come forward who claims he saw you and Dan Caine come out of Miss Gaudet's house on Church Street. He says your hands were bloody."

"When was this supposed to have happened?" Dan said.

"The night before last," Roche said.

"We were here, asleep in our beds at that time," Dan said.

"You can tell that to the judge tomorrow."

Crow said, "I sense Barton Clay's hand in this."

"So do I, and it stinks. Who is the supposed witness?" Dan said.

"A citizen by the name of Bobby Bates."

"What was he doing in Church Street?"

Roche hesitated and then said, "He's a small-time businessman."

"Then maybe he killed what's her name?" Crow said.

"I doubt it. Now you boys are coming with me. I have transportation to the courthouse jail waiting."

Dan rose to his feet and Roche slapped the Greener into a firing position. "Don't make me use this, Caine," he said.

"Barton Clay would like that, wouldn't he?" Dan said.

"I don't know."

"Of course, you know. Clay's the organ grinder and you're the monkey dancing to his tune. What tune is he playing now, Roche? The noose for Dan Caine two-step?"

"You're a funny man, Caine, but hanging is nothing to laugh about. Now hand over those gunbelts from the chair backs. No, wait . . ." He grabbed one of the diners by the collar of his coat and hauled him to his feet. "Bring the gunbelts to me."

Still chewing, the man, a young warehouse clerk by the name of Hopkins, spluttered pieces of chicken leg all over the table as he exclaimed, "This is an outrage!"

Dan said, "Do as he says, mister. The marshal ain't a one to tote a scattergun for show."

"Caine, you're as smart as a bunkhouse rat," Roche said.

"And you're as dumb as a snubbin' post," Dan said. "That makes us a mismatched pair, don't it?"

Roche nodded. "A good joke from a man who's gonna be hung."

"We all have to go sometime, I guess," Dan said.

"Ain't that the truth, but some ways of giving up the ghost are better than others. I'd put hanging way down on that list, right under getting gut shot." Roche let go of the drummer's collar and said, "Now do like I told you, sonny, and gather up them gunbelts."

Hopkins, now intimidated by the black eyes of the shotgun, did as he was told, and Roche slung the gunbelts over his shoulder.

"All right, let's go," he said.

"Just wait a dad-burned minute," Crow said. He grabbed a couple of slices of bread and made a sandwich of the chicken breast on his plate. "Now we can go," he said.

"And the condemned man ate a hearty meal," Roche said.

"Mister, that ain't funny," Crow said.

A moist-eyed Mrs. Dale rose from her chair and gave Dan a peck on the cheek. "So young to die," she said. "What a misfortune."

"It sure is," Dan said.

City Marshal Bill Roche grinned and nodded agreement.

CHAPTER FIFTY-EIGHT

"It worked with Wheeler's whore, it will work with Dan Caine and the breed," Barton Clay said.

"Why not let him go to trial?" Pete Clay said. "Either way he gets hung."

"I don't trust juries," Barton said. "There's no telling what they'll do. For starters, I don't think they'll believe a word Bobby Bates says."

"Pete," Ruben Webb said, "Bates is a smelly, drunken bum. Would you believe him?"

"No, I reckon I wouldn't. When do we do it, Pa?"

"Tonight. We can't waste time. I want it done and to see Dan Caine kicking at the end of a rope."

Barton was breathing heavily, sitting slumped in a chair by the hotel window. Pete thought his father looked unwell, but he wasn't about to mention it. "What about Roche?" he said.

"What about him?"

"Will he make a stand?"

Webb answered that. "He won't stand. He's a damn coward, and he'll step aside and hide behind his badge."

"Should we gun him?" one of the hands said, a tall, lanky man with mean eyes.

"No, we don't have to do that," Barton said. "A man who's forgotten how to say the word *no* might be useful at a later date."

"Roche has been that in the past," Pete said.

"He has, and he'll be useful tonight. All he needs do is to run away and hide in a closet until it's over. Pete, don't worry, when you burst through that jailhouse door, he'll figure he's looking into his own grave and skedaddle."

"Governor, how do we play it in the Lost Chance saloon?" Webb said. He smiled. "Spend money on the low-life trash that frequents the place and . . ."

"Break their hearts, you and Pete," Barton said. "Tell them and tell them again and again, it's a damned shame that the murderers of Paola Gaudet, a tireless worker for children's charities, will walk free. The killers are being sent back to Texas to stand trial and we know how that will end . . . with acquittals. Lay it on thick, boys. Tell them how Paola was savagely raped before she was strangled, and the money she planned to spend on schoolbooks was stolen. To hell with the schoolbooks, Caine and his breed spent the poor woman's money on whores and whiskey. Work them up, boys, get that unwashed penniless trash as drunk as pigs, before you call for a rope. Then lead your vigilantes to the courthouse, drag out Caine and the breed and hang them from the rafters of Tom Logan's livery across the street."

Ruben Webb and the gun hands greeted the speech with approving cheers tangled up with laughter.

"Pa, you're a genius, "Pete said. "But it all depends on Roche."

"He'll get over it. Later I'll tell him what a valuable

asset he'll be during my term as governor and in view of that I'll increase his stipend instanter! As much as any man, Roche loves his whiskey and whores, and that takes money. He'll sit still for a lynching so long as there's dollars in it. Trust me."

"You're a peach, Governor," Webb said, smiling.

"Roche made the arrests tonight at suppertime so I want the vigilantes in the jailhouse before midnight," Barton said. "Pete, you've got from now . . . let's see, it's eight o'clock . . . until say ten or eleven to get the riffraff good and drunk and baying for blood."

"What about when it's over? Have you thought about that yet, Pa?"

"Do you mean after Caine and the breed are swinging from Tom Logan's rafters?"

"Yes, I do."

Barton spread his fingers like fans and said, his face innocent, "Why, we tried to stop the lynch mob, but they overpowered us, says you and Webb and the gun hands. And I tried to stop them but there were just too many for me, City Marshal Roche says. Get my drift?"

"Sure do, Pa," Pete said. "It's golden."

"In the confusion it wouldn't hurt to gun a few of the mob, make it look good for the city." Barton said.

Webb nodded. "Leave that to me. I'll see what I can do."

"Then let's get started," Barton Clay said. I'll come see Caine when he's hanging by his neck. I wish Ben and Decker were here to see it."

"I'm sure they'll be watching, Pa," Pete said.

"Maybe," Barton said. "If there are windows in hell."

CHAPTER FIFTY-NINE

"Roche, you've locked up two innocent men," Dan Caine said. He and Crow were in a large holding cell behind the marshal's office, the only light in the darkened courthouse. "You've stooped mighty low."

"I know you didn't murder Paola Gaudet," Roche said. "You ain't the type." He nodded to Crow. "Neither is the big chief there. Why do you wear those braids on either side of your face?"

"They're Mescalero Apache. I'm partial to them."

"You're a strange one. You look more white man that you do Indian."

"That's always been my misfortune."

"It's dark in here, Roche," Dan said. The cell's only illumination was the pale light that came from the open door to the office where an oil lamp burned.

"So what? You figure on reading the Bible?"

"You're a daisy, Bill," Dan said. "Who wants us dead?"

"You know who, Caine. Hell, you gunned his oldest son."

"Barton Clay. How much is he paying you?"

"Nothing. This is official business."

"When's our trial?"

"You'll have a hearing tomorrow morning, and the date of the trial will be fixed then."

"You gonna hang us, Roche?" Crow said.

"If you're found guilty that will be my unfortunate duty."

"We'll be found guilty," Dan said. "Barton Clay's money will see to that."

"I have nothing to say on that subject," Roche said. "Except that there is an eyewitness. A man by the name of Bobby Bates saw you leave Paola Gaudet's house, and he says your hands were bloody."

"He's a damned liar," Dan said.

"I know that," Roche said.

"Who is he?"

"Bobby Bates is a bottle man. He collects empty bottles and sells them back to the saloons."

"Is he a drunk?"

"Of course, he's a drunk, the kind who sees a pink elephant in his closet."

"A fine, upstanding citizen then, huh?"

"Bates says he knows what he saw. But he's probably lying."

"Roche, you realize that you're a poor excuse for a lawman," Dan said. "If you were in Broken Back, I wouldn't hire you to sweep out the cells."

"I know what I am, so let it go," Roche said. "Anything I can get you boys?"

"I don't have the makings," Dan said. "They're back in my room at the boardinghouse."

"Les Jacobs down the Lost Chance saloon sells sacks of tobacco and papers. I'll get you some. You, Indian?"

"Yeah, a bottle of whiskey," Crow said.

"Alcohol is not allowed in the cells. Try something else."

"I don't want anything else."

"Les keeps a jar of hard candy, peppermint flavor, I think. I'll bring you some, Chief."

"Roche, you can stick your candy up . . ."

"No, Crow!" Dan said. "The marshal is only being nice. Bring him a bag of the peppermints, Roche. I'm sure we'll both enjoy them."

"I'll see what I can do," the marshal said. "I'm being right sociable toward you fellers, and I'm danged if I know why."

"Because you know that soon you'll hang two innocent men?" Dan said.

The big marshal thought for a spell and then said. "Yup, that's probably it." He closed the office door behind him and plunged Dan and Crow into darkness.

City Marshal Bill Roche was surprised. The Lost Chance saloon, the seediest, cockroach-ridden drinking establishment in town, a normally silent place frequented by numb, somber drunks, was roaringly busy, and as he walked closer Roche saw at least half-a-dozen shabby men elbow their way inside.

Roche stopped, adjusted the lie of his holstered Colt, and then walked into the saloon where he was immediately assailed by a wall of pipe and cigar smoke and the usual stench of piss, spilled beer, ancient sweat, and vomit.

As was his habit, Roche stood to the right of the door with his back against the wall and coldly scanned the scene in front of him. But it was Pete Clay's voice that caught his attention. The man was lost behind a wall of bodies and smoke and his voice was loud, almost shouting.

"It's a damned shame that a woman can be outraged and murdered in Tucson and her killers walk free."

That statement was immediately met by a drunken chorus of, "Damned shame." "Where's the law?" "Hang the rascals."

That last was music to Pete Clay's ears. "Belly up to the bar, boys," he yelled. "The drinks are on me."

Then Ruben Webb took his turn to yell above the din, "The killers are being returned to their native Texas for trial, and you know what that means, boys. They'll be found not guilty and an innocent woman's death will go unpunished." Then louder. "It's a damned disgrace."

Again, a noisy, drunken chorus of outrage and dire threats of shooting, hanging, and castration.

Roche heard the tone of the drunk, angry men change. A crowd yells, but a lynch mob snarls. He pushed his way through the boisterous crowd, grabbed Pete Clay by the arm and yelled into his ear, "Shut it down, Pete. It's getting out of hand."

Clay angrily pulled his arm out of the marshal's grip and yelled, "Get back to the courthouse, Bill. When we get there, leave right away and find a place to hide."

"Pete, what are you planning?" Roche said, moving closer to Clay, his eyes staring hard into the man's face.

Then loud, a shout, "We're gonna hang them two murderers who reckon they can escape the law. Ain't that right, boys?"

"Damn right," a drunk yelled, spokesman for a noisy, belligerent crowd.

"Pete, are you aiming to lynch my prisoners?" Roche said, alarmed.

Clay cupped a hand behind his ear and yelled, "What?"

"Are you aiming to lynch my prisoners?" the marshal shouted.

Pete was jostled by the crowd, and one drunk rooster shook his hand before he answered Roche's question. "Yeah, that's the plan. The governor doesn't trust the courts to see justice done."

"A lynching isn't justice, it's murder," Roche said.

Pete Clay smiled. "Bill, as lawmen go, you ain't the cream of the crop, and it's way too late for you to develop a conscience. Open the side door to your office and then fade into the sunset. You savvy?"

A ragged man wearing a battered bowler hat, barged past with a shot of whiskey in both hands. He grinned at Roche and yelled, "What larks!"

Roche said, shouting, to make himself heard, "Pete, look around you, these men are a drunken, worthless rabble. Stop what you're doing, and let the law handle this."

"Get out of here, Bill," Pete Clay said. "And take my advice . . . don't be in your office when we come a-knocking. And leave the cell key on the table, there's a good fellow."

Then Ruben Webb, emerged from the crowd and said to Pete, "Is there a problem here?"

"No, there's not. And the marshal is just leaving. See him to the door, Ruben. He's a little upset."

Roche stared at Pete until the man was pushed toward the bar and vanished into the crowd.

"Let's go," Webb said.

Realizing that more pleading was useless, Roche accompanied Webb to the door. Before he stepped outside, he said, "Webb, try and talk some sense into Pete. Let the law hang Dan Caine."

Webb shook his head. "I work for wages, but I'm not paid to give the governor's son advice."

When the saloon door shut behind him, Bill Roche realized he didn't get the makings for Dan or peppermint candy for Crow. But right then, that was the least of his problems.

CHAPTER SIXTY

City Marshal Bill Roche walked through a tunnel of darkness relieved by moonlight that lay on the gabled tile roof of the courthouse like silverplate. At a remove of twenty-five yards from the building stood a tree of large proportions, its trunk and two main branches making a perfect Y. Roche had walked past that tree a hundred times, but he still didn't know what kind it was. A live oak, he thought, or maybe a mesquite. Whatever kind, it was a perfect hanging tree, the branches high enough that a tall man could be hoisted up by a rope around his neck and there would still be plenty of room for him to kick.

Roche stopped and stood under the tree, and its branches filtered the moonlight, dappling the ground at his feet. The night was hushed, breezeless, as though holding its breath waiting for something to happen.

The exterior door to the law enforcement office was in the east wing of the building, a substantial portal of solid mahogany bolted from the inside. That was the door Pete Clay wanted unlocked.

Roche, a former guard in the Yuma Territorial Prison, had never before lost prisoners, discounting three or four he'd shot in the back when they'd made a run for it on a labor detail. Until now he'd no illusions about what he'd become. He knew he was no knight in shining armor riding around Tucson righting wrongs, but a court jester sitting at the feet of a cattle baron, living on scraps from the great man's table. He was forty-three years old, and some mornings he couldn't look at himself in the shaving mirror. He glanced at the shield on his shirtfront. Once, years ago, it stood for something, marked him as a man who upheld the law and protected the helpless, the weak, and the innocent. Young Bill Roche, in his wildest dreams, never thought there would come a time when he'd sink so low into the swamp that he'd hang blameless men because the baron wanted them dead. Legal murder it was. He couldn't escape that fact. He could only frame it and hang it up on his conscience. How many murders had he covered up for the Clay family? A dozen probably, the latest Dick Meadows, the Reynolds couple, Luther Wheeler and his whore, and Roche suspected that Barton Clay himself had killed Paola Gaudet, a woman he was known to frequent. And very soon Dan Caine and Crow would be added to that list . . . lynched by person or persons unknown. He knew the city fathers of Tucson wouldn't pry too deeply into the deaths of a couple of penniless Texans.

Roche, fear, worry, and remorse tying knots in his stomach, knew he'd reached a fork in the road. One route led back to Barton Clay where he'd trade abuse and servitude for double eagles. The other road led to . . . he didn't know, but a good guess was self-respect as a lawman and the very real possibility of poverty on a grand scale.

Bill Roche was still pondering his now very uncertain future as he walked into the dark courthouse, crossed the huge atrium, his boot heels thumping on the marble floor, and stepped into his office . . . and his destiny.

"Pete Clay is working up a drunken rabble and he's talking about a lynching, Caine," Bill Roche said. "And I don't know if I can stop them."

Crow said, "Unlock the damned cell and give me my gun, Marshal. I don't want to be butchered like a three-month-old hog in a slaughtering house."

"That goes for both of us," Dan Caine said. "At least give us a chance to fight for our lives."

Roche's face, the thin, sun-ravaged skin tight to the bone, revealed his distress, a weak, flawed man trying to be strong, going through the torments of hell. "There's a tree outside, and I think they reckon to hang you boys from it," he said. His warped, agitated mind couldn't hold on to a thought, and he said, "It's a live oak, I think. Or maybe a mesquite." He nodded. "Yes, I think a mesquite."

"Roche!" Dan yelled. He rattled the cell door, a sound like iron nails dropping into a tin pail. "Damn you, give us our guns and let us make a fight of it."

"So, what is the problem here?" the marshal said. "Let's get to the root of the dilemma like gentlemen."

"Roche!" Dan yelled.

"Yes, I have found the explanation. I will not let them take my prisoners. That's the answer in a nutshell," Roche said to no one but himself. "My dear sir, a lynching won't happen. The law says I am the protector of these two jailed wretches so protect them I must."

He crossed the room and took a Greener from the gun-rack. He opened a drawer, removed a box of bright red shells and fed two of them into the scattergun. "Now let 'em come by land or by sea," he said. "I'm ready to challenge Barton Clay. I'm ready to defy the devil himself. The bloodthirsty rabble wants to stretch some hemp, do they? Well, they won't. Not in my town."

"Roche, you raving lunatic, where is the key to the cell?" Dan shouted.

"The key?" Roche exclaimed. "No one makes a lock without a key and that is why there never was a problem without a solution." Roche said. He turned and stared at Dan. "Hark!" he said. "Do I hear raised voices in the distance?"

"Yes, you do and you're as crazy as a bedbug. Now unlock this cell and give us our guns."

"Fear not. I will protect you," Roche said. "It's not the Colt's gun that wins the battle but the hero's brave heart."

The marshal crossed the floor and stood about five yards from the heavy side door, the Greener up and ready.

Then the pounding began, and Pete Clay's angry yells demanded that Roche open the door. "Ye shall not pass!" the marshal answered. ·

There is no doubt that on the night of the intended lynching of Dan Caine and Crow, Bill Roche had a sudden onset nervous breakdown due to stress and almost immediately exhibited psychotic symptoms. Medical experts consulted by historians say that with rest Roche could've made a complete recovery, probably within a couple of weeks, but the events of the bloody night robbed him of that chance.

Dan Caine thought he heard voices inside the courthouse and again yelled to Roche for his gun. The lawman ignored him, his attention fixed on the door that was now splintering under the buffets of a battering ram, probably one of the heavy wrought iron–and-wood benches that had been set up in shady areas around the courthouse for public use.

It took several minutes to crash through the door, and it hung askew on its top hinge until the booted feet of cursing men kicked it aside.

From the cell, Dan Caine and Crow had a grandstand view of what happened next . . . actions and reactions so unexpectedly violent they could scarce believe their own eyes.

The first men to charge through the door were Pete Clay and Ruben Webb, Clay with a coiled, noosed rope hanging from his shoulder.

Bill Roche screamed words no one could understand and fired the Greener from the hip. The first load of double-aught buckshot hit Pete Clay in the chest and practically tore him apart. Webb cursed, drew with amazing speed and fired, his bullet slamming into Roche's belly. Big, strong, and enduring, his mind not quite right, the lawman took the hit and cut loose, his second whiff of buckshot slamming into Webb just above the buckle of his gunbelt. In the past, Webb had seen men killed by scatter-guns and he knew he would not survive such a wound. His legs collapsed under him, and he fell to the floor. "Damn you, Roche," he said. He lay on his right side and shot from that position. Two of three bullets crashed into the left of Roche's chest, smashed through the rib cage and wrought terrible damage to the lawman's lungs and heart. Webb saw the hits, grinned, and then died.

Roche fell to the floor like a felled oak, groaned and lay still. Beyond him, just inside the doorway, Pete Clay lay dead on the ground, the lynching rope still around his shoulder. His eyes were wide open, as though he was shocked at the manner and time of his terrible death.

When giving an account of the gun battle in the Tucson courthouse, demolished in 1929, Western men are always asked, "What happened to the drunken rabble?" The short answer is that they weren't expecting to be greeted by a loco marshal with a deadly scattergun and, panic-struck, they scampered, skedaddled, scooted, got the hell away from the courthouse and took refuge in the Lost Chance saloon where they drowned their trembling sorrows and told each other about their narrow escape from a murderous posse of lawmen armed with shotguns.

All except one, that is.

His name was Davy Lott and in his drunken state he figured there might be cash to be made by being the first to inform Governor Barton Clay of the death of his son. Lott was married, the father of seven children, but he disappeared off the face of the earth that night never to be seen again. An uneducated man, it's a pity he'd never read the advice of the ancient Greek playwright Sophocles who wrote, "Woe to the messenger who brings bad news."

CHAPTER SIXTY-ONE

"What happened here?" the man in the black frock coat said. He had gray, muttonchop sideburns and a perplexed expression.

"City Marshal Roche died trying to save us from a lynch mob," Dan Caine said. "It all happened about thirty minutes ago, so you sure took your time getting here."

The man ignored that and said, "Good heavens, what are you guilty of?"

"Nothing," Dan said. "We were wrongly accused by Barton Clay. That's his son lying in the doorway with the hemp rope over his shoulder he planned to hang us with."

The man stepped over to the door and when he returned his face was white as chalk. "Two dead men," he said.

"As I told you, Pete Clay is one of them, the other is Ruben Webb, the shootist. Bill Roche killed them both."

"And they shot him?"

"Yeah, Webb drilled him before he died."

"My name is Frederick Maish. I'm the mayor of this town. You are leveling a very serious accusation at Governor Clay."

"He's a murdering scoundrel," Dan said. "And his greed for power has now cost him three sons."

"Mr. Mayor, Barton Clay is a thoroughly wicked man who has no right to be the governor of the Arizona Territory," Crow said.

"He's sick, but he just told me he'll soon be well enough to sire more sons," Maish said. "I heard he's set on wedding and bedding another rancher's sixteen-year-old daughter. Why are you locked up, Caine?"

"Barton Clay got together with Marshal Roche and pinned the murder of a woman named Paola Gaudet on Crow and me. We'd never even met the woman."

"What was their evidence?"

"The testimony of a drunk named Bobby Bates . . ."

"The bottle man?"

"I guess so," Dan said. "He claimed to have seen us leave the dead woman's house and he said that we had bloody hands."

"Bates is a lowlife who will do or say anything you want, so long as you pay him. No jury in this, or any other town, would believe him."

"And that's the reason why Barton Clay arranged to have us lynched."

The mayor looked at Dan and said, "And your name is?"

"Dan Caine, I'm the sheriff of a town in Texas called Broken Back and this is Crow, my deputy."

"Crow?"

"I'm half Apache."

"I see."

"Mescalero."

"How interesting. Ah well, it's late," Maish said. "Once the bodies are removed you boys should get some sleep. I'll send someone with breakfast in the morning."

Dan was shocked. "Mayor, you're keeping us in here?"

"Only until I get to the bottom of all this and ascertain Governor Clay's involvement, if any. For all his boasting he'll need some time to grieve, poor man. Three sons gone." Maish shook his head. "How sad."

"Mayor, I told you Barton Clay is a cold-blooded killer and rapist and so were his sons," Dan said.

"Well, we won't speak ill of the dead," Maish said. "Get some sleep. Steak and eggs in the morning." He smiled. "Now there is bounty for you. Good night."

The mayor turned down the oil lamp as he left and plunged the marshal's office into darkness. The side door still hung open and Dan and Crow were still unarmed.

After Maish left and a silent, cadaverous undertaker removed the bodies of Pete Clay, Roche, and Ruben Webb, Crow's voice sounded unnaturally loud in the gloom. "I don't much fancy our chances, do you?"

"When I told Maish I was a sheriff back home in Texas he didn't seem impressed. So yeah, I don't fancy our chances either."

"Barton Clay could walk through that open door with a shotgun."

"Fish in a barrel, that's us."

"Maybe we should take turns staying awake."

"What good will that do?"

"I don't want to get shot in my sleep," Crow said. "I'd prefer to see it coming."

"I've been studying on it, and I reckon Barton won't come here tonight to do his killing," Dan said. "Even for him, that would be pretty obvious."

Crow rolled over on his cot and pulled up the gray army

blanket. "I feel like an empty shuck so I'm gonna grab some shuteye. If I get shot in my sleep, wake me up and tell me about it."

"Sure, I will. Sweet dreams."

The morning light brightened slowly in the windowless room, sneaking like a gray ghost through the wrecked side entrance. The workday had begun in the courthouse and Dan Caine heard the voices and footfalls of men and women echo strangely as they crossed and recrossed the atrium bound for the surrounding offices. Now and again the door opened, and a male or female head appeared, eager to glimpse the place where three men had died in a gunfight. They then stared at Dan Caine and Crow as though they were dangerous wild animals in a cage and quickly pulled their heads back for fear they might be bitten off.

The only bright spot in the gloomy morning was a visit from Bill Souter, the busy butcher. He wore his not-yet-bloody white apron and carried a smaller basket covered in a large blue napkin. "Breakfast, gents," he said. "Scrambled eggs and my best pork sausages."

Dan shook his head in wonderment. "Souter, do you feed everybody in Tucson?" he said.

"Sometimes it seems that way," the butcher said. "I'm thinking of laying on an assistant."

Crow said, scowling, "The mayor said steak and eggs."

"He misspoke himself," Souter said. "The jailhouse budget doesn't stretch to steak, but my sausages are a tasty substitute."

"Coffee?" Crow growled, determined to be cranky.

Souter waited until he passed two plates of food

through a small, rectangular opening in the bars designed for that purpose. Then he said, "Coffee I don't have, but there's got to be a pot on a stove somewhere in the courthouse." He smiled. "I'll be right back. Oh, here's news . . . Governor Clay has taken to his bed and is said by one of his aides to be very sick."

"No wonder he's sick," Crow said. "Marshal Roche gunned his only surviving son last night."

"He's not surviving now, is he?" Souter said. "Mayor Maish says Pete Clay was about cut in half by the marshal's shotgun." The butcher's smile fled as his face closed down. "The word is that Pete was fixing to hang you boys."

"The word is right," Dan said. "Marshal Roche saved us from a lynching."

"Too bad about Bill Roche," Souter said.

"Ain't it though," Dan said.

Souter's jolly smile returned. "Eat your breakfast, and I'll see about coffee."

"Wait. How sick is Barton Clay?"

"It was sudden and pretty bad, I'm told. So bad in fact that he may not be able to take up his post as territorial governor. Why do you ask?"

"Because I intend to kill him," Dan Caine said.

"Mr. Caine, don't put that about or you'll never leave your cell," Souter said. He stared at Dan for a long time and finally said. "Just keep that to yourself." His smile returned. "Now I'll go beat the bushes for coffee."

As the man turned to leave, Dan said. "Souter, what's your opinion on Barton Clay?"

"What I think of Barton Clay doesn't matter anymore," the butcher said. "On account of how they say he's no longer a man."

After Souter left, Crow did some thoughtful chewing,

swallowed, and said, "You plan to gun a sick man? That is if we ever get out of here."

"I reckon," Dan said.

"He could die."

"Yes, he could."

"Would you gun a dead man."

"Was Mary Jane Hillman dead when Barton hanged her?"

"Probably not."

"Then dead or alive, I'll put a bullet in Barton Clay. I hate him and all he stands for."

"You really hate him that much?"

"Every time I think of him, it's like swallowing poison."

"What made him sick, you reckon?"

"Probably hearing of Pete's death. His last son gone."

"He can't blame you for killing Pete."

"He can. If I wasn't here, Pete wouldn't have led a lynch mob and gotten himself shot by Bill Roche."

"If you hadn't come here, all his sons would be alive."

"And they'd be free to rape and murder, burn decent people out of their ranch, hang women, and torture old men for gold. The air is cleaner and the grass greener without their shadows."

"Well, then, we did what we came to do as vigilantes, avenge Dick Meadows." Crow smiled. "Time to go home."

"Not until Barton Clay is under the ground."

"Dan, all the poison you're swallowing could make you mighty sick and destroy you as a lawman. Ever think about that?"

"I'm not catching your drift."

"I don't want you to become too callous, too unfeeling. You have a little gal in Broken Back who needs you. But she needs you as you were when she fell in love with you, not the hard case you've become."

"Once Barton Clay is dead, I'll go back to my old self. If I can remember what my old self was."

"You were a real nice feller," Crow said.

Dan smiled. "And I'm not now?"

"No," Crow said. "You're not now."

Dan didn't comment on that last because Bill Souter stepped back into the office carrying two small china cups. "I found coffee in the city treasurer's office," he said. "Sorry about the cups, but the people who work in this courthouse are genteel folks." .

CHAPTER SIXTY-TWO

Dan Caine and Crow spent six days in the city jail before they were sprung by Mayor Frederick Maish, backed by several of the city dignitaries wearing broadcloth suits and glorious beards.

"Bobby Bates, known as the bottle man, recanted his story," Maish said. "He said he didn't see you the night of Paolo Gaudet's murder and he had the temerity to say that Barton Clay, formerly governor in waiting, paid him to concoct the tale, which is of course nonsense. The new city marshal was so furious he kicked Bates in the derriere and sent him on his way."

There was a chorus of "Served him right" from the dignitaries and one exclaimed, "Bravo new City Marshal Burt Alvord!"

Maish, like a medieval king handing out largesse, informed Dan that he and Crow would receive fifty cents a day to compensate them for their stay in jail. "Three dollars for both of you that can be picked up at the treasurer's office. Now that's benevolence for you."

"And they have nice cups," Crow said.

"What?" Maish said.

"Nothing," Crow said. "Nothing at all."

"Now, where is the photographer?" Maish said.

"Here, Mr. Mayor," a young man with a camera on a tripod said. It took him about fifteen minutes to set up, and then he said. "Now, don't move. Stand still and grin like you just saved two innocent men from the gallows. Smile for all you're worth, Mayor, and I'll tell you when the exposure is done, and you can start frowning again. You two desperate characters, please move to the bars so I get you in the photo. Yes, that's it. Thank you. Now scowl. Mayor, are you ready?"

"Ready." With a flourish, the mayor held up the cell key and smiled. After the picture was taken to the photographer's satisfaction, Maish turned the key in the lock and then the barred door squeaked open.

"You are free to go," Maish said, beaming. "Your guns and Texan spurs are on the table."

"Why the kid glove treatment, Mayor?" Dan asked.

Maish shuffled his feet and looked guilty, as did the dignitaries who turned their eyes everywhere except at Dan and Crow.

"The truth is, we came within a hair's breadth of hanging you both until City Marshal Alvord kicked Bob Bates in the rear and the man recanted his former falsehood." Maish sighed dramatically. "Oh, dear me, but you had a narrow escape."

"Well, Mayor, we'll get the hell out of here before you change your mind," Dan said. "And thank Marshal Alvord for us. He's true blue."

Dan and Crow picked up their horses at Josiah Crumb's livery, the bill taking up most of Mayor Maish's ungenerous stipend. They rode under a merciless noon sun that drove the good citizens of Tucson off the streets in search of shade. The adobe houses they passed looked as though they'd been molded by a giant hand, lying silent and still in the heat. A few had plaster exteriors that gleamed white as bone in the sunlight, and the air was dry and smelled of dust and was hard to breathe.

Following Crumb's directions, Dan and Crow rode toward the Palace Hotel and there had been no talk between them for many minutes before Crow said, "How do we play this?"

Dan, his face, hard and immobile, as though it had been hewn from a block of granite, gave no direct answer to the question. In fact, it was no answer at all.

"Crow," he said, "I won't leave the Arizona Territory while Barton Clay is still above ground."

"How do we play this?" Crow said again.

"You don't have to be a part of it," Dan said.

"What gives you the right to say that to me, Dan?"

"I have no right, and I'm sorry."

"Decide what you're going to do."

"Walk into the hotel, kill Barton Clay and walk out again, my step lighter and all the poison drained from my body."

"Will you tell Helen about it?"

"I'm not even sure that Helen will be waiting for me in Broken Back."

"She will. What will you tell her?"

"I'll tell her everything, about Toby and Ellie Reynolds, how the Clays nearly kicked me to death. I'll tell her how I killed Ben Clay, the worst of the brothers and about Mary Jane Hillman . . . I won't leave anything out."

"Bill Roche saved our lives. You can tell her that."

"Of course, I will. It ain't something I'm likely to forget."

"What will you tell her about gunning Barton Clay?"

"I don't know. It hasn't happened yet."

"He may have gunmen around him."

"That's why I have you."

"You know Mayor Maish will throw us back in jail."

"Good. It will give me a chance to tell him what kind of man Barton Clay really was."

"You're cutting it fine, Dan. We're walking in the shadow of the gallows."

"I'm going to end it today, Crow, one way or another. We'll take events as they come."

Dan and Crow rode in silence, each busy with their thoughts, until they reached the Palace Hotel. Dan didn't like what he saw. He and Crow tethered their horses at iron hitching posts painted to represent little black boys dressed up in jockey silks. There was no one around and none of Barton Clay's gunslingers were posted at the hotel door.

"Where is everybody?" Dan said.

"Siesta time, maybe," Crow said.

"Men like Barton Clay don't take siestas," Dan said. He drew his revolver and spun the cylinder, checking the loads, and then said, "Let's go pay our respects to the governor."

But he stopped in his tracks as a man stepped out of the hotel door. He was young, obviously a puncher by the cut of his duds, and he wore no gun. He stepped in front of Dan. "Stop right there. Where are you headed?" he said. There was no challenge in his voice, just a questioning tone.

"I'm here to see Barton Clay," Dan said.

"Name's Buff Grant. I am, or I was, the governor's

driver, only he ain't the governor anymore. Well, I put my name out, what's yours?"

"Dan Caine."

Grant managed a slight smile. "For a while there I didn't think you really existed. I reckoned you were some kind of boogerman."

"Pete and Ben and Decker knew I existed, and it killed them."

"Did you have a hand in Pete's death?"

"No, I watched him die from a jail cell, me and Crow."

"It was all Bill Roche's play?"

"Yeah. And he was as crazy as a loon that night."

"Roche killed Ruben Webb. That's hard to believe."

"Webb thought it would be easy. He sure didn't expect a crazy man with a scattergun on the other side of the jailhouse door."

"Who killed Bill Roche?"

"Webb did. Before he died, he got his work in."

"He had sand."

"Seems like."

"Why are you here?" Grant said.

"Cowboy, my name is Dan Caine. You know why I'm here."

"Mr. Clay is alone up there in his room. Everybody else deserted him except me. I figured I'd stay around if he needed to drive somewhere."

"Who's at his ranch?"

"No one, except for other ranchers who by now are biting off huge chunks of Lazy C range like sharks."

"What ails Clay?" Crow said.

Grant said, "You're the breed, ain't you?"

Crow nodded. "That would be me."

"Breeds bring bad luck. You ever hear that?"

"No, I never heard that. What ails Clay?"

"Apoplexy," Grant said. "Now that he can't be governor and can't hold onto his ranch, nobody wants anything to do with him."

"Is he conscious?" Dan said.

"Most of the time. Why?"

"Because I mean to kill him."

Grant's face lit up in a genuine smile. "Go right ahead, Caine. He'll thank you for it. Put him out of his misery."

"Put him out of my misery, you mean."

"Second floor, Room 21." Grant made a bow and swept out his arm toward the door. "Be my guest."

Dan looked at Crow who said, "Go ahead, Dan. I don't want to be there when you kill him."

Dan Caine mounted the stairs, gun in hand, and made his way to Room 21. The door was closed, and a tray of untouched food lay on the floor. It seemed that Barton Clay had lost his appetite.

Dan turned the handle of the door and violently pushed it open. He stepped to one side expecting a fusillade of shots. But none came. The carpeted hallway was quiet, and no sound came from Room 21, not even the tick of a mantel clock. Dan carried his hammer-back Colt high, up by his shoulder, when he stepped slowly into the room . . . and saw a sight that would haunt him for the rest of his life.

Like an unwrapped mummy, Barton Clay lay still in bed under a white sheet. Dan stepped closer. Barton was on his back, and the whole left side of his body was paralyzed. His stiff face was twisted, and his mouth drooped horribly. He tried to say something but couldn't form the words and produced only a tangled string of sounds that Dan couldn't understand.

But Barton Clay was aware. He knew what had happened to him. He faced the fact that he was a half-dead man and even if he recovered, he'd be forever as helpless as a day-old kitten, a deadweight that even kinfolk would shun. But Barton Clay had no kinfolk, and all his fine sons were gone. His brain was deteriorating rapidly, and he would not let himself live as a bedpan invalid.

He looked up at the hazy outline of Dan Caine who saw the terror in Barton's eyes and heard the pleading, impotent grunts and gasps coming from his numb throat. "Caaaine . . ." Barton Clay groaned, and his trembling right hand pointed weakly to the steamer trunk at the bottom of his bed.

Dan didn't move. "Get it yourself," he said.

"Caaaine . . ."

"All right, I'll do anything that will kill you faster, you no good piece of trash."

Dan already knew what he would find. He opened the trunk and under a musty pile of business papers, records of cattle sales and property deeds was a blue Colt with a walnut handle. Dan's hunch was correct . . . Barton knew that only a man who hated him would be prepared to end his misery. Dan picked up the Colt and one by one let four brass-cased cartridges drop to the floor so that the revolver's cocked hammer would fall on the fifth and only round.

His spurs chiming in the silent room, he stepped to the side of Clay's bed and said, "Listen up, there's one cartridge in the gun and you can use it to shoot me or blow your own brains out. Seems like you got a decision to make, huh?"

Clay's hand reached out for the gun and then he stopped, his eyes fixed on the corner of the room. "Ahhhhh . . ." a strangled wail of fear came from his grotesquely crooked mouth. He ignored the blue Colt and pointed into the corner. "See . . . see . . ."

"Who is it, Clay? Which one of your victims do you see? Is it Mary Jane Hillman, the woman you hung or maybe it's Ellie Reynolds, the old lady you burned to death?"

"Ahhhhh . . . mer . . . mercy . . . mercy . . ."

"Where are all your friends, you damn wretch? They should be standing around your bed, many of them, shedding salt tears. They've all deserted you. But look on the bright side, maybe the devil will appoint you governor of the lowest abyss of hell."

Barton once again reached out with a quivering hand for the Colt. Dan took the man's cold hand in his and shoved the revolver into his palm and made a fist of his fingers. He arranged Clay's hand on the pillow, his finger on the trigger, the Colt's muzzle shoved into his temple.

"One shot, Clay, use it wisely," Dan said as he backed away from the bed, hand on his holstered revolver.

He reached the door and said, "Heartbreaking, isn't it, Barton, that none of this would've happened if your sons hadn't murdered old Dick Meadows?"

Dan walked down the stairs to the door where Crow and Buff Grant waited.

"Well?" Grant said. "Is Barton Clay still alive."

A gunshot racketed through the hotel, and Dan said, "No. Barton Clay is dead."

* * *

"I've got the return train tickets in my pocket," Crow said. "Can we go home now?"

"Yeah, sure we can," Dan said, smiling. "I'm looking forward to Broken Back and a quiet life with Helen. That is, if she's still waiting for me."

But the fickle Wild West wasn't quite finished with Dan Caine and Crow. As fate would have it, a few minutes of hell-firing mayhem would force them to put their lives once again on the line as they came up against some mighty bad men.

CHAPTER SIXTY-THREE

The thirty-mile ride from the train depot in San Antonio to the outskirts of Broken Back happened in a late summer rain, and Dan and Crow wore slickers and wrapped themselves in silence. The sky was gray, the clouds black, and the air smelled of grass and wet earth. The only sounds were the creak of saddle leather, the hoof falls of the horses and the constant hiss of the downpour, like a bad-tempered baby dragon

In the gloomy distance, Broken Back huddled behind a curtain of steely rain and smoke from two-score of chimneys that refused to be pelted into submission and rose straight as strings above the roofs.

"Nothing's changed," Crow said, breaking the silence of the past two hours.

"Seems like," Dan said.

"I can see your house from here."

"It looks dark to me."

"Hard to tell from where we are."

"An oil lamp would light up the windows."

"Dan, the windows are to the front," Crow said. "You're

looking at the gable end of the cabin where there is no window."

"Yeah, you're right. How come you know gables? You lived in a tent."

"I must have heard some white man say it. White men say a lot of things like that around Indians. They don't want us to live in wikiups but in log cabins that can't be moved. That way we stay in one place and don't wander."

"Too bad," Dan said. "The Indians' way of life was a good way."

"Until it all ended with the slaughter of the buffalo," Crow said.

"Are you bitter, Crow? Sometimes I think you are."

"No, I'm not bitter, too much white man in me for that. But when I think about the buffalo it makes me downright sad. What are those fellers doing at the bank?"

Dan peered through the rain. "Some ranchers making a deposit?"

"Or some outlaw making a withdrawal. No honest man would ride in this rain, only lawmen and bandits."

"Let's go take a look-see. Within the town limits I guess I'm still the sheriff of Broken Back."

"You got your star?" Crow said.

"No. Do you?"

"Nope. I left it in the desk drawer in the sheriff's office."

"Right beside mine," Dan said. "Oh, well, let's go say howdy to those riders."

Some Western men still argue that Dan Caine did not expect a violent encounter that day, others that he'd opened his slicker ready to draw his gunbelt and was ready to get his work in if need be. The truth is Dan expected three ranchers doing bank business, a thing they did at least once a month. What he didn't expect were Clayton Bell, Milt Murdoch, and Snake River Ned Rising, a trio of the most vicious robbers and killers that ever terrorized the West.

Dan and Crow walked their horses toward the bank and then three things happened very quickly. The door slammed open and three men, two of them carrying bulging white money sacks, charged onto the boardwalk toward their waiting mounts. There was surprise on both sides, but Dan recovered quickly, drew his Colt, and said, "Stop right there in the name of the law." For an instant there was an impasse and both outlaws and lawmen froze in place. Then someone inside the building yelled, "Help! The bank is being robbed."

Clayton Bell yelled, "Shut your mouth" and fired a shot into the building.

The ball had opened.

Dan and Crow immediately cut loose and Ned Rising took a bullet that blew away his lower jaw and put him out of the fight. He would die three days later. Bell fired and Crow grunted in pain as a bullet slammed into his gun arm and for now stopped him. It was Dan's bullet that hit Rising and now he fired at Bell, scoring a solid hit to the man's chest. As he grabbed the reins of his horse, Milt Murdoch fired at Dan and missed. He swung into the saddle and Dan shot at him again, this time scoring a hit. His bullet slammed high into the back of Murdoch's shoulder, smashed his left collarbone and did severe, splintering damage. Then disaster struck. Clayton Bell had received a death wound, but the outlaw had sand and he fired at Dan before he fell onto the boardwalk and died. Dan felt a tremendous pain at the side of his head and found himself falling headlong into the muddy street. Dizzy, his vision blurred, he tried to get to his feet but immediately staggered and dropped to his knees. He'd lost his gun in the heavy fall from the saddle and now it was nowhere in sight.

And then he saw his death approaching . . . a man on a pale horse.

Milt Murdoch had galloped about fifty yards from the bank and had shot at people coming out of the mercantile who scuttled back inside. Then he did the unexpected. Blood and pain alerted him to the fact that his wound was a severe one and he swung his horse around, determined to kill the man who'd inflicted such a dreadful hurt on him.

Crow, his right arm useless, battled searing pain as he attempted, to no avail, to pull his Winchester from the boot with his left.

Murdoch, who had killed three men during his criminal career, came on at a walk through the teeming rain. When his gray horse loomed over the kneeling man, he thumbed back the hammer of his Colt and pointed his gun at Dan's head. "See you in hell, lawman," he said.

BLAM!

The flat statement of a Winchester echoed through the rattling rain and for a moment Murdoch stared at Dan, his face a mask of disbelief. But it was the expression of a dead man. The Colt fell from the outlaw's lifeless hand thudded onto the ground, followed by the louder *splat* of Murdoch, facedown, hitting mud. The back of his head was blown away, a testament to the raw power of the .44-40 round.

Dan blinked rainwater from his eyes, blinked again, as though he couldn't believe what he was seeing. But there was no doubt about it . . . the slender figure of his wife Helen emerged from the rain, a smoking Winchester in her hands.

She stopped and stared down at her husband. Tendrils of wet hair fell over her forehead and under the hem of her dress, mud stained a cascade of white petticoats and her high-heeled ankle boots.

"Helen . . ." Dan said, that single whispered word catching in his throat.

Helen Caine frowned. "All right, where have you been?" she said.

"Helen, you waited for me," Dan said.

"Since we have a baby on the way, did I have any other option?"

"I love you, Helen," Dan said, smiling. "And that's wonderful news."

"Look at you," the young woman said. "All muddy and bloody . . . you're a mess."

Helen Caine sat a porch rocker with two men she called her walking wounded. As an honored guest, Crow sat in the other rocker, his arm in a sling. Dan, a fat bandage around his head, made do with an uncomfortable straight-backed chair, his purring calico cat on his knees.

Helen dropped her crocheting into her lap and then picked up a small paper sack of motto candy from the table beside her. She selected a pink, heart-shaped piece and studied it.

"Well, what does it say?" Dan asked.

"It says, I love you," Helen said.

She looked at the candy for a few moments longer and then popped it into her mouth.

"Dan, if we have a girl, I'd like to call her Victoria," Helen said. "If it's a boy, I'll let you name him."

Dan said, "You know, I've always been right partial to the name Sammy."

Helen's eyebrows knitted together. "Well, that's something we'll just have to talk about, isn't it?" she said.

TURN THE PAGE FOR AN EXCITING PREVIEW!

On the wild western frontier, the three men known as the Jackals stand between the law and the lawless—delivering their own brand of justice with a fast draw, dead aim, and enough bullets to populate Boot Hill.

Johnstone Territory. Where Death Rides Hard.

Apache renegade Blood Moon plays a role in each of the Jackals' lives. To bounty hunter Jed Breen, he is a man with a price on his head. To retired cavalry sergeant Sean Keegan, he is a cellmate after a drunken brawl. And to former Texas Ranger Matt McCulloch, he is the key to a mystery that has long haunted him.

When McCulloch breaks Blood Moon out of jail, his fellow Jackals follow them into Mexico. Now, all four are wanted men. The U.S. Army and bounty hunters cross the Rio Grande in pursuit. Awaiting them south of the border are Mexican *rurales* led by Confederate expatriate Major Block Frazer seeking revenge against Blood Moon.

But nothing will stop McCulloch from completing his mission—to save his daughter from the Apache band that abducted her years before. Outnumbered and outgunned, the Jackals will stand together to free McCulloch's daughter— or end up hung, drawn, and quartered.

**National Bestselling Authors
William W. Johnstone
and J.A. Johnstone**

THE JACKALS
DEAD RIVER

Live Free. Read Hard.
www.williamjohnstone.net

On sale, wherever Pinnacle Books are sold.

Visit us at www.kensingtonbooks.com

PROLOGUE

From Box 31, Folder 7, Perdition County Archives,
Crossfire, Texas

Unpublished letters and manuscripts dealing with Purgatory City, other ghost towns, towns that merged with larger metropolises, and unincorporated towns, villages, way stations, and railroad sites.

They called my father a jackal. And that was the most polite word I remember hearing in Purgatory City, Texas. They called him a hard man. They called him lots of things. Well, so did I. There were times when I was a little girl that I thought my pa loved horses—mustangs, mostly—more than he loved me.

Much of my childhood has been forgotten, wiped out by a memory—a nightmare—I will not relate to you or anyone, though it still haunts my dreams. Often, I can't even remember the faces of my late, dearly departed brothers. Or even Mother's face. How beautiful I'd like to think she was.

Yet I just do not know.

But I remember my father.

I also recall vividly a wild Irishman, who loved to take a nip—oh, no, that does not do this man justice. He was a man who drank more liquor than could fill the tank on a fire wagon. He was a man who loved to brawl, no matter that he rarely won a round of fisticuffs, but he loved to fight. He would fight over a drop of a hat or a wink of an eye or just for a bet, even if the wager would win him only a copper cent.

They called him a jackal, too.

Yet I remember him with kindness. Stories around tell he once cared for a little baby in the jail that often served as his second home in Purgatory City. Most people thought this man would eat babies raw and spit out their tiny little bones. Did he? I never saw that. What I remember of this alleged jackal was a man who wore the uniform that freed the Negroes from bondage and prevented the dissolvement of our Union. Yes, I know. Here in Texas most of our great citizens pride those ancestors who wore the gray, who fought under John Bell Hood, Stonewall Jackson, Robert E. Lee, those who "saw the elephant"— as they like to say—in glorious battles at places like Shiloh, Chancellorsville, Seven Pines, Bull Run, Antietam, Kennesaw Mountain, Atlanta, Cold Harbor, and Gettysburg. But even those old soldiers, most of them all gone now, fought for Texas. And well, they also had a strong respect for the men they fought against.

Sean Keegan was one of those men. He also served in the frontier cavalry in Texas, fighting against the Indians that protested white settlers for taking over their country. Sean Keegan might have been branded a jackal, especially after he was court-martialed and drummed out of the service he so dearly loved, but I know this alleged jackal was tried and condemned for doing what any man, woman—anyone—would have done. He did what he had to do to protect the lives of his fellow soldiers. The men who rode with Sergeant Keegan on that day, I have to believe, would never have said anything derogatory about their gallant hero. Most likely, I think now with a great big grin on my face, they kept the man from County Cork filled with Irish whiskey and fine stout Irish beer.

A jackal? I call him a hero. I call him a man.

And I remember someone else, a man whose reputation was lower perhaps than that of my father. Especially after all the dime novels and picture shows and so-called factual accounts printed in newspapers like the one we have here in Crossfire—the county seat. Is it any wonder people frown at the very thought of a bounty hunter—a man who tracks down other men, not for justice, but for the money he might collect?

In this terrible calamity many are calling a Great Depression, I do believe the men sent by banks to foreclose on homes or to kick people off their properties where loved ones might be buried are much more vile than a man who had the courage to bring wanted men—some charged and condemned for the most wicked of crimes— to justice. Jed Breen was such a man, and while nobody recalls his name today, it was bandied around quite often all across this land we call West Texas.

Jed Breen was the third man termed a jackal in the roaring days of the town that is no more than a memory. Purgatory City thrived for a few more years beyond a riproaring, Hades-raising decade, till Progress—that awful thing known as Progress—doomed the city. It was nothing more than a few streets of mostly saloons and places of ill repute, when the railroad chose another path.

Fate—and the engineers who picked the path for the Great Texas and California Railway—is why Crossfire has become the seat of Perdition County. Fate is why this letter, this memoir, I write in my feeble hand will be posted to the Crossfire Public Library. And Fate is why Purgatory City is nothing more than a memory to most of us who remember it at all.

Perhaps this letter, these rambling thoughts of an aging Texican, will help people remember where they came from.

I am rambling, of course. I was writing about the third and last jackal, the bounty hunter Jed Breen. They said he had the blackest heart of anyone in the land—a black heart, they said, to contrast with his stark white hair. They said he never brought in anyone alive, but I can deny that as an ugly falsehood. Jed Breen brought in several men alive.

One of them was an Apache renegade named Blood Moon.

It strikes me as strange—no, it is heartbreaking and even numbs my very soul—the Apache Indian who terrorized both sides of the border between our United States and Mexico is the one whose name is remembered. Gridiron teams across the county are called Apaches, Indians, Warriors, Redskins, and I have seen my grandchildren shout, "Blood Moon! Blood Moon! Remember Blood Moon!" in pep rallies when their Cowboys, Cavaliers, and "Lions, Tigers and Bears" were going against schools with nicknames that recalled our Red Brothers. That is the only reason anyone remembers Blood Moon except for those

weary-eyed historians and old archivists who look through
volumes of bound copies of old newspapers, and maybe,
in ten or twenty years from now, will be reading this
letter . . . if anyone can make out my scratches.

I can barely see well enough to write.

The best historians will be able to tell you Blood Moon
was an Apache renegade who waged basically a one-man
war against Mexicans and Texans and federal soldiers in
the Southwest. He was so vilified and so terrified many
settlers the total reward offered for him was a staggering
amount today, let alone in the decade after the War Between
the States.

Blood Moon was a jackal, too, and perhaps he deserved to be labeled thusly.

Some men have even called another Indian, an Apache,
too, who lived most of his life in Mexico, and tried to
avoid most white people and most Mexicans, a jackal, as
well. Three Dogs, he was named. But if he were a jackal,
I never saw him that way. He was like a father to many of
his people, and he was like a father to me. For a long,
long, terrible while, he was the only father I had . . . or
the only one I remembered.

Until one day . . . or weeks . . . and then—

Well, this is no story to be told by an old person whose
memory is fading, whose hand has begun to ache, and
whose fingers are cramping.

Three men were called jackals in Purgatory City. Matt
McCulloch, a former Texas Ranger and a grand mustanger
back when wild horses ran free in this part of the state.
Sean Keegan, the former cavalry soldier and rumored
drunkard. And a bounty hunter called Jed Breen.

These white men were likely despised worse than the

Apache butcher we called Blood Moon. And the old warrior whose name was Three Dogs.

One more man from these wild and savage times needs to be remembered, though I cannot attest to his background except from what I've heard. He was a soldier of the Confederacy, too, and his name was Block Frazer.

The way I recall, from my old fading brain, this Block Frazer did not hail from Texas but from some Southern state—Mississippi, Louisiana, one of the Carolinas. I don't think it was as far north as Virginia or Tennessee. After learning the Confederacy was lost, he crossed the border with some of his men at the invitation of the ruler of Mexico. I don't remember that emperor's name, but you likely can find it in some history book. Perhaps even at the library.

I have read and heard stories that other former Confederate soldiers, their egos and will strong, also went to Mexico, refusing to admit defeat to President Lincoln's rule. Some stayed in Mexico, others grew tired or homesick after months or a few years, or they realized their welcome in that fine country was wearing out since Juarez had taken over the country.

Block Frazer, however, remained. I don't know why he stayed and I do not know why he hated Indians so much, but Block Frazer became—the way I remember things— a true jackal. He was an evil, evil, evil man, and he had his men do evil, evil, evil things.

Block Frazer was a jackal, though as far as I can tell, no one in either Mexico or Texas called him such.

I did not know Block Frazer. He came into my life just

once. I did not even know his name until months after I saw him try to kill my father.

Here, my dear readers, is what I know, and what I remember, and what in my aching heart is true.

Matthew McCulloch, Sergeant Sean Keegan, and Jed Breen are whom Purgatory City, Perdition County, Texas, branded jackals. But if it were not for those three men—and, I can say with a weak smile, one of them, in particular—I would not be here to write this piece of minor trivia, minor history.

Believe me or call me a fraud. That is your right.

McCulloch, Keegan and Breen were jackals to many, but they will always be heroes to me. And in their own way, Blood Moon and Three Dogs, were heroes, too. Block Frazer, well, he was a scoundrel and the vilest of men and though I should not think such thoughts, I hope he has been burning in Hell for many, many years. And that he will continue to rot in misery for he was a true jackal.

Note from J.S.T. Cohen, Archivist, Crossfire Public Library, November 13, 1936. This letter arrived on October 1, postmarked Crossfire, but with no return address and was not signed. While we are unable to verify the veracity of this—woman's from the look of the handwriting—account, research in our own archives has turned up some supporting evidence that warrant its claims.

An editorial from the Herald Leader *of Purgatory City— no longer, as the letter writer observed, existing—indeed ran a page 1 article in the [illegible] under this headline.*

THE TIME HAS COME
FOR OUR CITIZENS TO STAND UP
TO THE JACKALS OF WEST TEXAS
AND MAKE A STATEMENT
FOR LAW

The rest of the headline has been torn.

The editorial does, however, cite a Texas Ranger named Matthew McCulloch, a federal army sergeant named Sean Keegan, and a bounty hunter called Jed Breen as the so-called jackals.

If what the editorialist, one Alvin J. Griffin IV, wrote is even half-true, then it is my opinion that these men were indeed jackals, and that is an understatement.

Other articles found in various Perdition County newspapers from 1871–1883 (the last year was when the railroad bypassed Purgatory City that led to the town's collapse) have scant mention of McCulloch, Keegan, and Breen, but their names do pop up and sometimes they were still called jackals.

Letters to state archivists in the states mentioned by the anonymous letter writer regarding Block Frazer were returned with regrets that no one under that name for the period cited were found in city directories or newspaper searches or just not returned at all.

There are a few spotty mentions of one Blood Moon in Perdition County newspapers, but the National Archives and Records Administration said several pages of official military correspondence mention the name of the Apache Indian from as far east as San Antonio to as far west as Fort Inferno on the Arizona–Colorado border.

The Apache Indian named as Three Dogs has not been

found in history books on this library's shelves, and the archivist at the National Archives and Records Administration said no name popped up in a casual search.

We are waiting to hear back from the archives in Mexico City. [No record of any reply has been found as of this date, 7-11-1953, BKJ.]

Therefore, it appears three men in this county were known as the jackals, and they might rank up there with Jesse James and William Quantrill in their bloodlust and butchery.

It is, however, with deep regret that the person who wrote this account did not sign her (or his) name, but provided enough material and enough names and items that have been verified to make the staff and I believe this letter is worthy of being filed here.

But the county officials and the state archivists in Austin all stress that in no way are we endorsing this letter.

That is something we must leave to the individual readers.

CHAPTER ONE

Ugly Juan Maldado had put up quite the resistance in an arroyo near Devil Ridge, east of Fort Hancock, till a round from Jed Breen's Sharps rifle busted the murdering rustler's left shoulder. Although Breen cauterized the wound, he half expected Maldado to die before the reward could be claimed—especially when the soldier boys at Fort Hancock refused to take Maldado since he had never stolen government horses or mules. The post surgeon declined to operate on the badly wounded Mexican because he had not been wounded by a bluebelly or had ever worked as a civilian contractor for the United States Army.

The army boys decided to be uncooperative, Breen figured, because they wouldn't be claiming the reward on Ugly Juan Maldado, but that wasn't Breen's fault. Breen had earned this one, wearing out two good horses, spending six weeks sleeping—when he could risk sleep—in the scorching furnacelike heat, getting his fine new Stetson punched through the crown with a .45 slug that, two inches lower, would have blown off the top of his head.

He thanked the boys in blue for their trouble—at least

they hadn't denied him water or a sip of the surgeon's brandy—and pushed on.

Two and a half more days of traveling along the road that paralleled the Río Grande he finally reached El Paso.

Sheriff Burt Curtis shook his head when he examined Ugly Juan Maldado. "I'll be a suck-egg mule," he exclaimed. "This ol' greaser ain't dead."

"That's right," Breen said with relief. "Now if you'll just sign the affidavit that says he was delivered to you alive and well."

Curtis looked up, narrowing his eyes. "He ain't exactly alive, though. And sure ain't well."

"Not many men would be called *well* after having a Sharps blow out most of his shoulder blade." Breen extended the white piece of paper and pencil.

The sheriff looked at the paper without moving. "Why didn't you amputate?"

"My pocketknife was dull."

"You coulda took him to Fort Hancock."

"I did." Breen waved the paper. He wondered if Curtis was hoping the outlaw would die so he wouldn't have to sign the paper. Or maybe Burt Curtis couldn't read or write. "The good boys in blue declined to be of service." That proved to be the right thing for Jed Breen to say.

Burt Curtis, who had fought under John Bell Hood in the late War Between the States, began spitting out all sorts of profane thoughts about bluecoats and Yankees in general. When he finished, Breen still held that paper tightly so the wind wouldn't snatch it away and blow it to Mexico.

"Maldado's not dead," Breen said. "And that means

five hundred extra dollars." He held out the paper and pencil again. "If you'd do me the honor, Sheriff Curtis."

The county lawman rolled his eyes, spit onto one of Ugly Juan Maldado's brogans, and took paper and pencil. "Maybe the murderin' piece of scum'll live long enough to hang. That way the county gets paid for the gallows buildin', the printin' of the invites to the hangin', and the buryin' and such."

"You mean you get paid for all that." Breen smiled as the sheriff returned the signed document.

"But it ain't nowhere near as much as the extra five hunnerd you be gettin'."

Indeed. The Joint Citizens Committee of El Paso, Brown City, and Sierra Maloliente had specified that fifteen hundred dollars would be paid upon positive identification of Ugly Juan Maldado if the outlaw was dead. Another five hundred dollars if brought in alive. Breen wasn't exactly sure why. Bringing in a corpse would save expenses, so to a professional manhunter like Jed Breen it seemed more logical to pay more for a dead man than a fellow you'd have to feed and house and, as in the case of Ugly Juan Maldado, splurge on a doctor to keep the man alive long enough to be executed. Breen figured the citizens of El Paso, Brown City, and Sierra Maloliente wanted the honor of dragging the scoundrel through prickly pear and rocks before stringing him up. Maybe that was worth paying five hundred bucks.

"If he dies, you could still hang him," Breen said.

The sheriff looked up, eyes registering the truth of Breen's statement. "Reckon I could at that."

"But," Breen said, "maybe you ought to fetch a doctor to look at Maldado. See if he can't do a better job of keeping him alive to drop through that trapdoor." Feeling generous, he reached into his dust-covered vest, pulled out a half eagle, and tossed it to Burt Curtis. "Keep the change from whatever the sawbones charges you . . . I mean . . . the county."

Burt Curtis bit into the coin to make sure Breen wasn't cheating him.

"And join me at the Exchange Saloon when your prisoner is comfy in your best cell. I'll buy you supper and a bottle of rye to wash it down."

It paid, Breen had learned in his years plying his trade, to keep the law dogs happy.

Two weeks later, Jed Breen could hardly remember the last time he had felt this fine. He was riding back toward Purgatory City from El Paso on a fine strawberry roan won at a card table—aces full over jacks beating kings full over deuces—and had two thousand dollars in his saddlebags for turning in Ugly Juan Maldado to the county sheriff, alive and likely to live long enough to be lynched or tried and hanged legally. Breen's stomach was full from the fine cuisine one could find in a city like El Paso, even if that chow didn't taste anything like a man of means could enjoy in some real town with real class and real food—New Orleans or Kansas City or Memphis or St. Louis or Galveston—but it sure beat what passed for grub in Purgatory City.

Suddenly, Breen started thinking about taking a vacation or a leave of absence. Bounty hunting proved to be hard work, and often work that never paid much money. Plus, it was tough on one's backside riding hell-bent for

leather across the dusty inferno called West Texas. Unless
you were going after pickpockets or runaways, the job
could be downright dangerous, bringing in owlhoots who
did not want to spend twenty years in Huntsville or get
their necks stretched on the gallows or nearest hanging
trees.

*San Francisco perhaps. Hell, right now Fort Griffin or
Fort Stockton would feel like Paris or Rome.*

He stopped daydreaming and decided on something
more reasonable. When he got back to Purgatory City, he
would treat his friends, or the closest men that came to
being his friends—Matt McCulloch and Sean Keegan—
to supper and whiskey at the finest establishment in that
hellhole. That would likely set Breen back ten bucks. If
that. Depending on how drunk Keegan got or how many
fights he started. A grin stretched across Breen's stubbled
face as he pictured the look on Keegan's face when he
showed him the reward money.

An instant later, the grin died.

Jed Breen saw black smoke coming over the top of the
ridge. He reined in the strawberry roan, while reaching
down first for the Sharps, then stopping and dropping the
right hand to the butt of the double-action Colt Lightning
holstered on his right hip.

The roan snorted. Breen wet his lips with his tongue.
The wind blew hot, sending the smoke toward the east. He
tried to get his bearings, figure out how far he was from
Purgatory City, whose house or stagecoach station that
might be. But Jed Breen had never been known as neighborly and even the most God-fearing and generous Christian in that part of the Western frontier likely wouldn't feel

neighborly toward a bounty hunter, especially one known as one of the three jackals.

Matt McCulloch and Sean Keegan were the other two.

It wasn't a grass fire. Not smoke that thick and dark, and it wasn't like there was much grass this time of the year—or any time, really—to burn.

He listened, but heard only the wind. Then he clucked his tongue and gently spurred the roan. The hooves clopped and Breen drew the Lightning from the holster, keeping the barrel pointed at the ground and away from the roan's belly.

At the ridgetop, Breen reined up and saw the homestead about a quarter mile off to the east at the bottom of the hill. It was a dirt-and-adobe structure, so only the roof and door were burning, along with the privy over toward the corral. He saw a patch of white and blue between the burning home and the empty corral. Breen didn't know who had tried to homestead there, but he damn well knew what that patch of white and blue meant.

He thought about grabbing the binoculars out of his saddlebag or using the telescopic sight on the Sharps, but the sun was at ten o'clock or thereabouts, and he didn't want to risk the rays reflecting off the lenses . . . if anyone was still around.

For fifteen minutes, Breen studied the homestead and every inch of ground within a rifle shot. Finally, he kicked the horse into a walk, and tried not to hear the hoofbeats or the wind, but something else—the click of a weapon's hammer, the call of a hawk or raven, a coyote's yip.

A war whoop.

When he reached low ground, the roan turned skittish.

"Hell," Breen whispered. "I smell it, too, boy." His throat turned to sand.

Fifty yards from the flames, he pulled on the reins. The roan had been fighting the bit for about twenty-five feet, and Breen wasn't the kind of scoundrel to force a horse or anyone into the scene. Without holstering the Colt, he dismounted. Only after turning the horse sideways, keeping the ridge and road he had just descended to his back, did he holster the Colt and open the saddlebags—just not the one that held the reward money.

He found the hobbles and quickly secured the roan's forefeet. Rubbing his hands on the gelding's neck, Breen rose and looked over the saddle, staring at the surrounding countryside and the inferno beginning to burn itself out. He grabbed the canteen, uncorked it, took a mouthful to rinse out the gall and sand, and spit it onto the dirt. The next mouthful he swallowed.

The roan let Breen know he was thirsty, too.

"I know," Breen whispered, corking the canteen and wrapping it on the saddle horn. "But you'll have to wait."

He slid the Sharps from the scabbard and patted his trousers pocket. Three shells. Five already in the Colt, plus a shell belt filled with .38-caliber bullets. He tugged on his Stetson's brim to pull the hat snug before he moved off the road on the right, nearest the burning homestead, and crouching, he sprinted twenty yards, stopped, and dropped to one knee. Again, he studied the terrain.

If the fire was burning out, he told himself, whoever set it had to be long gone. That was common sense. Again, he wet his lips. Again, he remembered that common sense had gotten many a man killed in that savage, lawless country.

Men who took their time lived longer than men who acted recklessly.

For ten minutes, he moved little more than his eyes, although the wind blew his prematurely white hair, and he now wished he had told the El Paso tonsorial artist to take more off the length. He was paranoid enough from the smoke and stench of death that he thought his hair, especially white as it was, might be enough for some murdering prairie rat to draw a bead on. His stomach and nose began to protest the wretched stink. Looking at the roan, he wondered how long the horse would just stand there before trying to break free from the hobbles and gallop back to the gentleness and comforts of El Paso.

Another five minutes stretched past in agonizing silence.

Finally, Breen raced to the well on the western side of the burning house. The stench gagged him, and he pulled the bandanna up and over his nose. Wood and grass weren't the only things the fire was consuming inside, and what Breen smelled, he understood, was not a side of beef. Again, he looked at the patch of blue and white, clearer now, with a definite shape and form.

He held his breath and ran to the woman.

Choking down the bile, Breen made himself close her green eyes. Two arrows, shafts broken when she fell, remained imbedded in her back. She must have been running from the house for the corral when the Indian—Apache by the arrows—killed her.

The corral was empty.

A noise made him point the Lightning toward the line of scrub beyond the burning outhouse, and he almost put a bullet into the head of a mule. Breen's gun hand dropped like an anchor, and he struggled to catch his breath. He looked for tracks, but saw none, though the wind likely had wiped most of them out. He tried to think. Apaches or an Apache had killed the couple homesteading here. Why leave the mule?

At that moment, another noise tore through Breen's composure. He whirled around, and saw a juniper about thirty yards toward the east.

The crying sounded louder.

"My God," he whispered. Shoving the .38 into the holster, he grabbed his Sharps and ran to the stump of a tree, sliding, turning, and looking behind him before he glanced down at the swaddled infant. The green-eyed baby wailed as the mule stopped near the edge of the corral and brayed.

Breen glanced at the dead woman. Would she have run so far from the corral, left her little baby under the tree, then sprinted for the mule or horses? From where the body lay, it sure as hell looked like she ran from the house and was making a beeline for the corral or the scrub brush and arroyo beyond it when two Apache arrows had ended her life.

Breen tried to comprehend what all had happened, but before he could put together even one thought that made a lick of sense, he heard another noise.

One that practically stopped his heart.

Hoofbeats pounded the hard-packed road. The smoke stung his eyes as it wafted above and all around him, and he squinted, cursed, and saw the strawberry roan galloping up the road. On the back of Breen's horse sat a black-haired Apache. The very same red devil who'd killed the man—likely burning in the remnants of the home—and the woman. The miserable son of a cur had left the baby to die a slow death. Somehow, the Indian had managed to release the hobbles on the roan and keep the horse quiet. The Apache must have been a ghost, but a ghost Breen could see. The bloody thief was leaving Breen afoot.

And galloping away with his horse and his hard-earned two thousand bucks.

Connect with  Us

Visit us online at
KensingtonBooks.com
to read more from your favorite authors, see books
by series, view reading group guides, and more.

 Join us on social media

for sneak peeks, chances to win books and prize packs,
and to share your thoughts with other readers.

facebook.com/kensingtonpublishing
twitter.com/kensingtonbooks

Tell us what you think!

To share your thoughts, submit a review,
or sign up for our eNewsletters, please visit:
KensingtonBooks.com/TellUs.